BADU - BLADE OF THE NÖZ

A BACKSTORY NOVEL

TEMPEST RISING SERIES

MAX MOYER

JOIN MY MAILING LIST

Sign up for my mailing list for news, exclusive content and special releases and access. Also, for now, new subscribers receive a free copy of *Throne Born*, a novella that predates the events in *Zodak - The Last Shielder* by 200 years.

sign up and get your free book!

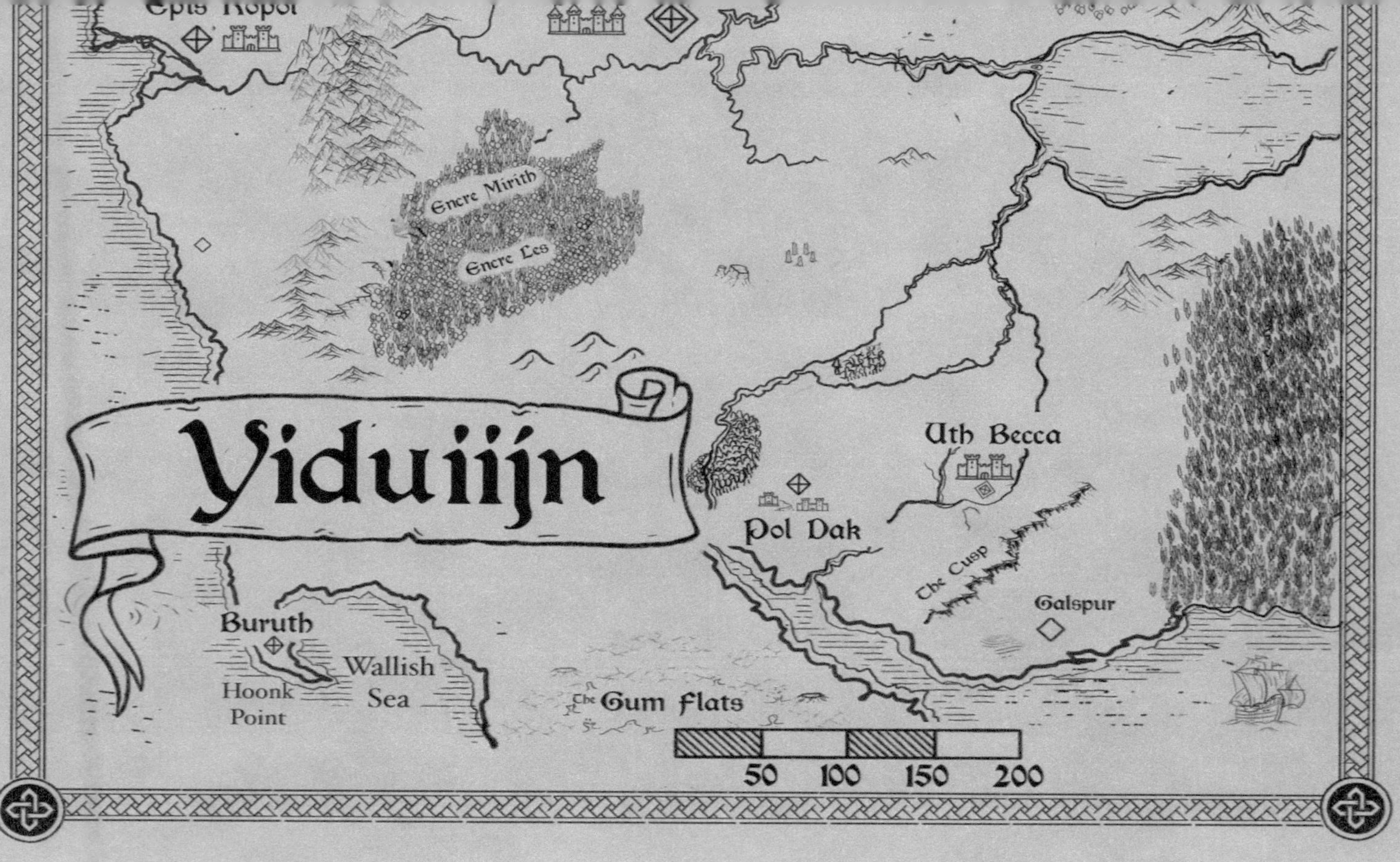

Yiduiijn
Epis Ropoi
Encre Mirith
Encre Les
Buruth
Wallish Sea
Hoonk Point
The Gum Flats
Pol Dak
Uth Becca
The Cusp
Galspur
50 100 150 200

Fahyzen Kingdom
Pi'b Bay
Fahyzen Ness
Gikland
Wyntis
Mis
Ohn
Helmun
K'andoria
Shadow Pass
FAHYZ
MEAD
NOST
SLAG

For my real-life nözan, the band of brothers by my side in life's adventures, as we each strive to be the heroes we revere.

Yiduiijn

(yid-wee-YIN)

Directions, Weights & Measures

Directions

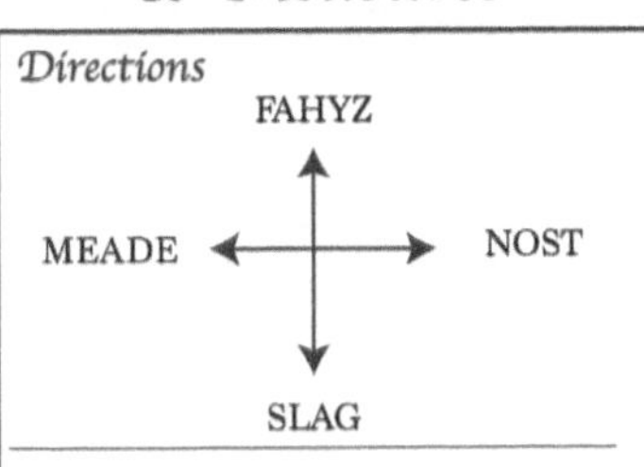

Measurements

jot - 1/12 an inch

inch - 1/12 a measure

measure - 1/6 a marq

marq - length of an average man

lynk - 9 marqs

cliq - 888 marqs: measured as the width of the mouth of the Swath (~ 1 mile or 1.6km).

span - 41 cliqs Standard; a day's journey on a galloping horse.

Kopolian Currencies

Kral	= 50 Bwua
Bwua	= 50 Agü
Daagü	= 2 Agü
Agü	= 10 shalip
Shalip	= (roughly) 1 corq
Yinga	= ½ shalip
Mika	= ¼ Yinga
Pimika	= 1/10 Yinga

Weights

crimp	= 1/7th chip
chip	= 1/13 dok
dok	= 1 wellish shell (1 lb)
chub	= 1 1/5 dok
dokkert	= 7 dok
slab	= 77 dok
wagon	= 11 slabs

maxmoyerwrites.com

NOTE FROM THE AUTHOR

First, thank you for being here. It means a lot that you invest your time in a story I've created. I truly, truly hope you love it.

With this story, I invite you, the reader, to step into Yiduiijn (yid-wee-YIN), into the world of Mind's Eye.

Badu - Blade of the Nöz is set in the same world as *Zodak - The Last Shielder,* 50 years earlier. It's an origin story for the beloved old mystic Badu from Zodak. Enjoy!

TEMPEST RISING SERIES

Suggested Reading Order:

Throne Born (a prequel novella)

Zodak - The Last Shielder (<u>Book 1</u>)

Badu - Blade of the Nöz (a backstory novel)

Series Book 2 (Coming)

Series Book 3 (Coming)

Please visit www.MindsEye.site to stay up to date on what's next.

Thanks again
   - Max

CONTENTS

PROLOGUE

Sporadic cries and shouts of hate rise all around me. I've been moved outside, though beneath the musty cloth, everything remains black. The breeze carries the smell of the sea, mixed with wet stone. It's a welcome relief to the stench I've been living in. As the guards rip off my hood, blinding lights sear my vision. This place is new to my eyes. I've seen very little of the cursed castle, which is just as well. After they kicked me awake, they marched me up a never-ending flight of steps out of the rotting dungeons that have been my home for days, or has it been weeks? Where exactly I stand now, I can only guess.

Hunger racks my insides, and every cough—every deep breath, even—sends a stabbing pain through my wrecked body. I have broken ribs, bruises, and one eye swollen shut. The wound that used to be the two fingers on my right hand hasn't started to heal as much as fester. Yet, I will show no pain. No matter how they try to break me, these svin will see no hint of defeat in my eyes.

They didn't earn the screams they sought in the torture dungeon. I stared ahead, fixed like stone, unshakeable until I lost consciousness. *Do they not know the Eiklin of the Eikstrand? Do they not know my kind? I am no common thief from the streets. I am Rune Langkar, commander of the Skvar. I have slain hundreds in battle. My people have survived in the barren and ruthless Fahyzen Ness for centuries. My ancestors were warriors from birth. These rass know nothing of our traditions, our strength. They don't know what it means to be Eiklin.*

As my eyes begin to adjust, I see we stand in an open stone courtyard, splayed beneath the sinister glare of the black castle. To my left stretches the ocean, sparkling and infinite. Immediately a deep peace washes over me. I have looked upon this view since boyhood. The glassy sea below owns more of my soul than this svin in the golden mask could ever take from me. *When you reach the end,* I remind myself, *find the horizon where sea kisses sky.*

To my right stand six other prisoners, four men and two women, none of them Eiklin. *An efficient way to send a message,* I suppose. The two priestguard soldiers holding me are the same rass that have been my dungeon nursemaids. *Violent, abusive nursemaids at that.* My mouth creeps up in the slightest of grins at the thought. I stare death in the face, and yet I smile. This is the defiant pride of the Eiklin.

The figures marching at the far end of the courtyard catch my eye. Two guards ascend shallow steps to take position on a raised platform, one on either side of a worn stone block. These are not the regular priestguard. I recognize their kind. I've only encountered them in the flesh once, but these massive, looming figures are unmistakable, their ashy gray skin, long ragged white hair and beards, piercing blue eyes under heavy brows, ever draped in piles of furs: Tszoi warriors from the Tszox Range, the wild mountain people from my childhood tales.

My people are tall, rugged warriors, but these Tszoi each stand a head above me and outweigh me by half. I cannot begin to fathom how this false god had persuaded these savages to play castle guard.

A thin line of people continues to trickle in behind me, twenty, perhaps. Not the hordes I've heard flood the castle on their feast days.

Among them stand half a dozen wearing red and black flowing robes, the same colors worn by the priestguard. They have bald heads and dozens of fresh, pink scars crossing their downturned faces. *Servants? No, these are the priests. The pitiable fools who have swallowed the lies of immortality and the power of a counterfeit god.* They are skeletal, and as my eye traces the raised ribbons of scar on their faces, I recall stories of how the devoted priests were recently commanded to disfigure themselves out of reverence for their leader. A Tszoi could break one of these spindly men in half with his bare hands.

A dozen thick stone columns decorate the space, each topped with a copper dish burning with too purple a flame to be natural. The acrid blue smoke rises from the columns, some settling and swirling around us. Flashes of past battles, of death, pulse in my mind. Frantic, angry thoughts flicker within me faster than I can snuff them out.

Something is not right. I am Eiklin, master of my mind, of my emotions. But ever since we stepped out here, I could feel it. *The smoke. It must be the smoke.* It pulls threads of thought in my mind, stirring up my anger, like the fjörbite leaves our warriors chew before battle. *More of the fraud's tricks.*

The Eiklin never believed in this false god. We never will. Our clans have inhabited the brutal Fahyzen Ness for centuries, beholden to none but the hundred gods atop Himmel Peak. Our elders still keep stories of the elves' founding of this golden city of Epis Kopol over four hundred seasons ago. It was once a great city. Now it rots from the inside.

Such events were long before this imposter, who calls himself the Farish, or "chosen one," took the seat of power. His devout followers claim him to be the same Far Seer Priest from centuries past, but such a claim is foolishness.

I recall his army marching on my people. I can still see the swarm approach, staring down the throat of death itself. I thought it was to be my last hour, and by the gods, how I wish it had been. We took hundreds upon hundreds of the attackers to the grave, but victory was never ours. The Tszoi fight like those possessed. Before the blood-red sun dipped into the sea, they had slaughtered most of us and captured the rest.

Svin! I spit now on the stone at the memory, earning a reflexive slap from the guard beside me, his metal gauntlet sending a stab of pain through my face and a flash of yellow light across my vision. *Add it to the bruises, you rass.*

Thudding drums break me away from my wandering memories. The small crowd starts moaning and wailing softly. Motion catches my eye.

There he is, the Butcher. The Kopolian general who slaughtered my comrades, one after another, seeking to find our commander. He would have gone on slitting throats methodically had I not finally stepped forward, identifying myself as the leader. I did it just to stop the bloodshed. I should have kept quiet.

The Butcher stopped, stared at me from behind his coward's helmet, and then ordered the execution of all fifty Eiklin prisoners. I shudder for the thousandth time at the image of my beloved Aada standing proud as they cut her down, even as I silently begged Skaldhar, the divine Bard of Miracles, for one more.

In a rage, I broke free, stealing a blade and sending two more to the grave before they stopped me. I had hoped to join my Aada in glory, but two fingers on my sword hand were all they would take from me.

The Butcher emerges from the open mouth of a castle gate, clad in glistening silver armor shimmering in the morning light, leading a pair of priestguard. Behind him follow two more Tszoi and another half dozen priestguard. The Butcher fixes me with a stare as he passes. I give him nothing.

The wails of the disciples rise to a crescendo, and drums thunder. From the back of the raised platform across the courtyard, a priest emerges through a passage followed by the Far Seer Priest himself, hunching slightly as he passes through the doorway. The god behind the golden mask. He seems to float rather than walk forward.

The Far Seer Priest stands as tall as the Tszoi but is a bony willow of a man, a stark contrast to the beefy brutes. A dark elf, some call him. One of the original Keepers embodied, say others. A cursed wretch, if you ask me. His buffed golden mask wearing the permanent scowl sparkles in the bright sun. It hides fresh scars from some wench, they say.

The drumming and wailing stop when the Farish takes his seat on the stone block atop the stage. The hollow scraping of a dozen torches burning in the wind is the only sound. A spidery bald man in a scarlet-and-maroon robe with an absurdly tall collar takes his position at the base of the stage, a few steps below the seated Far Seer Priest. *The chief priest,* I conclude.

"From history past to futures untold, may he lead," squawks the chief priest, bowing low and putting a palm to his forehead.

"Kilzhet has taken human form," dozens of voices reply in unison.

Kilzhet? King of the ice, I translate the name with amused disdain. *Now, he claims to be the Ice King incarnate? The principal and powerful evil entombed in the Wyther Downs? Is there no limit to this man's arrogance?*

"May the Farish walk. May he rule. All he knows. All he sees."

"To his favored, Kilzhet the mighty shows mercy," cries the chief priest.

"On his enemies, he breathes justice," replies the crowd.

Ha, justice! It has another name: tyranny. I roll my eyes. The Butcher snaps his gaze to me, or I think he does. It's hard to know exactly what's happening behind the black slit in his helmet. I meet the gaze.

"Before the Farish, upon this very altar, stand such enemies. Enemies who oppose his glorious seat." The priest waves an arm at the six of us. "Enemies who wish him harm, who wish him dead." A pious and offended gasp escapes the faithful. It is true. I have envisioned the death of the false god many times.

"But the Farish knows mercy, even for those who have opposed him." The chief priest turns to face us. "Even now, he offers you each a chance to repent, to give yourselves to him. Step forward to be spared the darkness."

I don't look at the other prisoners, but I can feel their fear. I can sense their resolve crumbling like a sandcastle in the tide. At least one has soiled himself already.

After a long pause, one of the wretches steps forward on unsteady legs, followed by another, a third, and finally a fourth. What a pathetic sight we are. A few beatings and bruises, and these rass have lost their very souls. They are weak, broken.

The only other prisoner who has not stepped forward is a proud-looking dark-skinned man with a barrel chest. He stands defiant. With long black hair and beard, the thick warrior with the scar running down the left side of his face and tattoos is unmistakable. He is one of the fierce warriors from the Guti tribe to the slag of the city. I have heard of these warriors. If the stories are true, then, like me, this man will never break.

The four who have succumbed to terror are led to the steps before the Farish.

"Beg for the mercy of the Farish!" demands the chief priest. I see a flicker of hope in the eyes of the captives as they exchange brief, questioning looks before the first drops to his knees at the feet of the false god. The man cries and moans and kisses the boots of his captor. The others do the same. Beaten dogs, desperate for salvation. They don't know the Far Seer Priest like I do. I shake dark thoughts from my head.

The drums begin again. The wailing of the disciples rises. Even as the repentant prisoners kneel, I see the Tszoi move up behind them. The Butcher nods, and in a flurry of struggle, Tszoi blades flash and the prisoners crumple, their throats slit. Blood pools on the shallow step before the Farish.

The Butcher looks at me again. Behind that helmet, I know he wears a sadistic grin. *If that was mercy, what waits for me?* I crush the thought as soon as it arrives.

The Tszoi mechanically drag the dead prisoners across the courtyard to a circular stone pad beside the seawall encircled by burning torches. There they drop the bodies in a messy heap.

"For the unrepentant, submission comes from sacrifice," bellows the chief priest so all can hear.

"Might we all seek sacrifice to Kilzhet," answers the crowd.

The Butcher nods again, and my captors and those holding the Guti warrior begin marching us toward the pile of freshly slain bodies.

"Not him!" cries the Farish, stabbing a bony finger at me. "I have something else for him."

I'm yanked backward. The Guti tribesman is loosely shackled to a stone column. This will not go well for him, I know. Yet, there is no fear of death in his eyes.

Servants hoist poles with thick bundles of red dried swampleaf into the fires. The flames burst from blue to purple, thick smoke billowing into the sky. The drums begin to beat softly at first, then grow to a booming crescendo. I notice the guards beside me glancing nervously at the sky. I follow the gaze, and high above, I spot them. Tiny specks appear against the blue, shapes slowly grow as they descend. No. *Impossible. They can't be.* But somehow, they are. Dragons. Priests, zealots, and guards scatter, and I'm jerked toward the castle doorway with new urgency. Even the Tszoi retreat.

My mind reels. Dragons are myth, yet as sure as I breathe, they circle above. There is no mistaking these creatures: long serpentine necks, thrashing tails, and taut batlike wings. I am startled again when they dart from the sky, for they are much closer than I first thought, and smaller. Their bodies are no bigger than oxen. One of the beasts grabs a limp body from the pile and flies off. Another pursues a fleeing priest, but the man drops to the ground, barely evading the long, groping claws.

I see the tribesman standing defiantly even as the first dragon crashes into him, claws out. Somehow, he manages to evade the beast with only a flesh wound. When it circles for a second pass, he crouches and then leaps with catlike speed. He is suddenly atop the creature, wrapping a muscled arm around the scaly neck. The warrior in me cheers at the sound of the neck snapping, but before the pair hit the ground, a second dragon strikes, and then a third.

It was a hero's death. His clan would be proud.

The feasting frenzy continues for many long minutes when the torches burn blue again, the dragons begin to fly off, some carrying bodies or parts of bodies until the sky is clear. The chief priest gingerly returns to the platform, summoning the Far Seer Priest. The dark lord creeps from the safety of his stone passage, glancing once into the sky before resuming his regal posture and striding slowly back to the stage. The circular stone pad is now solid red with blood and the remnants of the feast. Again, I am dragged before the fraud.

The Farish stands and faces me. *What will he do with me?*

As if reading my mind, he speaks: "For you, I have something... else; something special." The chief priest carefully lifts something from a large wooden box cradled by a pair of minions and drapes it around the Farish's neck. When the servants shuffle aside, I see the false god now wears an elaborate ornamental necklace. A masterfully carved lattice of gold webbing cradles something at the center, hidden beneath a black cloth.

"I have great plans," says the Farish. "Kilzhet is building armies. I need another general."

The box-toting minions move toward me. Heavy hands clamp on my arms. A guard kicks me behind my knees, and I fall, striking the stone with a painful thud.

I snort mirthlessly. "I will never serve you." I glare up in defiance. "I'd sooner offer myself to your dragons." The Farish says nothing, his golden mask unreadable as the chief priest approaches.

The priest removes something else from the box. It resembles a dull bronze helmet. I see a flicker of red stone set in the forehead. Heavy hands push my head into a bow.

"May he live," shouts the chief priest.

"May he live forever!" answer the zealots who have returned to their places and call out with a growing, hungry intensity.

As the helmet is crammed onto my my head, pain lances behind my ears and shoots across my scalp. I refuse to wince at the pain. The Farish takes an awkward half step toward me and then freezes. A wail rises from the crowd.

"He's calling the dark spirit!" someone cries.

"Come, Kilzhet! Come!" declares the chief priest in a loud, dramatic cry. The other priests now kneel, foreheads on the ground, each reaching his hands forward like madmen stretching toward a fire yet trying not to be burned. The guards at my side kneel now as well. All faces are fixed on the ground.

Simply theatrics, I tell myself. *He is no god, just a wicked tyrant.* My gaze darts around, seeking some escape. The low seawall catches my eye. Certainly a better departure from this life than whatever is coming. When the hysteria reaches a fever pitch, the drums pounding and the air thick with the acrid smoke, I prepare to run. A swift punch to the neck of the distracted guard beside me and I can sprint for the wall. Perhaps I can take one or two over the edge with me.

I tense my muscles, readying myself for the moment of action, and then... nothing. My body simply doesn't respond. Not a muscle twitches below my neck. For the first time in my life, I am not my own master. Fear screams from the back of my mind like a madman rattling a cage as I try to break from this invisible prison. It is no use; I am frozen.

I feel a trickle of something wet behind my ear. The helmet has punctured my scalp. My heart races as the wind whips through the courtyard. Even as an icy claw of terror grips me, I show nothing. I recite the Skvar war chant in my mind, something to steady me.

Before me, the Far Seer Priest seems to grow in stature as everyone else shrinks. Even the Tszoi are on bent knees, eyes to the ground. *How can these proud mountain warriors bow before a man?* The Farish's long, bony white hand reaches for the necklace and rips the black cloth away. Immediately my eyes shoot to the center of the exquisite pectoral, fixing on the long, jagged, hypnotic blue stone glowing at its center. A flicker of warning deep within urges me to look away, but I cannot. I don't want to.

Instead, everything within me, every fiber of my being, wants that stone. I want to drink it, to lose myself in the blackness of navy sky that swirls beneath its surface. My head burns like fire within the helmet, and then a chilling sensation covers me like thick, cold molasses. It starts at the crown of my head and washes down over my entire body. A sickly, dark, and sweet feeling envelops me as the blue stone before me seems to grow, filling my vision. Nothing else exists before me or around me. All that matters, all that has ever mattered, is the blue infinity of that precious gem.

Into the deep blue darkness it pulls me, carries me. I am gone for a time that cannot be measured, swept into currents of time and space that know no bounds. Within me builds a dark excitement, a hungry joy. The feeling grows until, without knowing when, I realize the sweet, dark delight has soured, rotted. All wonder vanishes, and my joy turns to suffering. A thousand points of jubilation become a million needle pricks of body and mind. The suffering is great, even for an Eiklin. The rapturous escape deep within this place with no name has turned to haunting, and I have become a prisoner, locked in the clutches of death itself. A thousand years of a thousand night-mares assail me at once.

From the prison of this pitch blackness, the Far Seer Priest walks into view, a singular figure against a sea of blackness. There is nothing here, no one but the two of us.

"I can make it stop," says the Farish, waving a hand. Imme-diately my torment ceases. "But you must join me." I am eager, no, desperate, to end the suffering. But there is more. I am flooded with dark desire: All I want is to serve him. "Kneel and kiss the ring." The Far Seer Priest's demand is at once both a soft, soulful entreaty and an irresistible command. I fall to my knees and eagerly kiss the red ring on his hand. I was once a man who knew resolve, a fierce and noble warrior. I am now a worm. The thought flickers away and is lost like smoke in the wind.

"The Concession!" booms the Farish. "Repeat it: 'I surrender my body to the Farish. I commend my soul to Kilzhet.'"

"I surrender my body to the Farish," I repeat, my voice quiv-ering like that of a child after a scolding, defiance an impossi-bility. "I commend my soul to Kilzhet." And with those words, something snaps within me. My very soul is rent as rushing darkness surrounds me, covers me.

The blackness lifts, and I am again in the world. When I emerge from the pit of darkness, part of me has died. My soul feels old and weak, ravaged for a lifetime. *What sorcery is this?*

As my vision returns, I hear a chorus of bellowing and chanting. The soft, reverent moans have grown to desperate cries. Still, every face is bowed low to the ground. The hollow eyes of the golden mask are fixed on my own.

"Welcome, brother," says the Far Seer Priest. "You are now a serpent in the palm of the Farish. My Adder."

"His soul was given to Kilzhet! His blood given to the Farish!" cries the spidery priest, now sounding far away.

"His body was given to the Farish. His soul given to Kilzhet!" the people chant.

The Far Seer Priest beckons me, and without a shred of resistance, I rise on my own and walk to the throne. I take my place beside the Far Seer Priest, my Farish.

"Now, my Adder, what shall we do with the troublesome Eiklin?" asks the Farish, waving off toward the fahyz.

"Bleed them," I reply.

1

———

NIGHT RAID

Badu crouched in the darkness, leaning against the rough oak siding of the bunkhouse, his form lost in the purple shadow cast by the chunk of pink torchstone lashed to a post. The silhouette of the patrol guard came into view, just measures from his hiding spot. The guard wiped his mouth with his sleeve, tossed something out into the grass, and turned to continue his languid pacing, pausing only momentarily to scratch himself.

This was no deadly priestguard from the grand castle of the Far Seer Priest. Instead, castoffs and thugs patrolled the manor house and its sprawling compound grounds. This sentry, a man of average build, outweighed Badu by a dozen doka, yet Badu had made his assessment: the creased and cracked leather at the back of the man's boots showed him to be someone who stepped in before they were fully untied: *lazy, hasty.* The food waste he threw landed only a couple of marqs away: *left-handed, undisciplined, not athletic.* The spear remained in the crook of the guard's off-hand as he turned: *unprepared, lackadaisical.* Badu could detect the faint smell of unburned ferikökü root, a

13

mild sedative when chewed but a powerful hallucinogen when dried, ground, and smoked: *numbed, bored, mildly defiant.*

Badu had seen enough. His finger touched a metal vial inside his cloak, then the soft feather-tipped throwing dart. No, this man warranted nothing so exotic. As soon as the guard turned to continue pacing, Badu rose.

He moved at a measured, almost casual pace, stepping silently behind the man. In a swift motion, he yanked a flap of fabric from a pouch on his shoulder, draping it over the guard's head as he brought his arm across the guard's neck, clamping down on the fabric and windpipe in one movement.

"Huh!" The guard's knees buckled. He jerked and clawed furiously at the shroud over his head and the arm on his throat.

Badu gripped the guard's flailing spear and leaned back, out of range of the man's thrashing head. The guard spun and lurched spastically, struggling against the unseen attacker.

The man was likely stronger than Badu, but it was no even match of strength. Surprise and naked terror fought alongside Badu. The cloth soaked in yumak oil had begun its work already. Badu released the frantic guard's windpipe just enough to permit a deep breath. Air raced into a thousand chambers in the guard's lungs along with the tranquilizing yumak vapor, entering the bloodstream nearly instantly. The struggle lasted only a few seconds before the guard's muscles slackened.

"Sleep," said Badu quietly.

He lowered the semiconscious guard to the ground. Heavy steps sounded on the bunkhouse's roof as Kafa, the muscle-bound, jovial brute with the heavy Guti tribal accent, abandoned his silent creeping for exaggerated stomping along the building's spine. Shouts rose from inside the bunkhouse, and within moments, the bedraggled and disoriented guard on sleep shift stumbled outside, sword in hand.

His eyes widened in terror when he spotted Badu crouching over his fallen comrade. His gaze flicked up to the silhouette of the oversized intruder perched above him, framed against the moonlit clouds.

"Hallo," called Kafa with a good-natured wave.

The pale guard shot a hand to the whistle hanging around his neck, but the wood never reached his lips. A third figure rose from the shadows behind the guard, clamping a gloved hand over his mouth and delicately pricking a feathered needle in the guard's neck. The guard crumpled. Faroz, the well-built katana, or second-in-command of the Nöz, laid the man on the stone ground. The three men, Faroz, Badu, and Kafa, formed attack team Kirzi.

Despite his heft, Kafa dropped like a cat from the roofline, alighting on the doorframe and then a hinge before dropping to the ground, only slightly slower than a freefall.

Badu spotted movement in the open doorway. He met the wide eyes of a middle-aged woman beside a young child, maybe five seasons old. Badu put a finger to his lips.

"We are here to help," said Kafa, flashing a broad smile.

The alarmed woman nodded stiffly. The child beheld the three assailants and fallen guards, opened his mouth to scream, and then fainted.

Objective one: free the children.

It was no secret that Gorev, the tyrannical baron who controlled the large ore mine dug into the foot of the Shizah plateau beside the town of Helmun, kept dozens of child slaves. Badu couldn't hear the stories of this monster without spitting on the ground. This night was long overdue. *Gorev deserves worse, much worse,* Badu had thought a hundred times. On night missions like this one, against a true villain, Badu bristled against the Code of the Nöz. *Justice demands this pislik's blood, doesn't it?*

After hearing the briefing, Badu would have happily delivered the death sentence, but the Code prevailed. "We do not take life. It's what makes us the Nöz." Garris Vayagür, the chief of the Nöz, had reminded Badu many times over the years since he first folded him into the group as a boy. "We are a lever for justice. The vurmak: a silent fist, not a blade." The vurmak was in Gorev's compound, clenched, ready for the strike.

Badu and Faroz streaked across the field toward Gorev's manor house. Kafa remained behind to shepherd nearly twenty child slaves and their captive caregiver through the vineyard and out the access door in the compound wall. The pair paused in a sparse grove of copner and pecan trees a stone's throw from the manor house wall to listen. Despite the late hour and the clouds that now shrouded the moon, the world looked bright, awash in an orange hue, the effect of the sightstones Badu and the other nözan had swallowed before departing on the mission. The odd effect of the kestra berry seeds was known to few.

Faroz swiped two fingers across his nose. Badu smelled it, too. Freshly disturbed earth, animal, and the unmistakable reek of carrion. A newly erected pen stood at the corner of the manor. Badu didn't recall that building on the structure map they had meticulously studied for days.

The banter earlier in the night as the six men rode to the manor now tugged at Badu's mind.

"Dugan said the baron keeps a gorgol chained up in there," Ferat, the kinder and gentler twin brother of Faroz, had said as the group sped toward the manor in the dark, each astride a giant flightless choluk bird, as the ground slipped beneath them like a rushing stream. *Impossible,* Badu had thought. Nobody he knew had ever seen a gorgol, the massive, scaly monster with a sunken head, arms as wide as a man's waist, and fists like molasses barrels that could crush a soldier in a single blow.

"I heard it was an orc," Kafa had said. Badu caught the mischievous smile on Kafa's face. *Ever the instigator,* Badu thought, grinning in the dark.

"A pile of trollbohk," Garris had exclaimed from the front of the group without looking back. "Fairy tales. Time to lock in. The manor is a cliq ahead." Garris, the resolute rock of the Nöz had earned the streaks of gray in his long black hair. He led the group well.

"There are no orcs mead of the range," Faroz had barked dismissively, refusing to be pulled into fanciful imaginings. "Besides, no man keeps an orc, or gorgol, for that matter."

"Not one who plans to live past sundown," joked Kafa. A couple bursts of nervous laughter followed.

Shaking off the memory and returning to the manor grounds, Badu tried to brush away the terrifying image of the gorgol. From scraps of stories, orcs weren't much better. Smaller, yes, but more man than beast in mind and hate, with a taste for human flesh. *Stop!* he commanded himself as his thoughts spun with images of ghouls. Sezlik merkaz: find the center. Calm and command. *The new building is probably just a pig pen,* he assured himself, glancing again at the structure.

Faroz motioned for them to move. At ten measures tall, the wall around the manor house would keep the children and beasts out, but it better served as a vantage point than a true deterrent for any real offensive. The baron's hidden vault behind the back wall of the pantry was a poorly kept secret, too. Like many in his position, Gorev overestimated his power and the loyalty his wealth could buy. Instead of months of spying, it took Garris only two weeks to find Bullah and convert her from kitchen maid to spy. She had served faithfully, but none in the party had heard from her in almost a fortnight. Garris and Faroz discussed canceling the mission due to her absence.

Faroz reached the base of the wall and crouched. Badu spotted the soft glow of a lantern and the glint of metal as a guard moved in their direction along a catwalk on the front wall. As the guard reached the near corner, he turned and lethargically began ambling away again. Badu found Faroz's eyes and made an X with his crossed arms. *Go!*

Faroz widened his stance, bracing his elbows on his knees. Badu jogged forward and leaped up, planting a foot on Faroz's back. He catapulted himself up to one of the flat teeth on the edge of the wall, landing in a crouch, his eyes roving. The meandering guard continued to plod away. Badu unclipped a coil of rope and dropped it over the edge. Fifteen counts later, he was coiling it again, Faroz by his side.

"Keep your eyes open," snapped Faroz.

Why does every word he speak to me sound like he's scolding a child? Badu took a calming breath, putting away his anger that burned against the katana. This was not the place.

Badu signaled toward the wall guard, who had nearly reached the far end of the catwalk, and then pointed to the shape of the snoring guard in the long, open courtyard below. The manor house occupied the left half of the walled interior, with the baron's living quarters atop the tower rising three stories. Faroz gave the signal and dropped lightly into the court-yard. If the pair moved quickly, there was no need to engage the wall guard.

Badu snapped the coil of rope to his belt and bent to drop from the catwalk when movement caught his eye. Atop the flat roof of the tower, where Gorev spent most summer evenings sipping fine, aged yasbandi wine and watching the sun set over the valley, four figures now struggled in short, stilted movements.

It was Team Mavi: Garris, Sevin, and Ferat, grappling with a fourth. Badu gave the dove-whistle call, pointing to the roof. Faroz looked up, annoyed, halting just a few paces from the sleeping guard. He chopped the air silently. Faroz was right, of course. The wall sentry had to be dealt with.

Without hesitation, Badu bolted down the catwalk toward

the front of the manor compound. The wooden slats creaked beneath his quickening paces; speed now prized over stealth.

"Who's there?" came the guard's alarmed cry as he peered into the darkness, torch aloft. A shout from the tower pulled his eyes away. Badu closed quickly, swinging the slender chain of the dikeni, or star thorn, as he ran. As the Code demanded, he had replaced the lethal sharpened pyramid weight at the end of the dikeni chain, with the hefty leather sphere filled with small stones called the acorn.

The distraction from the tower was all Badu needed. He launched himself into the air, cutting the corner of the catwalk. By the time the guard heard the flapping of canvas in the air and spun, it was too late. The acorn slammed him in his head as he turned. Badu landed lightly on the catwalk beside the collapsed guard. He spun the dikeni, whipping the acorn around his body and back into a tight circle, preparing to deliver a second blow, but the guard was out.

Springing to his fallen body, Badu removed a slender, spiky stalk of yumak from a bundle in his cloak pocket. He snapped the tip off the plant and carefully squeezed a streak of its gelatinous insides onto the guard's top lip. He glanced down to see Faroz doing the same to the sleeping guard.

"Knocking your opponent unconscious is not difficult." Garris's lesson echoed in Badu's head. *"But how do you ensure he won't awaken and take up arms or sound the alarm?"* Enter the yumak plant. The direct application of the yumak was not as fast or effective as processed oil, but this guard wouldn't wake until dawn.

Muffled shouts from the rooftop continued as team Mavi dangled the hefty baron over the edge of his lavish sunset patio far above the jagged rocks below.

Objective two: deliver the message to the baron.

The silhouette of the portly man flailed in distress. *I think he's getting the message.* Badu smiled.

2

EXTRACTION

Faroz and Badu moved silently into the manor and down the small, blue-tiled hallway to the kitchen. It was exactly as Bullah had described it. The false wall at the back of the pantry slid smoothly aside to reveal a set of three steps down into an opulent hideaway. A fine Ohnian woven rug covered the stone floor, and among the golden and bejeweled chalices, vases, and treasures, rested stacks upon stacks of paper trading notes from Epis Kopol, the staple currency in the Mead Kingdom.

"Do you see what I see?" asked Badu, tilting his head to a shelf in the corner, piled with glowing white stone bricks.

"Sokel! Beautiful," said Faroz over his shoulder as he swept piles of the trading notes into a shoulder bag and threw a second to Badu.

Shuffling footsteps sounded, and Badu whirled to the entrance. Sevin, the slender young scout with the fair skin and blue eyes, appeared, trailed by Ferat and Garris. *Team Mavi.* Badu released a breath.

"Excellent," said Garris. "We've no time to waste, though. There may be other guards. Collect payment and we go."

"There's a lot more here than three dokkert," said Ferat, staring at the precious stacked sokel bars like a child peering into a sweets shop. The treasure could buy a whole village.

"All of the notes and two bricks per man. Nothing more," commanded Garris.

The men quickly emptied the shelves of the paper money and slipped milky-white glowing bricks into packs and pockets, leaving a small fortune of the coveted mineral behind.

Kafa rumbled into the secret room. "The children are gone," he said, taking two bulging sacks from Sevin and pocketing two sokel bars.

Objective three: secure the wages.

"Good," said Garris, his voice firm with the edge of authority. "Out."

Each man shouldered his bag and moved in unison. They cut across the kitchen and out into the moonlight. Stiff grass crunched underfoot.

Garris made a slicing motion and raised a palm. "Fan out. Convene at the vineyard—"

"Stop! Thieves! Drop what you've taken!" came a trembling voice from the shadows beside the manor. A slender, bedraggled figure stepped out into the light—no, two figures. A gaunt, wild-eyed man with a nest of tousled hair held a knife to the neck of a bewildered child.

"You came for the children, didn't you?" The man's eyes darted about. He wore a plain linen sleeping gown. *The baron's steward,* thought Badu. "Don't want to watch one die now, do you?" The man shuffled beside the newly erected building, keeping his back to the wall.

"We've left plenty of sokel in the vault." Garris spoke in a calming tone.

"Ha! No thief leaves sokel behind," barked the man. "You killed the master!" His voice rose with the accusation.

"No," said Garris. "He's alive and well. Soiled his fine silkeen robe I'm afraid, and he's likely still whimpering in the corner, but I think you'll find the baron to have had a... change of heart."

Kafa gave a deep chuckle.

Ferat gripped a parumak, sleep chaser, and edged closer to the man. The long, flexible wooden fighting staff ended in a hardwood bulb. "None," Ferat said quietly, confirming he had no clear shot on the man.

"Stay back!" The man's eyes shot up at Ferat, and he slammed the wall of the enclosure at his back with the knife butt. The pounding echoed loudly, answered almost immediately by a deep growl and shuffling within. Badu's heart leaped. The vision of a massive, hunched gorgol sprang to mind. *Just fairy tales,* he reminded himself.

"You'll be sorry you came here!" hissed the man, groping blindly behind for the latch that secured a door to the enclosure. Something within slammed into the wall with a resounding crash and strained against the door.

"Run! You must run!" squealed the captive child, his eyes pleading. "It's Olukahz!"

"A gorgol?" Ferat blurted, his eyes wide.

"Step away from the door!" Garris ordered.

"Olukahz knows no pity," replied the man, his hand visibly shaking.

"I have a shot," said Badu, training his yeeliku, a small handheld crossbow, on the man and fingering the trigger.

"No!" ordered Garris.

"I have a shot," repeated Badu.

"Stand down, runt! That's an order," Faroz snapped, dripping with contempt.

"It's not the Code," Garris said.

"Shivv the Code!" quipped Badu, but he removed his finger from the trigger. As he did, the frail, harried man flipped the latch open.

"Back!" shouted Garris.

The slatted door on the enclosure burst open as if blasted by a ferocious squall. A black shape the size of a slender pony shot out, knocking Ferat to the ground. The servant screeched and ran, releasing the boy as he fled.

The bonehound snapped its long, narrow jaw lined with rows of gleaming teeth down at Ferat's face. Ferat jammed the parumak up into those crushing jaws. The bonehound paused, momentarily unable to close its mouth, but with a shake of its great head, it wrenched the parumak from Ferat's hands and snapped the wood in two. *No!* Badu silently screamed.

Garris whipped a boomerang at the bonehound, catching it squarely in the face. The animal staggered backward, shaking its long, shaggy neck and head. Lowering yellow eyes on Garris, it growled, crouching low. Garris removed two dagnek from his belt. He was an expert with the dense wooden fighting paddles, each as long as a man's forearm. Badu had seen Garris disable a trained guard in seconds with the dagnek, but they were never meant to kill, and certainly not a bonehound.

The beast pounced on long, springy legs, covering the ten measures with alarming speed. Garris swung the dagnek, catching the bonehound under the jaw with a crack, twisting its head aside and stalling the attack. The beast paused and then sprang forward, whipping its long, muscled neck back and slamming its skull into Garris's temple. Garris fell to the ground, unconscious. The bonehound opened its massive mouth and bellowed a choppy, guttural howl.

Badu took careful aim with the crossbow, the sound of his rushing blood deafening in his ears. Garris forbade Badu from carrying the yeeliku, or little snake, but Badu always smuggled it with him. Each of the bolts of the fatal implement was dipped in poison. In past raids, he had used it to send a rope over a branch or to create a distraction, but he had never fired it in battle. He released one calming breath and fired the yeeliku.

His aim was true, and the bolt slammed into the back of the bonehound's open maw. The animal screeched and thrashed, shaking its head wildly.

Kafa's massive frame crashed into the bonehound, tackling the beast. In a flash, three more men were upon it, punching, stabbing, and beating the monster with knives and short gozy clubs. After a flurry of flailing, snapping, and clawing, the bonehound lay still.

"Aaagh," came Garris's moan from the darkness. Badu helped their groggy leader to his feet.

"The boy?" asked Garris, rubbing a temple and surveying the dead beast.

"He's safe," answered Sevin. "Fled toward the bunkhouse."

"You almost got us killed," Faroz snapped at Badu, cuffing him on the head as he passed. Badu clenched his teeth, the swarm of curses rising within.

"Move!" ordered Garris, shaking his head and blinking slowly. "We've stayed too long."

Carefully slipping between buildings, the men silently exited the compound, untied their choluk, and gathered below the crumbled incline leading up to the Shizah Plateau.

"Look, Bizhak! They're off," said Kafa, using Badu's nickname of "the Blade." He pointed to the silent procession of a few dozen children hurrying out the access door in the compound wall. Badu spotted a small straggler running across the moonlit vineyard to join the group and nodded to himself. *They have been through the unimaginable,* thought Badu, pushing away the dark edge of his own childhood memories that crept to mind.

"Up," ordered Garris, and the men spurred their choluk ahead. The giant, flightless birds, each carrying a man atop a twin pommel saddle, began to pop up off the ground, springing from one boulder to the next as they ascended the crumbled section of cliff.

"A word," Garris called to Badu. Faroz smiled smugly as he passed. *Was that a wink? Shivv!* Badu silently cursed. *The day is coming,* he thought. With his eighteenth birthday only days away, Badu would finally be able to openly challenge Faroz in nishpat omak, the call of defiance. Badu relished the thought. In many groups, challenging a superior officer could get him expelled or even killed. The Nöz had its own rules, though.

Without a word, Garris held out his hand. Feeling like a chastized child, Badu fished out the yeeliku and handed it over. He shook his head.

"We'll discuss this further," said Garris, and with a kick, his choluk leaped up on a pile of boulders, alighting from one to another. Badu tried to ignore the burning pit in his stomach, the shame and humiliation. *This is injustice! Didn't I save them all?* Faroz's jeering face flickered in his mind. He spat on the ground and kicked his choluk forward.

THE BELLS IN THE TALL, stately tower in the center of Helmun rang, shattering the deep, still night. Azman instinctively rolled over, feeling for his wife. She was beside him.

"What is it?" she asked groggily.

"I do not know, Imiin. They never ring it at night," Azman answered, already sliding into slippers and robe, reaching for the club he kept behind the bed. Imiin was also up, moving cautiously into the entry room of their small home.

"Careful," called Azman over his shoulder, straining to reach the club that had fallen behind the bed frame. Imiin's sudden scream sent a shock through his body. Grasping the club, he raced into the front room, weapon raised. As he entered, he froze.

Imiin knelt, prostrate on the bare dirt floor, wailing loudly.

Her hands cradled the feet of a dazed child in a tattered sleeping gown. Oman, their nine-year-old son.

Azman dropped the club and raced to the boy. "Babak! Babak!" he cried, snatching the child up and twirling him. Imiin was now on her feet, groping for the lost son who had been ripped away from her by the baron's thugs eighteen months before.

In the midst of the tempest of tears and shouts, Azman suddenly thrust the boy into the arms of his mother, grabbed the club, and stormed outside. The billowing rage of a father now replaced his joy and amazement. His club would deliver judgment to the baron's contemptible thugs for the many long months of agony, consequences be damned. But the streets were empty. A thin trickle of bewildered children dispersed to the buildings they once called home. Sporadic shouts of joy from the reuniting pricked the sleepy night as the bell tower continued its melancholy song.

Azman scanned the dark town square for answers. He spotted a strange shape beside the long-dry fountain. Was it a person? A body? He approached cautiously, club raised. As he drew near, he saw the shape was not a body but three large sacks. He ripped open the nearest one, spilling its contents out on the cobblestone. Azman drew back, frozen in awe at the sight: piles upon piles of shalip, agü, and other Kopolian trading notes. In the entirety of his life, he had never seen so much money.

He tilted his head to read the note pinned to one of the bags:

A gift from the baron to the people of Helmun.

3

THE CODE

Stooping low, Badu grabbed the chain and yanked the heavy iron dart from the red circle painted on the shredded soma tree stump. He backed up four paces, resumed his wide stance, and dropped the dart. Just before the tip hit the ground, he stepped forward and jerked the thin chain. As the heavy triangular star thorn rose, it paused, weightless, beside his face. Badu snapped the line, sending the dart twirling around his torso.

The moment it thudded into his side, he whipped it back and spun it around his arm. His feet fluidly shifted pose, and the projectile was spinning again. This time, it circled behind his neck and back again. He traced a figure eight in the empty air, drew his left knee up as the line tightened around his body once more, and then surged forward, extending his hand. The line unwound, and the dart shot out as if fired from a crossbow, slamming into the center of the red target fifteen paces away.

"Impressive." Garris clapped slowly, emerging from the shadows of a copner tree into the secluded grove. "Your practice has served you well."

"The dikeni suits me, Ussa," answered Badu, dipping his head.

"Ussa? I suppose I am, for a little while more, anyway. You reach full manhood before next mooncycle, as I recall. After your gecit marking ceremony, will you call me uyesi, brother, or simply Garris, as the others do?" The older man smiled. It was true that none in camp used the formal title of teacher or master, yet Badu had preferred it over the more casual monikers. Years ago, when he first discovered that Garris's title of "uncle" reflected a deep friendship with his father rather than any blood connection, Badu stopped using that name, too.

"Your position commands respect," replied Badu, eyes still lowered.

"Your discipline serves you well. But there is freedom in this camp," said Garris.

"But, Ussa, you say freedom can be dangerous," Badu replied quickly.

"Hmm." Garris tossed his long dark hair over a strong, sloping shoulder. "Walk with me," he added, striding ahead into the soma trees without waiting for an answer.

Badu coiled the dikeni and clipped the chain to his waist. He hurried to catch up with Garris, who walked purposefully but without haste out of the colonnade, as they called the grassy patch dotted with crumbling ancient columns interspersed among the soma, copner, and oak trees.

"Is that how you saw the Code during the raid? As dangerous?" asked Garris when Badu drew up beside him. Garris walked using the tall mizrak, a spear with a massive spade-shaped blade, as a staff.

"I... The Code..." Badu floundered for words and finally dipped his head. "The mission was a success," he said without looking up.

"It was," replied Garris. "Yet you brought a forbidden item with you." He glanced sidelong.

"Yes." Badu paused. "But it saved the company," he added.

"It did," conceded Garris. "And without it, perhaps the bonehound would have done more damage."

"It could have killed someone—"

"Freedom," interrupted Garris, "courts danger. You have freedom within the Code."

"I did not break it, Ussa," objected Badu.

"No, this time you did not," replied Garris. "But what if that were no bonehound but an—"

"Orc?" Badu cut in. "The Code doesn't apply to margoul." His voice carried an edge of defiance.

"No, it does not." Garris squinted, wrinkles like cracked pottery framing his searching eyes. "But what, then, if it were just a strongman? Or a Tszoi fighting slave?"

"Then you would be glad I had the yeeliku," said Badu.

The two had reached the glade's edge where a rocky cliff wall rose fifty measures from the forest floor. Garris pushed ahead, disappearing behind a thin slab of rock. In silence, the two men ascended the narrow, hidden path that wound up the face of the rock. At its crest, the passage opened to the Ridge, the rocky promontory overlooking the sea.

The Nöz called the forest glade that housed their camp, the Skyrt. It was an oblong stretch of land, half a cliq long and a quarter of that from front to back running along the shoreline. The Skyrt was comprised of grass and woodlands sunken into the rocky cliffs rising from the sea. A tall cliff running up the Tenner Mountain Range formed the back wall of the Skyrt, and the thin Ridge separated it from the ocean, creating a hidden pocket of forest safe from prying eyes. Garris liked to say the Skyrt was the footprint left by Yuz the almighty himself as he walked among the rocky cliffs before time. Badu liked the image, but few of the nözan shared Garris's faith.

Sitting on a boulder with the butt of the mizrak planted

beside him, its wide spade-shaped blade glinting in the sun, Garris looked like a king taking his throne. Badu sat beside him.

"From here we can see it all, with such clarity," said Garris, gazing at the sweeping view before them. "Epis Kopol, in her grandeur, looks serene from here. The ocean and Scattered Isles viewed as they were intended at the inbreathing." It was true, the vista stretched for hundreds of cliqs in each direction out to sea. To the left ran the shoreline and open plains before meeting the sprawling city of Epis Kopol, with its hunched pale-yellow domes, spidery network of bridges among the splintered islands of the river delta, and glittering gold temple towers. The severe, rocky shoreline drove slag past the heart of the city where it relented, forming a crescent cove near the Fisherman's Quarter. A white, sly smile in the water marked the thin reef line protecting the cove.

"The Code is good and useful," said Badu, "but I just—"

"You just don't trust it," Garris finished the sentence.

"I..." Badu began. "There must be exceptions," he said. "What if the baron *did* keep a Tszoi warrior slave? It could have wiped out our whole party."

"Kafa was raised on skirmishes with those brutes," said Garris. "But you're right. At times, the Code demands... creativity, sacrifice even. The reverence for sentient life is a narrow path."

"Some deserve no such reverence," said Badu. Garris raised his eyebrows. "And Code or no Code, on the day I find myself before the Far Seer Priest, I'll have his blood."

Garris sighed, nodding as he looked out over the sea. "There's rumor of nishpat omak. You will challenge Faroz after your gecit? Once you've been marked?"

"Is it so obvious?" asked Badu. Garris only smiled. "Ussa, you've seen the way he torments me."

"I only wish you two could find peace."

"Perhaps we will..." Badu said, imagining the day Faroz would address him as his superior.

Garris snorted. "Conflict breeds conflict, son." He shook his head. Silence swept over the pair, and both men turned to the water. Garris suddenly pointed to the glittering waves far below.

"I see them." Badu smiled at the great pod of silver bowfish, each as long as a child, darting through the water and launching into the air from the crests of the waves. There were hundreds of them, no doubt feasting on a swarm of chit chit, the small, winged crustaceans that hatched from the sand. Yet even as the men stared, captivated, a long dark shape slid from the deeper water into the shallows.

"A buyuk's spotted them," said Badu.

The silver shapes of the bowfish, engrossed in their feeding frenzy, flashed around and above the slow shadow, oblivious to its presence. With a sudden rush of movement and an enormous splash, the water surface exploded in white as the great body of the buyuk surged out of the waves, snatching three thrashing bowfish in its massive jaws. With another great splash, the enormous monster slapped back into the waves and slunk into the deep to feast.

"Want to go for a swim?" Badu gave an exaggerated smile.

Garris chuckled. "Legend has it that larger things lurk beneath those waters."

"The moloth?" Badu snorted, rolling his eyes. Garris only smiled. Most coastlanders had heard the children's stories of the moloth, a giant ray a cliq wide that slept on the ocean floor until the day it was awoken. On that day, the tales went, it would rise, surging out of the water and into the sky, blotting out the sun. "You're starting to sound like Oster," Badu added and then quickly looked away.

"You know we have a new member joining us?" Garris asked. Badu raised his eyebrows. It had been three seasons since anyone new joined the Nöz, and that was just Salik and Täs, a pair of young brothers abandoned by the world. "A very skilled warrior, I'm told," Garris continued.

"To replace Oster?" Badu blurted the question without thinking. He saw pain dance across Garris's face. Little had been spoken of Oster since his capture in one of only two failed Nöz raids. Even now, months later, the beloved nözan with the gap-toothed smile and bellowing laughter crept into Badu's thoughts during the day and haunted his dreams at night.

"No. Who could replace Oster?" Garris replied, his eyes drifting off. A thick silence cut like a blade between them. Badu had spoken too openly. He knew Garris lived with the guilt of that failed mission, and what must have been a horrible death at the hands of the Farish. They had unsuccessfully scouted the Far Seer Priest's body dump pits for weeks in hopes of retrieving Oster's corpse for a proper sea burial but had never found anything.

"But the new recruit," Garris finally spoke up, "is aligned with us. United against the Farish."

"How did this man find us?" asked Badu, glad to move on.

"There were whispers among the web in Epis Kopol," said Garris. "I asked Shuuv, from the Saffron Crescent, to drop a careful clue to this man, Cor."

"But you've not met him?"

"Not yet," answered Garris. "Faroz, Efe, and I will meet him in Kursa in two days' time." That was, of course, the proper delegation, yet Badu felt a quiet stab of jealousy. Efe was the camp's elder, and Faroz the katana, number two. Still, Badu longed to be in the inner circle.

"It will be good to strengthen the Nöz," said Badu, his mind abandoning the envy and racing ahead with a new thought. *What might a new warrior do to the balance of power? Could this Cor unseat Faroz as katana one day?*

"As long as the group Cor joins is not fractured," Garris said as if reading Badu's mind.

"You don't want me to challenge Faroz? To issue nishpat omak?"

"These things must be weighed carefully," answered Garris. "You've become a strong fighter, but leadership is so much more than battle. We adopted nishpat omak as a last resort. To avoid bloodshed. Take Kafa. He grew up watching the much bloodier methods of the Guti."

"Yes, he's said they lose many good warriors to the infighting."

"It's why we fight to submission only. Still, Faroz is a skilled warrior and a good leader," said Garris. "If you challenge him, you must be ready to lead, not just to fight."

"I can lead," Badu replied.

"Can you? Can you put your anger aside and lead from behind?"

Badu was quiet.

"And if you challenge and lose, you know the cost."

"Yes, I know." The familiar fear stabbed him. "Servitude for a full season and a mooncycle in solitude."

"You don't need to rush into nishpat omak on the day of your marking." Garris patted Badu's leg. "Pass the gecit, then earn the trust of the men. Otherwise, you lead from weakness."

"But Faroz will make my days miserable."

"Hear my voice. If you stay your hand, I will move you from Faroz's team and I will speak directly with him. A good leader is the servant of all. Faroz must know that."

Badu nodded in reluctant acceptance. It wasn't the triumph he dreamed of, but perhaps Garris was right. Silencing Faroz would be its own victory. *Nishpat omak could wait,* he thought with a sigh.

"Besides," added Garris, "we share a common purpose."

"To defy the Far Seer Priest," answered Badu.

"Every man in the Nöz has reason to stand against the Liar. It's the common bond of the nözan. We use that contempt as fuel. Every mission we carry out disrupts and defies his crooked rule. But our refusal to live by the bloodlust that controls the Farish is as much a part of our defiance as our missions."

"But it *is* his blood I want," said Badu reflexively. "He took everything from me. He crushes the heart of the people."

Garris paused. "There's another tenet on which the Nöz was first built. Deeper than respect for life. Stronger." Badu groaned inwardly. "The Nöz owes its foundations to Yuz, the life giver himself. Maker of Color."

"I know, I know. The Nöz was once a fanatical religious sect." Badu's words carried more of an edge than he'd intended.

"Not a sect. Not a religion. A rebellion. A rebellion against the Liar and his defiling of the truth and the Color," said Garris. "And a rebellion we remain."

"But we're mercenaries now, not some shivven priesthood." He'd spoken too brashly. "Forgive me, Ussa," he said quickly, glancing up at Garris.

"No." Garris wagged a finger, ignoring the blunder. "Mercenaries fight and kill for money. We fight, yes, and we collect our fee for the group's survival, true, but there is so much more to the Nöz. We won't spill a man's blood for a shalip. Yuz creates life. Yuz should take it."

"There aren't many in this harsh world who believe that," answered Badu. "And there must be exceptions."

"The margoul are an exception," said Garris. "But when it comes to man, to foreigner, to Tszoi—that's not our decision to make."

"And what if it costs us our lives?"

"So be it."

Badu sighed in exasperation. "There is evil beyond margoul, Ussa," he said. "Evil in the hearts of men. Look at the lords of Epis Kopol. Look at the Farish. Think of Oster. Some deserve the ultimate judgment."

"I have seen many who have chosen the path of delivering that kind of judgment," replied Garris. "But like your father—"

"My father was a coward!" snapped Badu.

"A coward?" Now Garris turned to the boy.

Badu shook his head, not meeting Garris's eye. "The day you rescued me... He could have stopped it, Ussa. He could have fought. Downs, he could have fled. They might all still be alive."

"He fought... resisted in his own way," said Garris.

Badu snorted. "That's not fighting."

"He fought for the Code," Garris offered. "He helped create it, you know."

"That man was nothing but codes, and principles, and foolish faith in the invisible. Moaning and wailing in his closet as the Liar's thugs took everything he had."

Garris was quiet. He tilted his head. "You know you've never spoken to me of that day," he said finally.

"And I shouldn't have now. Forgive me, Ussa."

"You carry a bitter seed in your heart, curled like a serpent. Every day that you feed it, it grows."

"And grow it will until the Farish has breathed his last."

"And you have a plan for that, do you?" Garris rested a hand on Badu's shoulder. "A plan to kill the Kopolian deity in the fortress on the hill?" He winked.

"He's no god."

"Are there any in your world?"

"I may not share your trust in Yuz, Ussa, but I have faith in vengeance. The Liar will bleed. I don't care if he's lived for a hundred seasons or a thousand. Elf or man or spirit from across the sea, the Far Seer Priest will die, and I will kill him."

"Or die and kill your soul in the pursuit," added Garris.

"So be it."

Garris sighed. "If we're opening doors to the past, I must say, you have your mother's fight in you."

Badu looked up, brow furrowed. "Fight? What do you mean? When did she fight?"

"When did she not?" Garris chuckled. The wistful smile faded. "It was her fight that started it all."

"What?" Badu pulled back. "It was my father that brought the guards. His blind devotion to the forbidden gods."

"No," said Garris softly. "Many prayed to Yuz in those days, some openly in the streets. It's the reason the Farish gave, but not the true cause."

"Tell me!" said Badu. "I need to know."

"I was going to wait until your marking," said Garris. "But I suppose you're ready." He stood and began slowly pacing on the rock bluff.

"You've waited eleven seasons to speak of my mother?"

"Where to begin?" said Garris. "As all know, the Farish has his harem." Badu's head whipped up, and he rose. "Easy, son." Garris patted the air to calm the boy. "Your mother wasn't among the one hundred virgins kept for the Farish." Badu returned to his seat, his jaw still clenched.

"Nonetheless, her beauty was legendary. When she was invited to serve in the Lotus Temple in the slag of the city—an invitation that is never turned down, mind you— she accepted against the pleading of your father. It was a chance to improve the family's fortunes, and it saved her delicate hands from the spider claw that beset nearly all the spinners at the weaver's mill.

"For a while, fortunes did improve, certainly. The home you remember was a palace compared to the hovel you never knew. All living under your roof were happy except your father."

"She served the Liar?" Badu blurted.

"Only indirectly. The Farish rarely visited any of the seven city temples. Most who served there would never even glimpse him outside his fortress. But for reasons I cannot explain, that changed one day. The Far Seer Priest himself arrived unannounced at the Lotus Temple for the Bishmat, the washing ceremony. And there he spotted and immediately coveted your mother."

Badu dropped his head.

"With a hundred virgins at his fingertips," Garris continued, "each cloistered for a full season in preparation for him, the Farish still chose Damla, your mother."

Badu spat on the ground, mumbling.

"Two days after the Bishmat was all he would wait. The priestguard arrived at the Lotus Temple and escorted your mother out—against her fiery will, I might add."

"He took her?" Badu clenched his fists.

"None refuse the Farish," said Garris. "At least, none had until Damla." Badu looked up. "That's right. Not only did she refuse him, she also raked him across the face with a heavy pewter candlestick."

"No!" Badu exclaimed in wonder.

"Before he met your mother, the Farish wore no golden mask." Badu's eyes were wide, his mouth agape. "And so, as punishment..." Garris closed his eyes and shook his head.

"Why did they proclaim it to be my father?"

"The Farish claims to be a deity. How could he admit to being rejected and scarred by a commoner? When he learned of your father's... devotion to the forbidden ways, it was all the excuse he needed."

Badu stood slowly. He strode across the top of the rocky ledge and gazed down the sheer cliff face that terminated a hundred measures below in jagged rocks, jeering up at him like a broken-toothed smile. *Jump, pislik.* The taunting voice seemed always to be there. Just boyish impulses, he knew. *No. Revenge first,* he silently told the voice. His gaze lifted from the frothy crashing waves below to the quiet and still horizon.

"I can't believe it. She *was* a fighter," he said to no one.

"Release the hate," came Garris's voice at his back. "Live with eyes forward, up. Not looking back into your swirling, hateful past." He rested a hand on Badu's shoulder.

For a flicker of a moment, as Garris touched him, Badu thought he glimpsed something, felt something. A flash of light and hope. Could freedom truly reside within those simple words? An image flickered in his mind's eye: his father reaching for him in robes of white.

Badu shook the vision away. *Your hate gives you strength,* came the prompting. *Yes.* He clenched his teeth and turned his gaze to the slag, to the bulbous domes bubbling up from the delta into the grand city of Epis Kopol. Then he glanced past the city at the dark, looming shape of the Far Seer Priest's castle, shrouded in mist and perched like a black raptor on the cliff above the city.

"Not today, Ussa. Not today."

4

THE WRESTING

E *leven years earlier*

Shouts from the front sitting room pounded relentlessly like waves on a beach of broken rocks, tearing Badu from his pleasant dream of petting a strange, shaggy animal he had coaxed out of hiding. Before opening his eyes, he just listened. The comforting weight of his older sister Ildemala's arm draped over him, and a leg of one of the younger twins crossed his own. For as long as he could remember, he and his three siblings had slept in a "pig pile," as his mother teased. But even in this place of respite, atop the newly stuffed sleeping platform, he could feel it. Something was wrong.

Muffled cries escaped adults in the sitting room. He couldn't make out what was being said, so he searched for the meaning behind the words as his mother had taught him. From this practice of okuma, reading body language, pauses, and pitch of conversation, he could derive as much information as words conveyed, sometimes more. At seven years old, Badu had far from mastered okuma, but in this case, the meaning was clear: danger. He carefully untangled himself from his siblings and crept to the door to the living room.

"You must take them! Go now!" Roshan, the kind neighbor and lifelong family friend, urged Badu's father, Asil. The men stood in the flickering light of a freshly lit lamp, the lingering smell of a flint strike barely detectable behind the scent of burning seal blubber. Roshan, sleeping cap in hand and hair ruffled, looked to be on the brink of tears, his strained face tight with fear.

"Arrested?" Asil spoke the question slowly and calmly. Everything he did was measured. He faced Roshan, a hand resting on the man's shoulder.

"Yes! And they're coming here."

"Can you be sure? You have seen them yourself?"

"Seen them?" Roshan shook his head, his shoulders sagging. "No, but my Eseemi heard it all. She said the Farish... he was full of rage. Something Damla said or did, I'm afraid."

Asil sighed. "I see."

Badu's mother, Damla, spent the mooncycle in the Lotus Temple, the grandest of the seven temples dedicated to the Far Seer Priest in Epis Kopol. While Damla seemed to find favor with the priests, Badu knew his mother to be anything but devoted to that fraud, as she called the Farish behind closed doors.

"Thank you for your warning, Roshan," Asil said suddenly. "I know what we must do. Please take good care and embrace Eseemi for me."

Roshan closed his eyes in apparent relief as he nodded vigorously. "Very good. My sister can arrange the back room of her shop if you need quarter once you're gone."

"Quite kind," said Asil as he and Roshan each clasped the other behind the neck in a farewell embrace. "You are a true friend," he added, pulling back and meeting the man's gaze. "Istak tevin, go with light," Asil spoke the forbidden blessing.

"Hear my voice. Be careful, my friend," said Roshan, meeting Asil's eyes once more before rushing out.

"We're in danger, Papa?" Badu's voice quavered as he stepped from the shadows onto the woven carpet covering the open living space of their modest home.

"Roshan seems to think so," said his father calmly. "But we will fight!"

"We will?" Badu's eyes widened in surprise. His father was many things and highly regarded by nearly all who knew him. But a fighter?

"Yes! Come," said Asil, picking up the lamp and taking Badu's hand in his own as he swept across the sitting room.

Badu's gaze flitted up to the family sword hanging on the wall. The glinting relic with the ebony handle had been passed down through his father's family, but Badu had never seen it removed from its perch other than to be polished. Asil passed the sword without so much as a glance and walked toward the far wall. He carefully drew back a hanging tapestry, revealing a hidden room. Ducking inside, Asil pulled Badu behind him and let the tapestry fall in place. Badu's excitement fizzled. He knew this sacred spot.

"This isn't fighting," he said disappointedly, the grand images of an imagined battle dissipating.

"No, not with swords and steel," said Asil with a twinkle in his eye. "But with something much more powerful!"

The cramped room was only a few measures wide, barely long enough to hold a man lying down. A knee high wooden plank table rested on stone supports at one end of the room, spanning the narrow space. His father's worn copy of the Colorsong Scroll stretched across the table. A large, threadbare cushion sat on the ground, and incense and candles covered the tabletop. Hanging the lamp on a hook, Asil dropped to his knees on the cushion.

"Baduh'oan Chrintzu," Asil said, staring intently at the boy and using his full given name. "You must trust in Yuz. There is nothing he cannot do. His power exceeds that of a thousand armies." His father often used the shortened, familiar name for Yüzrenek, the Colorgiver, the creator of all.

Badu only nodded, his heart now racing. With that, Asil turned and dropped his face to the floor. From his prone position, he started speaking, crying out. The words slipped into song, a sad and deep note, that grew to a moan and then back to a cry. The cry turned to forbidden prayers from the scroll of Colorsong. A string of pleas and cries rose and fell like the dawn trumpeters ringing out over the sea from the Farish's castle on Bishmat celebration.

After watching his father for a moment, Badu finally lifted the lamp from its hook and slipped out of the prayer nook, pausing in the sitting room to listen. *Will there be trouble?*

His siblings were stirring, and the night had lifted by a few shades as dawn crept over the city's rooftops like a hunting cat. Looking to the sleeping room and then back to the prayer closet, where the tapestry muffled his father's cries, Badu wasn't sure what to do. Roshan was insistent, adamant even, yet his father seemed not to care at all about the supposed danger.

If Papa isn't worried, I will not worry either, he finally decided, feeling brave and a bit defiant. "Fe-al Yuz," Badu said to himself. Faith in Yuz. He made his way to the kitchen and laid a small fire to boil morning water. *What had happened with Mother?* She could be fiery; this he knew well. *"Put a sword in her hand on the wrong day and look out,"* his uncle, Garris, had once said. Badu laughed to himself at the image of his graceful and beautiful mother, Damla, with her long dark hair, swinging the huge blade that hung on the wall.

Carefully lighting a twig on the lamp, Badu touched it to

the teepee of kindling. The dry sticks sucked the flame in and soon glowed with growing heat.

"Is there tea?" Ildemala staggered into the room, her hair a nest. At thirteen, Ilde, as Badu called her, was the eldest sibling and the unquestioned leader of the home when Damla was gone. Even Papa deferred to her in many domestic matters. She would be beautiful like her mother one day but still wore some of youth's softness. She poured water into a kettle as Badu poked the fire.

"What's Papa doing?" Ilde suddenly stopped and cocked her head.

"Just his prayers," answered Badu, blowing on the embers.

"Those aren't his usual..." Her voice trailed off. Badu caught her concerned look as she strained to decipher the muted cries. Her eyes widened.

A shout burst from outside. With a great crash, the front door flew open, cracking off its top hinge. A massive guard dressed from head to toe in flat black scaled armor that seemed to suck light from the room entered, followed by three huge priestguard. They all had swords drawn. Ildemala screamed and dropped the kettle. Badu felt faint.

"Where is Asil Chrintzu!" demanded the demon in black. His helmet had only a small slit at his eyes, and the top bore the unmistakable shape of a striking viper.

A stab of terror lanced through Badu, and he froze.

"What is the commotion!" Asil called, throwing back the tapestry. When he saw the soldiers, he stopped. "I see," he uttered in a strange, resigned tone.

"Asil Chrintzu," said the black soldier in a grating voice. "You are hereby charged with insurrection, conspiracy, and betrayal of the priesthood." He spoke in monotone, sounding almost bored at the declaration. The black serpent man moved toward Asil.

"I've done nothing of the sort!" insisted Asil, raising an accusing finger at the soldier. "I demand an explanation!"

Without slowing or breaking stride, the soldier in black slammed Asil across the face with a backhanded blow, sending him sprawling. Ildemala screamed again, and Badu cried as he stood trembling helplessly. The guard ripped the tapestry from the wall and peered into the space.

"A seditionist, all right," he declared. "Take 'em outside!"

Get up! Badu silently urged his father. He looked up to the sword on the wall. *How can I reach it? How can I get it to Papa?* But even as he wondered, the guard in black hauled the disheveled Asil to his feet.

Another guard grabbed Ildemala by the hair, against her shrieking and kicking, and a third stormed into the sleeping room, returning with the six-year-old twins, Mossa and Emila. The room became a sudden blur behind Badu's tears. *Escape!* demanded a voice inside. Without thinking or questioning, he ducked low and scrabbled toward the kitchen, aiming for the side door through the pantry.

Badu jerked up as he nearly collided with the maroon-and-scarlet chainmail skirt of a towering priestguard. A steel grip clamped on his arm.

"You come with me!" barked a gruff voice, dragging Badu to his feet. Instead of leading him to the front of the house with the others, the guard pulled Badu toward the pantry.

"No! Stop!" shouted Badu, kicking, screaming, and pounding uselessly on the guard.

The guard clamped a hand over Badu's mouth and pulled him into the pantry. Once inside, the man dropped to a knee and pulled off his helmet. Badu turned to spit in his face and stopped abruptly.

"Uncle Garris!" he exclaimed.

"Quiet, boy!" scolded Garris. "You want to live, you do

exactly what I say!" His voice was harsh, almost angry. Badu had only ever heard kindness and laughter from Garris.

Badu nodded quickly, fighting back tears. Garris replaced his helmet and pulled him through the pantry and out the side door. They burst onto the cobblestone alley that ran through the Red Quarter. To the left, the alley opened into a wide street and market square. Badu looked that way, and his heart froze.

A knot of a dozen more guards, including a few of the huge Tszoi warriors from the Inner Sentry, flanked the unmistakable silhouette of the Farish's shiny black chariot. It rarely left the castle, and the Far Seer Priest himself was never seen outside the gates of his compound unless visiting a temple. Even his grand addresses, made twice a year on Byran Hanu, Feast Day, were given from the balcony of his great black castle, speaking down on his Kopolian subjects.

Badu spotted a hunched figure kneeling on the ground before the devil in black. He knew that figure: Damla, his mother. The guards threw Asil down on the pavement beside his wife and began lining up the children.

"Not that way!" Garris pulled Badu away from the city square, hugging the right side of the alley.

"But the others!" cried Badu.

"It's all I can do. Keep your eyes forward, son!" Garris ordered. Badu's head spun, and splotches of gold danced across his vision. The ground tilted and lurched. "Almost there," said Garris, his voice tense. Garris glanced back down the alley again and rushed across its cracked, bleached cobblestones, pulling Badu toward the dark passage between two buildings on the far side.

Disobeying Garris, Badu looked back down the alley once more. In the morning's first light, he glimpsed the silhouetted shape of the soldier in black as the demon raised a large blade over his mother's head and swung down. A strong tug pulled Badu from the alley into the dark.

5

———

NISHPAT OMAK

Badu stabbed the twisted fingers of the long oak pole into the vat of boiling water and fished out a plump thwicket. He plunged the game bird into the cold tub and, after seven counts, removed the bird by its long neck and began plucking its purple and blue feathers. Some of the nözan complained about their rotations in the meal hut, but Badu found the repetitive and menial tasks of food preparation relaxing. He let his mind wander as his hands worked. Today, like many days, he dreamed of an encounter with the Far Seer Priest.

His fantasies always took him inside the Farish's massive black castle, though his knowledge of the place was built on scraps of rumor from the occasional merchant and overheard conversations. Situated toward the back of the castle grounds, against the seawall, was the Altar, as it was called. Every Kopolian knew of this place. For each mooncycle, smoke rose from the Altar, drawing dragons from the mountains. A ritual of some sort. Some said the Far Seer Priest sacrificed prisoners to the dragons, and others claimed he drank human blood himself to gain immortality.

"Not real dragons," Heffel, the ex-castle guard, had said in a recent debate with Kafa. "Just those skittish, harmless drakes that buzz around the top of the Tenner Range." All in camp had spotted the elusive shapes in the wild, flitting in silhouette up in the mountains. When fully grown, however, the drakes reached only the size of a large cow; these were not great dragons from legends. They never ventured near any human civilization except at the castle.

"If they're harmless, why so many stories of them ripping the Farish's prisoners apart on the Altar?" objected Kafa. "We've seen them above his castle when the smoke turns purple."

The Altar was where Badu and the Farish faced off in today's imagining. *Sun glints off the Farish's golden mask, the proclaimed deity stands two measures over Badu, his thin, skeletal frame resembling a man stretched in the dungeon racks for years. Long, bony fingers grasp the handle of his infamous scythe, its red blade glowing while purple smoke billows behind him. Badu stands unwavering, jaw clenched, dikeni in hand, ignoring the swarm of dragons circling above. Decades of hate have solidified and sharpened this moment into piercing resolve.*

"I've waited for you," croaks the Farish.

"Not as long as I," quips Badu. The fantasies always carried some amount of banter. Badu would try a new line, dramatically revealing his identity as the son of Tanrila Kisi, marker of the god, the priestess who left the Farish scarred and masked. Sometimes, Badu would reveal his vivid memory of the day the Farish slaughtered his family. Today, though, the dialogue was cut short. *The Farish is agitated. He wants blood. Badu is happy to oblige.*

When twenty birds had been plucked, cleaned, and skewered, Badu rubbed them with oil and spices, and delivered them to Eldiven, the poet who leaned on a crutch while tending the roaring fire. Eldiven still recovered from a snapped ankle a mooncycle ago. He and Efe, the camp's elder, were now permanently stationed in the meal hut preparing food. If either objected, it didn't show.

Like most of the structures in camp, the cooking fire was situated on the nost edge of the Skyrt, built into the cliff wall furthest inland. An ancient shaft cut into the cliff face carried smoke up and away from the Skyrt to avoid drawing unwanted attention.

There were theories about the Skyrt's origin, but nobody knew who originally built the simple structures that now comprised the Nöz camp. The crumbling columns in the colonnade, located almost exactly in its oblong center, seemed to have once marked a sacred space, evidenced by worn ceremonial stone basins and a raised platform. Stone paths, most covered by grasses, roots, and brush, fanned out from the colonnade in every direction like spokes from a wagon wheel or rays from the sun.

Most of the nözan ignored the paths, roaming the Skyrt as they pleased, but not Sevin. He rarely stepped off the worn stone paths in the center of the Skyrt if he could help it. Whether it was out of reverence, superstition, or something else, Badu couldn't recall. Kafa delighted in shoving Sevin off the narrow walkways whenever he could.

The slender Midlander paid more heed to the unseen than most in camp. Sevin's mother, a servant of the Far Seer Priest captured in the kirmak, had the gift of niz göru, or night sight. She saw clear pictures of the future in her dreams. Sevin had ignored his own night visions for many years, but eventually, the inescapable link between dream and reality couldn't be dismissed.

"Twenty?" said Eldiven in feigned surprise. "Twenty thwick, a lot for a yeeli, yet they should make a very good meal-y," he sang the impromptu song.

"That's your worst one yet!" Badu smiled and rolled his eyes, ignoring the playful taunt. The title yeeli, meaning "boy" or "young one," served as a constant reminder of Badu's impending gecit, the marking ceremony that would usher him into manhood. While the prospect of advancing filled him with a sense of pride and excitement, it also carried a prick of dread. Kafa liked to remind Badu of how tame the gecit was compared to the manhood ceremony of the Guti tribe.

As a boy, Kafa had to navigate the fifty cliqs from the coast back to his native village with nothing but a bone knife, and if he didn't return with the carcass of a leopard, it would be for naught. Kafa's success was met with a "marking" of his own. A thin scar running from his forehead down his cheek to his jaw split the intricate tattoo on his face. *"To symbolize the river between life and Awan, the afterlife,"* Kafa had told him.

The Nöz gecit borrowed from many traditions, including an ancient Kopolian manhood ceremony. Gathered around a bonfire, Badu would recite the pledge and deliver a life sacrifice to the fire—typically a rodent or game bird killed earlier that day—then each member of the Nöz would deliver an open-handed strike on the face, beating childhood foolishness from him. Most would deliver a symbolic blow short of a full swing. Faroz's strike would be a different story. He had promised as much.

Only then would Garris brand Badu's dominant arm with the crossed symbol and welcome him to walk through the hol a uyesi, or hall of brothers, the tunnel created by two rows of initiated nözan, each holding a fist aloft, touching that of the man across from him. The brothers Salik and Täs, the two boys in camp younger than Badu, would not participate but would undoubtedly be among the most attentive observers of the ceremony. Täs had four seasons until his own marking, but Salik was only two seasons off.

When he had passed through the hol a uyesi, Badu would join the Nöz fully, not as a yeeli, but as a man, a marked. He would be permitted to grow his hair long like the others and would truly be one of them. It was only as a marked, as a full nözan, that he could issue the nishpat omak.

"Yeeli, the pine nuts!" shouted Efe, tending to a boiling pot of his own. Badu jerked, leaving his daydreaming to return to the smoking pan of grains and nuts. He jumped up and stirred the mixture. "The men hate them burned," added Efe, the group's elder and the last sitting chief before Garris took over. Efe now held the venerated role of akili olan, thinking one, not a position of power, but of influence. Now boasting a head of white flowing hair, he had long since stopped going on missions yet remained a rock of experience and wisdom among the men.

"Right," said Badu. "Thank you, Efe. You've saved us from a fate worse than death: burned nuts." He smiled playfully at the elder.

"You need to keep your head where your feet are, yeeli," said Efe, his tone unamused as he returned to the boiling broth. "Yuz wakes each dawn without your advice." Badu's father used to recite the same Kopolian proverb long ago. Shame needled Badu with the rebuke from the camp's venerated akili olan. He batted the feeling away.

The evening was warm, and the men lounged under the fading light, well-fed and contented to listen to Sevin play the stringed skimalt as Finnur, the only other light-skinned Midlander in camp, sang a tune from another time and place. On a clearer night, they might hike up to the Ridge to watch the sunset over the sea, but thick clouds had moved in, ushered along by a building warm breeze.

"You fought a bonehound?" blurted Täs eagerly as soon as the song had ended. His brother, Salik, rolled his eyes at the tactless outburst.

"Bizhak shot the herfing thing down the throat," said Kafa, wiping goat milk from his mouth. Badu knew Garris didn't approve of Kafa's nickname for him, *the blade*. Blades were implements of death.

"Badu broke Code," snapped Faroz, fixing Badu with a glare.

"It has been addressed," Garris cut in.

"And then what happened?" asked Täs eagerly.

"Kafa happened!" declared Salik triumphantly. "He tackled it!" Having not been in attendance, the boy could only parrot the story he had heard earlier in the day.

"Your memory is amazing, yeeli," teased Badu. Salik shot a playful glare back at Badu.

"That beast took us all by surprise," said Garris. "The enclosure was newly constructed, a new defense."

"I fear Gorev discovered our spy Bullah," Faroz said. A heavy silence swept across the group, a closing memory for the courageous kitchen maid.

"Lot of good it did the fezzi," Ferat said finally, breaking the quiet. "You should have seen the face of that rass when Garris hung him over the rocks." Laughter spread around the fire. "Offered us a dozen children each, the pislik." As if on cue, the men all spit into the fire in unison.

"Surprised you could hold him up," Kafa rumbled. More laughter.

"Old man strength." Garris winked. Efe laughed.

"The mission was spoiled," Faroz said, staring at Badu. The laughter died.

The familiar angry wave rose within Badu. "And what did you do?" he demanded. *You should stop,* a voice inside urged, but fire now coursed through his veins. "You can whine about the Code, but I saved your herfing life."

"Badu!" Garris snapped. Badu knew his disrespect for rank would earn him some sharp words later or worse.

"You don't *think*, yeeli!" snarled Faroz. "You're just a boy playing with fire. And one day, you'll get us all killed." Badu jumped to his feet, and Faroz did, as well. Despite the five seasons that separated them in age, Badu was as tall as Faroz and stared at him eye to eye.

"Quit!" shouted Garris.

"Yes, quit, yeeli," said Faroz, pushing Badu backward. The shove wasn't hard, but Badu's foot caught one of the logs jutting from the firepit, and he fell to the dirt. A few men called out objections. Faroz wore a look of surprise.

Bubbling rage exploded inside Badu. In a flash, he was back on his feet. He lunged at Faroz, swinging for his face. Faroz blocked the attack with a deft swipe, but Badu's other hand shot out, releasing a fistful of ash and dirt.

"Aaagh!" cried Faroz, coughing and pawing at his eyes. Abandoning reason, Badu braced his legs and shot both palms into Faroz's chest. Teke, ramstrike. The blow knocked Faroz backward. He stumbled and would have fallen if Kafa and Heffel hadn't caught him. Badu could feel the eyes of the men on him.

"You!" seethed Faroz, hate burning in his red eyes and the veins in his neck bulging.

He lunged, but Kafa and Heffel held him back. Badu stood like an oak, fists clenched at his sides, chest heaving.

"That is enough!" roared Garris, pounding the butt of his mizrak on the stone.

Thunder rumbled from the darkening sky above. Silence swallowed the group, the crackling fire the only sound.

"I will not stand by as you two—"

"Nishpat omak," growled Faroz, interrupting Garris. Someone gasped.

"What?" asked Badu.

"I call for nishpat omak," said Faroz loudly.

"But he's not marked," said Ferat.

"The pislik can't call it, but nothing in the Code stops me."

Badu's mind whirred. *What? He's challenging* me? *It doesn't makes sense. I have no rank.*

"But he's not ready," objected Garris. "And if he loses..." His voice trailed off.

"If he loses, he'll be disgraced," answered Ferat, a tone of defeat beneath the words. "Yeeli for another two seasons."

"So, he can't complete the gecit?" asked Salik, wide-eyed. "He won't be marked?" The group fell silent again.

Garris suddenly brightened. "But he doesn't need to accept the challenge—"

"I accept," Badu cut in, eyes still leveled on Faroz. All voices sounded far away, echoes behind the blood pumping in his ears. Rage owned him.

"Son, we spoke of this!" Garris snapped. "You have nothing to gain. You can't take the katana seat before you're marked."

"I accept," Badu repeated.

"The sun rises, it shines, it sets. So, it is. So it must be," spoke Efe. Garris looked to Efe and then back to Badu, a silent plea in his eyes, but there was nothing he could do.

Nishpat omak: challenge issued, accepted, and sealed with a proverb.

The rumbling sky above belched again as the storm swept in, pushing a sheet of icy rain.

6

———

THE CAPTIVE

Dawn came fast and hard, ripping Badu from a conversation with his father in a lush, sun-drenched garden, awash in brilliant colors and sweet, earthy aromas. He had dreamed it before, and it always left him with a lingering wash of joy and peace. Badu hated the feeling. He hated the lie. As he rose to consciousness, he reached for the jagged truth, the black rock that anchored his thoughts and mind: his father's betrayal. There it was. Cowardice cloaked in blind faith. Badu breathed deeply, sweeping away the foolish serenity and settling on anger. He felt grounded again.

"Awake?" asked Salik in too-eager a voice. He stood with Täs in the opening of the yeeli tent. Each of the nözan had his own quarters, a small canvas tent that held a straw sleeping mat covered in furs, and a trunk for personal effects. The ivory tents, arranged like teeth along the wall of the cave, each aligned with one of the many ancient depressions scooped out of the cliff face, creating the semblance of a room within the enclosures. Badu, Salik, and Täs shared a larger tent arranged off to the side.

The barracks had a spot for a small fire for the winter

months, and a large canvas tarp jutted out from the cliff wall, extending the living spaces and providing shelter from the sun and heavy rains that blew in from the sea. The canopies, painted to match the surroundings, helped to obscure the camp from the rare intrepid interloper on the clifftops above and could collapse in a matter of seconds, covering the entire living quarters with what appeared to be scrub brush and rock, causing the camp to disappear.

As he gathered his senses, Badu recalled what drew the boys. *Nishpat omak.*

"You hoping to be the next man marked?" asked Badu sleepily as he stretched and rose from his mat.

Salik laughed self-consciously, his tanned cheeks growing red. "No, Badu, we're here to help." Täs looked up at his brother with a question in his eyes that told Badu all he needed to know. Of course, Salik wouldn't be able to ignore the possibility.

"You may yet pass me, Salik, but you'll have to wait until after breakfast to find out."

Another awkward bark of a laugh from Salik. "We brought you nightbalm," he offered. The compound, made from seal blubber, fragrant herbs, and a few drops of yumak, soothed sore muscles and readied the mind. Badu sat permitting Täs to massage the salve into his knotted shoulder muscles. Salik and Täs owed Badu no such servitude, but the three yeeli shared an unspoken bond as the only unmarked in camp.

"Will it be the dikeni for you?" asked Salik.

"Yes. That and a pair of dagnek, I think," replied Badu. The casual reply belied the hours he had lain awake carefully considering the question and imagining a million permutations of the contest.

The dagnek were a good choice. At a distance, the dikeni would give him the upper hand, as its reach was longer than any staff or baton, however, in close combat, he would need the fighting paddles. Each paddle was just over a measure in length, with straight shafts rising from the handle and one rounded edge, resembling a wooden sail or half a leaf torn down the center.

In the contest, they would, of course, use sparring tools: padded dagnek, and they would replace the hard acorn at the end of the dikeni with a softer, leather ball. The nözan took nishpat omak seriously, but damage to one's honor would be the extent of the permanent injuries.

"Careful with those," said Badu. Täs had removed Badu's dagnek from their stand and twirled and chopped the air, lost in his own world.

"You couldn't beat a one-legged thwick with those things," teased Salik.

"Could too!" Täs shot back, swinging wildly at Salik's torso.

"Easy," barked Badu, but Salik effortlessly dodged his younger brother's clumsy assault.

"What if you lose?" Täs panted, relinquishing the paddles to Badu.

"If I lose, I lose," answered Badu.

Badu knew he trained harder than any in the Nöz. None could match him with the dikeni, certainly. Faroz would choose another sparring weapon, likely a spear.

When Badu used to imagine calling nishpat omak, he thought even landing a single blow on Faroz would be worth it. Just standing across from Faroz in battle as a marked equal would bring a measure of justice. If he lost, the penalty would be tolerable. Now, though, everything had changed.

"But if you lose, you can't be marked," said Täs. Salik looked away. The unspoken thundered in the small space.

"Well, then, your brother will have to be the next to face the gecit testing." Badu offered a smile but quickly flushed the thought from his mind.

If he was defeated, then for two excruciating seasons he

wouldn't be permitted to grow his hair long or sit with the men in the ring at firecall. It would be a bitter bile to swallow, being passed over by Salik, one of the "littles" as the nözan called the brothers, while Badu was forced to follow Faroz like a shadow, serving his every whim for two seasons, would be a bitter bile. Faroz would ensure it was unbearable.

Is there still time to back out? No! That would be worse. *And what if?* The thought pricked. *What if I actually win?* Beyond just glorious retribution, victory would mean Badu would take the seat of katana as soon as he was marked, second only to Garris. Faroz had shocked the Nöz two seasons earlier by invoking nishpat omak, at the time a nearly forgotten section of the Code, challenging Heffel and winning the seat of katana. Badu could still feel the hot envy that burned in him, watching Faroz land the decisive blow, toppling the stolid and respected Heffel.

Badu gathered his things and slipped through the back of camp, avoiding the growing knot of men at the morning breakfast gathering, though the aroma of fried cheese and fresh bread made his stomach rumble. He continued to the colonnade. Separated from camp, the sparse section of woods was quiet, interrupted only by the occasional birdcall. The night's rain had cleared, leaving the clearing fresh and bright under the diffuse morning light. A soft ocean breeze rolled over the Ridge, fluttering the papery leaves atop the trees and ferrying in the spiced aroma of soma wood and sea salt.

Badu tucked the pair of dagnek in his belt and slowly unwound the dikeni chain. He closed his eyes and breathed deeply, commencing his regular morning ritual. Slowly he practiced his steps as the clinking dikeni tipped with the acorn, began a lazy arc around his body. Faroz's face sprang to his mind, wearing the jeering expression that now seemed permanently affixed.

Slow, practiced movements grew faster until Badu whirled

in the glen, following his mastered routine. With a lunge, the acorn shot out of his hand and thudded into a knot on a copner tree. The full force of the acorn could crush a man's skull. *What will the training ball do if I land a shot?* he wondered. In nishpat omak, points were awarded for any strikes landed, so participants often softened their blows. Badu had no such intention. The stakes were high, and he'd receive no mercy from Faroz.

Badu wrapped the acorn around a low branch, simulating a snag or opponent's catch. Abandoning the dikeni, he dropped the chain and rolled to the side, pulling the two dagnek paddles as he did. Crouching in a defensive position, he paused, eyes on the copner tree that now wore Faroz's face. Then he sprang, delivering a six-strike attack with the fighting paddles—ear, rib, knee, knee, sternum, jaw—and dropped back to a crouch. Faroz was faster than Badu with the paddles, but if he could land just two successful strikes with the dikeni, then he would need only one final, victorious blow with the dagnek.

"Badu! Badu!" Täs's unmistakable, prepubescent voice pierced the glen and shattered the imaginary battle raging in his mind's eye.

"What is it?" Badu stood to recover the dikeni but noticed the frantic look on the boy's face.

"It's the... We must go—" A loud, clear horn blast came from camp.

Strange. Why not strike the gathering gong for nishpat omak? wondered Badu. "I know, I know," he said, sighing. "I'm coming."

"No... Not the contest. It's something else. There's trouble!"

Badu frowned, coiling the dikeni as he trailed Täs back to camp. The entire group gathered by the cold firepit. Maroon battle paint streaked across Faroz's face.

"... we learned of this urgent matter," Garris addressed the seated nözan.

"What is it?" Badu cut in as he drew near.

"The recruit," answered Garris. "We were to meet him at a tavern in Kursa at midday. But there's been some sort of attack."

"An attack?" asked Badu. "On the recruit?"

"An ambush from the sound of it," replied Garris. "Tin-men," he added, using the nickname for the priestguard soldiers.

"Shivv!" swore Ferat. "Does he know the camp's location?"

"No, not our location. This was to be our first meeting," said Garris. "But he'll know more about the Nöz than we'd want to share."

"How did the Farish learn of this meeting?" demanded Faroz.

"Might be the Adder," said Heffel. "The Liar's lapdog has been searching for us for seasons now."

"We don't know," replied Garris, "but Tilmer, the stable keeper, rode hard from Kursa with the news. He said the priest-guard plans to execute the recruit after extracting whatever information they can."

"Shivv!" cursed Ferat again.

"We've got to stop it," said Finnur, standing, his frame tall and slender.

"We can give 'em a nözan welcome." Kafa grinned widely and lifted a tall spear.

"But are we marching into a trap?" asked Faroz.

"Cor, the recruit, doesn't know the camp's location, but who knows what else Shuuv might have told him," said Garris. "I don't see that we have a choice."

"How many are there?" asked Sevin.

"Tilmer counted five soldiers."

"Five?" scoffed Kafa. "Send Täs alone." Someone chuckled.

"It does seem light," replied Garris. "I've asked for more information. Tilmer will meet us at the grain mill outside Kursa."

"What about the nishpat omak?" asked Täs, earning a slap on the head from his brother.

"It must wait," declared Garris, looking up at Badu and then at Faroz. "I need you both riding with me as one."

Something inside Badu relaxed, but Faroz only scowled and shook his head, smoldering eyes fixed on Badu. *It will pass,* thought Badu, already thinking of Kursa. Like most of the nözan, he relished above all else the chance to fight priestguard soldiers.

"No visions?" asked Finnur, nodding in Sevin's direction. "No dreams?" Finnur was among the few in camp who considered Sevin's night visions truly prophetic.

"I..." Sevin looked up out of the corner of his eye. "No, I don't think so. More of the same – a jumble of blurry night terrors I've had for weeks."

Faroz batted the air dismissively.

"So be it," said Garris. "Forward team, depart in a quarter hour." A collective grunt answered as the men dispersed. The forward team included every member of the Nöz other than the littles, the frail Efe, and the hobbled Eldiven.

"You're lucky, yeeli," came a voice at Badu's back. He spun to face Faroz's boiling eyes.

"I guess you put on your makeup for nothing," said Badu. Faroz lunged forward, raising a hand as if to strike. Badu didn't flinch. *He won't, not here,* Badu guessed. Sure enough, Faroz stopped his hand a measure from Badu's face.

"Saddle up!" Garris barked at them.

"Your time will come, yeeli," hissed Faroz.

"Or yours will." Faroz spun and stormed off. Badu's heart thundered.

"What a whiny rass," said Täs. Salik burst out laughing and covered his mouth at the insult. Faroz glared back over his shoulder.

"Tish!" Badu scolded the boy. "You don't speak that way of

the katana!" Täs looked down, cheeks flushing, and Salik fought against his giggling. "Whatever else he is, he's your superior."

"Why does he hate you so?" asked Salik. "He's the one acting like a yeeli."

"That's for me, Salik. You may be his direct soon, so you'd do well to keep those thoughts to yourself," Badu replied. "Go! Saddle the choluk." The pair scurried off.

Once gathered and astride the choluk birds, the forward team departed through the tunnel that ran under a cliff at the far edge of the Skyrt. They emerged out into the meadland plains through an opening obscured by overgrown vines and strategically arranged scrub brush. Rolling waves of sea oats and tall grasses stretched from the foot of the Tenner Range that housed the Skyrt all the way to Epis Kopol, fifty cliqs to the slag. The group rode inland, skirting the base of the Tenner Range, around the Callis Foothills before turning fahyz toward Kursa. The animals ran swiftly in formation, and within two hours, the town's outline came into view.

Kursa was a sleepy village marked by a cluster of buildings surrounded by a smattering of farms and homes. For unknown reasons, an elaborate ancient stone temple stood at the center of the village. The temple sat empty most of the time, though the few devout followers of the Farish assembled there for holy days and festivals. From afar, Badu thought the monolith looked ridiculous. It towered over the sleepy village huts and buildings like a bejeweled priest, lifting his robe to avoid a dirty flock of chickens.

Outside of town stood a faded blue grain mill, the aged building groaning with each steady turn of the waterwheel. The group approached slowly.

"Mr. Garris!" a voice came from the shadows of the building beside the massive rotating wheel.

"You two," said Garris to Faroz and Badu. Badu frowned but followed. Faroz shook his head in disgust, as he dismounted.

"Thank you, Tilmer," Garris spoke to the frail man with the crooked back and darting, birdlike eyes, pressing something into his waiting palm. "What have you seen?"

"Still just the five guards—"

"Are you sure?" cut in Faroz.

"Yes, yes, sir." Tilmer bowed to Faroz as he spoke, glancing up askance. "Just the five. They have the prisoner in the back room of the inn. First floor, nost side."

"Excellent," said Garris.

"Is he hurt?" asked Faroz.

"That I don't know, sir," said Tilmer. "Haven't gone inside. Haven't gone close. But the sooner those fezzi are gone, the better." Tilmer spat on the ground, then looked up with sudden concern.

"Very good, Tilmer." Garris placed a hand on his shoulder. "You've done well." Tilmer nodded, blinking and smiling expectantly. With a roll of his eyes, Garris fished out another coin.

"Very generous, sir. Very good." Tilmer nodded and bowed as he backed into the shadows and then was gone.

"Five guards?" asked Faroz. "To ambush the Nöz?"

"Perhaps they underestimate us?" offered Badu.

"The priestguard are as arrogant as they are hateful," agreed Garris. "Perhaps they believe us to be common brigands. They rarely encounter any resistance of any sort in Epis Kopol."

"Still, it seems a... miscalculation." Faroz shook his head.

"They will learn," said Badu to no one in particular.

~

A SLENDER MIDLANDER in a long blue riding coat holding a walking staff stepped from the dusty road and entered the only inn in the town of Kursa, pausing on the threshold to adjust his eyes to the dim light. The door closed behind Finnur.

"Five counts, and we move!" came Garris's call from his hiding spot beside the inn's long front porch. Badu crouched at the side of the building beside a group of stately black horses draped in the priestguard colors that now grazed freely behind the inn, their reins cut. Kafa hunched beneath a window, holding the end of a cord lashed to the latch of the closed shutters.

Two, three, four... Crash! Shouts erupted from within. *Here we go!* Badu nodded to Kafa, who jerked down hard on the cord, ripping the shutters from their hinges. The crash scattered the startled horses. Badu darted forward and leaped off Kafa's back, swinging into the room and landing in a crouch.

Before him, two priestguard soldiers faced off against Faroz and Finnur in the doorway, their backs turned. A third lay on the ground. Another guard stood with his sword drawn, backed into the corner to Badu's left behind a hooded figure sitting tied to a chair. The guards facing the door spun at the crash and sudden blast of sunlight. As Badu reached for his dagnek, Faroz and Finnur pounced on the distracted guards from behind.

The attack ended swiftly, and the two guards slumped to the floor, unconscious. Badu spotted the body of the fifth man on the ground outside the door.

"Stop! Stop or I'll do it!" the last standing priestguard screeched in a shaky voice, holding a sword to the neck of the captive. "Stay back!"

"Wait. Friend," said Badu, holding up his hands, "you've misunderstood." Someone grunted, and the guard looked up. "I have papers from the Farish," said Badu in a calming voice.

"What? What papers?" demanded the guard. His eyes darted around the room. "You've killed them!" His voice cracked. Badu flinched at the soldier's broken decorum, betraying unusual weakness.

"We haven't killed anyone," said Badu, still calm. "Look, I'll show you the order straight from the Farish." He slowly reached into his sleeve. With a snap of his wrist, the dart shot through the air and stuck the guard in the throat. Shock plastered the man's face as he jerked a shaking hand up to the feathered end of the needle protruding from his neck.

"Not paperssss—" The young man crumpled.

"What?!" groaned Kafa indignantly as he squeezed through the window and thudded to the floor. "None left?"

"Sorry, friend," said Badu. "They fell like skupp."

"Too quickly," snapped Faroz.

"Next time, I come in first, Bizhak," growled Kafa. Badu patted him on the back. Finnur cut the ropes binding the captive.

"Cor," said Garris in a slow, clear voice, moving to the prisoner. He untied the hood from the captive's head and lifted it off. "You're safe. We are the—" He jumped back. The men gasped.

The prisoner lifted her head, rust-colored hair falling to her shoulders. Bright hazel-green eyes blazed defiantly.

"Who are you?" asked Garris.

"I'm who you came for," said the woman, rising and rubbing her wrists.

"No, I'm afraid we came for... someone else. A man named Cor."

"You can't fault Shuuv," she answered, looking over the group. "The tavern owner didn't know. I prefer it that way."

"We came for a recruit, not someone's mistress," Faroz groaned.

Cor shot a hard glance at him. "Hey, fezzi, catch," she called, tossing something at Faroz. Even as he reached to catch the bundle, the woman slid to the floor and spun, sweeping Faroz's legs. As he fell backward, she brought a leg down over his torso in a fluid motion, slamming him hard to the ground and pinning his arms. She leaned an elbow on his head and whipped the dagnek from his belt, pushing it down on his windpipe.

Badu watched in awe.

"I *am* Cor. Corvina. And I'm nobody's mistress," she hissed before Kafa brought his fist down on her head, knocking her out cold.

7

FOLDED IN

F*our years earlier*

BADU SAT on his hands to silence their irrepressible fidgeting. He must not let Garris see the nerves that crackled through him like an approaching summer storm over the ocean. Never before had his uncle asked him to join a mission, never before had he been brought along with the men.

"So, you understand the plan?" asked Garris, who sat beside him on the coachman's bench of the wagon, guiding it expertly down the pocked dirt road.

"Yes, Ussa," replied Badu. "When the men—when you all, I mean—get out, I take the wagon past the mill, turn to the slag, and double back to the feeding troughs behind the fairgrounds." He had practiced the line a hundred times in his head.

"Good," replied Garris, stealing a look at the boy from the corner of his eye. "And if anyone stops you?"

"Oh, yes," stammered Badu. "I tell them that I'm bringing

supplies for Odenji Kumkalla, and I show them the crates in the back."

"And..."

"And if they appear to escalate," Badu continued, "I give them the bundle of agü notes in the felt bag."

"Excellent." Garris smiled and Badu breathed deeply. "You'll make an excellent nözan one day."

"If he's not captured by the tinmen and made to dance for the Farish first," came a voice from behind them through a dark opening under the canvas tarp stretched across the back of the wagon.

"Oster, do not give the boy more to worry about than the task at hand." A series of chuckles rose from the dark void but no more taunting. Badu tried to remind himself that the six men under the tarp were friends, allies. But he knew they were dangerous, too. He had seen them spar, heard the stories of their raids. At fourteen seasons old, Badu often found himself staring in wordless wonder at the towering, fearsome warriors he called family as they trained or fought or even strode through camp.

"There in three," called Garris to the back. "Checkpoint approaching. Two tinmen." The group had stopped a few cliqs up the road to cover the wagon, and all but Garris and Badu had squeezed under the tarp. The soft, muffled chatter of the men under the tarp that had been constant background noise now stopped. Badu's stomach twisted at the sight of the pair of priestguard soldiers standing beside the dusty road at the checkpoint ahead. The large soldiers in the polished armor would kill him without hesitation if they knew who he was. Beyond the checkpoint, the road wound down into the low-slung valley town of Baszhär. The town was nestled between the blue hills, known for their abundant crop of pike melon and ground corn that grew to amazing sizes here beneath a waist-high carpet of sapphire brillflowers. From here, the valley below looked like a painting.

"What brings you to Baszhär?" asked one of the guards as Garris pulled the wagon to a stop.

"Heard his lordship caught some of those filthy savages," said Garris without pause, adding an accent Badu had never heard before. "Want my boy here to see the power of the Farish's justice."

"Ya see," said the closest guard to the other—tinmen, as the Nöz called them. "This is the kind of Kopolian we need. Good for you, Baba," said the guard, looking back at Garris, his gaze drifting casually to the wagon behind. "You teach him well. What's in the wagon?"

"Couple tubs of squash from the garden, but mostly empty crates. Hoping to fill up with the heavy crop of ground corn I heard came in."

"Indeed."

"You listen to your old man," said the other tinman, addressing Badu, "and one day, maybe you could even join the guard! Bet you'd like to see the inside of the castle, wouldn't you?"

Badu nodded dumbly and attempted a weak smile, his whole body shaking.

"'O' course he would," answered the first tinman. "Every boy's dream."

"Not 'a them Guti savages," said Garris.

"Gah!" The guard drew an arm up. "Which is why the lord's gonna teach 'em a lesson."

"Watch 'em all lose their heads," added the other.

"Get what they deserve." Garris spat on the ground. "Noon in the middle of the sparring grounds, right?" he asked casually.

"Yes, yes. Make sure to be up a row or two in the decks to get a good view," the tinman said. Like all priestguard, their faces were hidden behind helmets, but Badu could just feel the smile. The beheadings. It was why they had come. Public execution of five Guti warriors captured in a skirmish.

"May the Farish shine for a thousand seasons," said Garris with a short bow.

"And thousands more," replied the guard in the practiced retort, waving the wagon ahead.

Behind the horse stalls, when Garris was sure no eyes were on them, he quickly drew back the canvas covering the wagon, and the men piled out. Each man wore nondescript robes and traveling garb. Immediately they began to disperse, casually walking off in different directions. Within thirty counts, it was impossible to identify them as a group, and within sixty counts, the men were gone.

Badu realized with a start that the plan was underway. The group's grace and fluidity in executing just the first step had him mesmerized. He hurried over to the driver's seat, picked up the reins, and clicked his tongue, urging the horses forward. Trying to act casual, Badu steered the wagon around the mill and turned back through the vacant buildings to the town's center. He spotted the long lines of feeding troughs in the shadow of a sagging wooden wall that marked the edge of the fairgrounds, just as Garris said.

Today there would be no fair, Badu knew. The singular attraction of the day, which appeared to have emptied the entire town of its occupants, was a show of force by the Farish. A punishment for those who dared to defy his rule. Four men and a woman were to be beheaded before the entire town and nearby residents as well. Judging by the empty homes and shops he passed and the muffled sounds of a crowd coming from the other side of the wall, the Farish's promise of a week's rations of trading notes for all who attended had produced the desired effect.

Garris had debriefed the nözan just a few days earlier.

After a group of priestguard had severely beaten a young Guti girl who had strayed too far from camp, the Guti attacked. War drums sounded in the night, and torchlight dotted the hills above Baszhär before a small band of warriors attacked the priestguard outpost near the edge of town. The Guti were fierce warriors, more than a match for a priestguard, but the entire setup was a trap. Priestguard reinforcements hid in ambush, and when the tribesmen closed in on the outpost, the trap was sprung. A dozen Guti were killed and one priestguard. Four warriors were taken captive, a woman and three men, including the Guti chief's son, a mountain of a man.

Badu tied the wagon as far as possible from the line of stately black castle horses that munched hungrily at the feeding trough. The crowd swooned on the other side of the dilapidated wooden wall. He knew he should stay with the wagon, but curiosity burned within. Badu crept to the wall and tried to peer through a gap in the wood, but all he could see was the underside of a platform and shadows of bodies.

Stepping back, he eyed the rudimentary feeding platform where an attendant would stand to drop corn down the chute to fill the feeding trough. The top of the frame of the platform rose above the wooden wall. Glancing around, he began climbing.

Badu had never seen so many people in one place outside of the city. People filled the rows upon rows of crude wooden stands, and in the center of the dusty bowl, surrounded by a sea of onlookers, was the sparring ring, a slightly raised platform that regularly hosted minor feats of strength and competition. Despite a brilliant blue sky, the scene had a dark, ominous feel. An executioner dressed in black, with a black mask, stood holding a huge axe beside a massive tribesman lashed down to a stout wooden block. Four more Guti stood off to the side of the platform, chained together and flanked by three tinmen.

Badu counted four more at the edge of the platform keeping the crowd back.

A priestguard addressed the crowd, reading from a short scroll. Badu couldn't hear him well, but he appeared to be done speaking because he closed the scroll and turned back to the executioner with a nod. The crowd let out a desultory cheer. The cheer died out as the crowd sucked in a collective breath. The executioner drew the huge axe high into the air, its curved blade glinting in the sun. Badu's stomach turned, and his hands started shaking.

With the axe flying high overhead like a war banner, the executioner suddenly froze. One hand released the axe and pawed at his neck. The heavy axe fell from his other hand, crashing on the platform, followed by the thud of the executioner's limp body. At exactly the same time, Badu caught sight of a flicker of flame from the far side of the platform as something burst into flames.

"Fire!" came a muffled cry. The confused murmur of the expectant crowd exploded into a roar as mass panic spread like a bushfire. Badu glanced back at the priestguard on stage, who had dropped the scroll and now dashed toward the bound prisoner, drawing his sword to finish the executioner's work. But even as he ran, a cloaked figure sprang from the crowd onto the platform, catching the tinman from behind. Badu recognized the way the figure, the way he moved, the strong sloped shoulders. He spotted the man's quick jab to the priestguard's neck. Garris. The priestguard spun, swinging his sword wildly, but Garris parried the blow with a dagnek fighting paddle. The poison dart did the rest. Before the guard could swing again, he staggered backward and toppled off the stage.

Badu wanted to shout a warning when he spotted three priestguards pushing through the current of panicked onlookers to reach the stage where Garris had begun to free the prisoners. His futile shout would have been lost in the din. Like phantoms from the mist, cloaked figures emerged from the crowd, each pouncing on a tinman. Before Badu's eyes, the detachment of feared and formidable priestguard soldiers was reduced to a dozen red crumpled shapes, their stately crimson capes trampled by the muddy boots of commoners.

His heart still racing, Badu quickly climbed down and untied the wagon. On cue, Garris appeared with the line of Guti prisoners as Heffel gathered the priestguard horses. The other nözan had suddenly materialized and began climbing into the wagon.

"You must go now!" Garris instructed the large Guti warrior as Finnur cut the last ropes binding the other prisoners.

The warrior spoke something in his native tongue to the other prisoners. Each in turn pressed their palms over their eyes and bowed low to Garris. Then, without a word, they began to run away toward the hills.

"Wait, the horses!" called Heffel. He, Ferat, and Faroz each held the reins of the dozen priestguard horses.

"You may take them," offered Garris.

"They do no... need," said the large man. "Run fast," he added, throwing an arm toward the freed prisoners. And indeed, the four warriors were already a hundred measures away and picking up speed as they raced for the blue hills and the dense forest beyond.

"You take a horse," offered Garris to the man. "Bring it to your father. The chief is a friend."

Of course, this man is the chief's son, thought Badu. More than the impressive physical stature, the way he carried himself betrayed his lineage.

The large man waved a hand. "No. I not leave."

"We should move!" came Eldiven's urgent call.

"Mount up. We'll take the horses. Meet at the Crescent," called Garris over his shoulder. "We need to go," he said patiently to the chief's son. "You are free."

"Kafa is no free," said the man. "Kafa is slave. You new master. Blood owing." Kafa pressed his palms to his eyes and bowed.

Garris's shoulders rose and fell with a deep sigh. "Gah. I was afraid of this," he said to nobody in particular. "Very well. We will discuss. But we leave. Into the cart." Garris motioned to the coachman's seat. Without hesitation, the huge man sprang like a cat up into the wagon. Badu staggered back a step, startled by the motion. Garris only gave him a wink and jumped up to the driver's seat, motioning for Badu to get in the back. Galloping echoed as the nözan thundered away from the town of Baszhär on the swift castle horses followed closely by the wagon.

"Think the tinman nearly wet himself when the chopper went down," roared Heffel as he lifted a tankard high, receiving clanks of a half dozen mugs.

"Well planned and well executed," added Garris.

"Any sign of Oster?" asked Finnur after taking a draw.

"Think he was caught?" asked Badu. The thought of capture was the stuff of nightmares.

"No, not Oster. He's probably out running that horse ragged chasing game," said Eldiven with a chuckle. "You know how he loves to be out in the open."

"Or chasing ladies," said Heffel.

"Fall off his horse if he caught one," said Finnur, and the group burst into laughter. Badu took his cue and laughed along with the men. In the quiet that followed, Badu's gaze drifted over to the Guti warrior. The huge and imposing man somehow looked small in the corner of the private room in the back of the Saffron Crescent. He hadn't said a word since they left Baszhär.

"Why won't he go home?" asked Finnur, the light-skinned Midlander, nodding toward the tribesman.

Again, Garris sighed. "The blood debt. We freed the other Guti prisoners from peril, but we saved his life. So, he's pledged himself as a slave."

"They were *all* going to die," objected Faroz. His brother, Ferat, nodded in unison with his twin.

"Not the way the Guti see it," said Garris.

"And what if you just say no?" asked Faroz.

Garris was shaking his head. "If I refuse to accept, he's required to finish what I interrupted."

"He'll kill himself?" asked Badu, eyes wide.

Garris nodded. "Their customs are strange." He turned to the Guti. "You are called Kafa?" The big man nodded, his wide eyes flitting around the circle of men. "I am Garris. We are called the Nöz." The man nodded quickly. "We are glad to have you with us." The tribesman smiled widely. "But you cannot be my slave."

Fear filled Kafa's eyes. "I... am slave," he grunted urgently. "Pononga." He held his wrists up in surrender.

"No," said Garris, shaking his head. "The Nöz has no slaves, only brothers. If you stay here, you will stay as a brother." The tribesman looked confused. "Garuncha," said Garris. With the last word, Kafa's eyes lit up.

"Garuncha pononga?"

Garris nodded. "Garuncha. Brother." Kafa nodded slowly, too. Garris stood. "Uyesi," he spoke loudly and raised a mug. "Meet our new brother, Kafa. We will begin his training right away," added Garris. The men joined in the toast and banged on the table. Kafa's eyes shot around the small room from man to man.

"What did I miss?" The beaded curtain to the private room flew aside as Oster burst in, his gap-toothed smile stretched wide.

"I told you he'd come," said Eldiven with a look of smug satisfaction as he leaned back with his tankard.

"Where have you been?" asked Ferat.

"Yeeli was getting worried," added Faroz with a wink at Badu. Badu blushed at the attention.

"What's he doing here?" Oster nodded at Kafa.

"Our newest recruit." Garris smiled.

"He's a mountain!" Oster exclaimed, nodded approvingly as he slid into the bench beside Ferat. "Ok," he began excitedly as he poured himself a drink. "I've got it!" The men waited in silence. "A way to kill the Farish."

"Shhh!" snapped Garris, his eyes wide. "You can't talk like that, even here." Oster dipped his head slightly toward Garris.

"Again?" teased Finnur.

"No, this is it!" continued Oster enthusiastically. "Let me tell you a story..." A collective groan came from the men. But Oster was already on his feet, tankard in hand.

"Three generations ago, an army from across the ocean— the Sea Wolves—landed on the shores of my ancestors' village of Freemal, full of death and conquest. Even back then, all knew of the brutality of the Wolves and the terror and destruction left in their wake, but this was different. A vast army had arrived." Oster swept his arm as if to summon the image of thousands of men on the shore. "Villages up and down the coast had been ravaged by the marauders, and a mention of the Sea Wolves struck fear in the hearts of the strongest."

"Wait, is this the giant stingray story again?" said Faroz. "The moloth?" Another groan from the men.

"We all know the fable you tell of your great-grandfather and how he saved the village," said Heffel, rolling his eyes. Badu had heard the story twice before, but he couldn't get enough. He hoped Oster wouldn't be deterred.

"Yes! My great-grandfather Pachra. Exactly." Oster beamed. Badu knew that look. The story would go on. "How Pachra first learned of Uzgül, the king of moloths, I do not know," Oster continued. "But what I do know, and what every one of the elders in my village will swear, is that one terrible night there was an army of death at its doorstep, hundreds of boats moored in the bay, and a thousand tents littering the beach. The people braced for death that night. But in the morning, there was…" He paused. "Nothing. No tents, no horses; even the dense stands of palms were gone."

Despite themselves, some of the men leaned a bit closer at the retelling. In a hushed voice, Oster shared how Pachra had learned the secrets of awakening and commanding the monster from an old net weaver. If the great creature was nearing the end of its century-long slumber, a spike or harpoon planted deep in the flesh behind the skull would awaken the hibernating moloth, swore Oster.

"Brightly burning stacks of yellowflare grass draw the moloth like a needlefly to a candle," said Oster dramatically, "and, if arranged in a circle, the fires can actually cause the monster to attack whatever lies within the burning ring."

"Trollbohk," coughed Finnur and the men laughed.

"Pachra—a pearl diver, you know—swam to the depths, hour after long moonless hour, harpoon in hand, coming up only for air," said Oster. "Some would have given up, but not Pachra." He paused, letting the tension build. He drank a swig from his mug.

"Yuz smiled on my people that night. As his brother, Mavra, dutifully kept watch from the shore, torch in hand, hidden in the scrub brush outside the Sea Wolf camp, something happened. The waters began to boil. A geyser rose from the blackness as the mighty Uzgül broke the surface and took to the sky." Oster now stood on the bench. "All was quiet as Uzgül circled high in the night sky. Mavra hurried to light the fires, ever evading the Sea Wolves.

"Hours passed with nothing. Mavra thought they had

failed. As the fires grew dim, there came a thundering sound from the clear sky. A rushing wind. The moon and stars were blotted out for a time. The great and terrible Uzgül swooped down and swallowed the whole army of Sea Wolves in a single breath!" Oster leaned forward as he spoke, his eyes wide with excitement. Many of the men leaned forward, too.

"When the sun rose, the beach was empty." Oster finished in a whisper and sat back, a look of satisfaction on his face. Badu's mind spun.

"Why do you tell us this story for the fifth time?" asked Faroz, shattering the moment.

"Only five?" teased Heffel.

Oster said nothing for a minute; then his voice softened and he leaned in. "What if, uyesi, we could find and wake Uzgül?"

"To swallow the Farish's army?" laughed Heffel.

"Not an army." Oster's eyes lit up. "A castle."

"He's gone mad," said Finnur, his blue eyes wide.

"You asked where I had been today." Oster sat and reached for his riding satchel. "I've been with Andri, my father's uncle. Now a frail old man. Not far from the Garden." Oster fished in his bag. "But he discovered this among some old relics and urged me to take it."

"Your sanity?" laughed Eldiven.

"Look!" Oster produced a yellowed leather scroll. He unrolled it before them. A faded ink drawing covered the scroll. It looked like Epis Kopol Harbor to Badu, evident by the distinctive jagged cliffs and terraced slope of fishing huts down to the water. However, the city was different. More like a provincial town than a metropolis. On the horizon, a great shape, like an enormous stingray, splashed into the waves just in front of the reef, marked by a black triangle of rock known by the Kopolians as the Shark's Tooth.

"Listen." Oster flipped the leather over and read from the script on the back:

"Its shape blotted out the bloody morning sun. We fishermen saw it. To our graves we will swear to it. A monster from the heavens within our very reef. Down into the depths it plunged. None of us will fish near the reef again, but never has the spirit been seen again. Yuz has put it to sleep. Just as well, for few believe our account. But we believe. We have seen. And with my final breaths, these twenty seasons later, I tell what I know.'

"It's dated 345 post establishment." Oster looked up at the group. "Andri said the Sea Wolves came when Pachra was a young man of twenty seasons. He was born around 305. The timeline works."

"This is madness," said Finnur, rising. "I'm off to bed, brothers." He patted the shoulders of the men as he squeezed out of the tiny room. "I'll get the full debrief in the morning," he added with a playful smile and left.

Garris reached for the scroll, turned it back over, and studied the ink drawing again.

"You truly believe this Uzgül exists?" asked Ferat. "That he's still down there? On the seafloor in the bay..."

"The kings cried a hundred tears, the moloth asleep—"

"A hundred years," Badu finished the line of the childhood rhyme. Every man, woman, and child in the city could have done the same.

"Even in your fantasy world where any of this is true," said Garris, rolling the scroll and handing it back to Oster, "the Code forbids us to kill a man, much less the thousands that would perish if your impossible dream were ever to come to pass."

"But, Garris, imagine if we could—" began Oster.

"We must remember who we are," Garris cut in, standing. "We are the Nöz. The vurmak, a silent fist, not a blade. We stand in defiance of the evil one who corrupts the heart of this city. And we fight." He looked each man in the eyes as he spoke.

"We fought today. But not this way. Our time is better spent freeing more prisoners and bringing justice to the suffering, not on whimsical dreams of revenge. Remember, uyesi, 'revenge is a snake that constricts the heart.'" He spoke the proverb and turned to Kafa. "Please, friend, come with me? I will get you a room for the night."

Kafa stood silently and followed Garris. Wordlessly, Ferat and Faroz rose and left behind him.

"It's getting late," offered Eldiven, and he patted the dejected Oster on the shoulder as he left.

"Sorry, old friend," said Heffel, rising. "I want his blood as much as any." He started moving toward the exit. "It was fun to imagine. But I'm afraid it will take more than fairy tales to kill the god on the throne."

"Badu," came Garris's sharp voice. Badu jumped up, offered Oster an apologetic smile, and slipped out.

8

NEW BLOOD

"**B**ut who *is* she?" pressed Sevin, addressing the group of nözan seated on stout stone pillars surrounding a dormant firepit in the clearing at the camp's center. Garris occupied the venerable seat of the Sefa, flanked by Faroz and Efe and facing the rest of the members arranged in a semicircle.

"And how did she end up with those sherking tinmen?" Finnur, tall and trim with washed-out blue eyes and sandy hair, looked like he could be Sevin's older brother, though the two weren't related other than by distant ancestors.

"She must be an enemy of the Farish," offered Badu. "Doesn't that make her an ally?"

"Does she know the recruit?" asked Salik.

"She *is* the recruit," Garris replied, shaking his head, staring vacantly at the cold, charred wood in the center of the ring.

"Lured us all out like a pack of howling fezzi." Faroz rose from his stone perch beside Garris and paced. "How did this happen?"

"We've been fooled." Kafa grunted.

"The innkeeper couldn't have known," answered Garris. "Shuuv spoke with reverence, almost awe, of a daring warrior who fought like a lion and escaped the Farish. A fighter who wore the scars of capture and burned with fire against the Farish."

"A lion who made Faroz look like a kitten," Kafa said, beaming his broad, contagious smile. Badu looked down to hide a smile of his own.

"Her skill *is* undeniable," added Heffel. "I've never seen a woman move like that."

"Have you seen a man move like that?" asked Sevin.

"She caught me... unaware," barked Faroz defensively, still pacing.

Made you look like a rass, Badu wanted to say. He told himself he wouldn't have been caught off guard like Faroz, though he wasn't sure.

"She was supposed to be an ally. And a man!" Faroz added.

"She surprised us all," offered Garris.

"It's clear she's well trained," said Badu, who stood with Salik and Täs just outside the circle of seated men. "And she hates the Farish."

"Thousands hate the Liar," said Heffel. As an ex-priest-guard, Heffel had encountered this hate for the Farish a hundred times over.

"But her skill is undeniable," said Badu.

"What are you saying, yeeli?" Faroz turned on Badu.

"She bested *you*." Badu shot a challenging look. "Maybe she could join?" The group erupted in objection.

"Impossible," declared Garris.

"We know you've never seen a woman up close before, yeeli, but try to keep your mind clear," said Faroz.

Badu clenched his jaw. His cheeks burned. The quickening rose, the heat. He recalled the averted nishpat omak and suddenly longed to be in the ring.

"Among the Guti, any can fight," said Kafa. "All who make a

first kill and pass the ujan testing join the warriors, man or woman." Garris shook his head.

"Maybe she does deserve a chance," said Ferat. Badu sometimes wondered how the mild and friendly Ferat, so quick to trust and kind to a fault, could have shared a womb with Faroz.

"We saw the way she fought," added Heffel. "The way she moved."

"Even if she were the strongest and best of us all, her joining would still shatter the balance," said Faroz.

"Like soma roots growing through shale," offered Eldiven, the poet. His hair just beginning to earn streaks of gray, Eldiven was the second most senior member of the Nöz behind Efe and just a handful of seasons older than Garris.

"Faroz is right," added Garris. "It would disturb the Nöz. It could destroy us. No women. Period."

"But there once were," said Efe, the last of the "faithful fathers," as some called the original Nöz members. Efe alone carried the memory of the group's beginning.

"The Nöz has changed," replied Garris. "We're not the faithful sect from so many seasons past."

"We are warriors," said Faroz. "We are uyesi. Brothers."

"If she wants to help, perhaps she could spy for us in Epis Kopol," offered Sevin.

"If she can be trusted," said Faroz, returning to his seat on the worn rock beside Garris.

"Shuuv says she can," said Garris.

"Shuuv thought she was a man," snapped Faroz.

"Shuuv drinks too much of her own ale," said Kafa with a chuckle.

"When the yumak wears off, we will speak with... Cor," said Garris with finality. He nodded to Efe.

"Together, we come," said Efe, rising, his eyes closed.

"Come as one," responded the men in unison. Badu, Salik, and Täs stepped forward to join the ring of seated members.

"Together, we stand."

"Stand in defiance." The men raised their right fists beside their heads.

"Together, we fight."

"We fight as uyesi," responded the men, each reaching out to touch the shoulder of the man to the right.

"Together, we come."

"We come as one."

~

"You hold it out like this." Badu extended his arm, bent at an angle, creating a fulcrum for the dikeni chain to orbit. Täs and Salik watched intently.

"Let me try," said Täs impatiently. Badu handed him the chain. On the first pass, Täs hadn't let enough chain out, and the orbiting training ball thudded into his arm.

"Ow!"

"Just be glad it wasn't the thorn." Badu smiled. "Try again. More chain."

"One more, then it's my turn," said Salik.

Täs wound the chain and spun it again. This time, it caught and snapped back, gaining speed.

"Good. As it comes back, spin it around your body," said Badu. "Like this." He demonstrated. Täs repeated the motion, successfully completing the arc and circling his torso.

"You're a natural!" said Badu.

Salik jumped up and snatched the dikeni away. "Can't be that hard." The older boy assumed the stance, trying to replicate the movement, but only succeeded in hitting his elbow. He tried again and hit himself on the head. On his third attempt, he lost his grip, sending the practice bulb flying into the nearby bushes.

"It's okay. That happens," said Badu, retrieving the weapon.

He pressed the smooth leather handle studded with textured nail heads into Salik's waiting hand. "Try again."

"The boy needs a wider stance," came a voice from behind, startling the trio.

Badu spun. "Uh... You're awake." He stammered. Corvina rested on a pile of grain sacks arranged against a tree in the training clearing fifty mounts from the camp's center. The three yeeli were charged with watching her. *"Not guarding her, exactly,"* Garris had said. *"Just watching over her until she's awake. Then alert the group."*

"You're an observant one," she jabbed, a wry smile forming on her delicate bow-shaped lips.

Badu found his heart suddenly racing. "Run, gather the others," he ordered Täs. The wide-eyed boy dropped the stick he had been playing with and raced from the clearing.

Cor had awoken silently. She had none of the frantic, disoriented jerking or panicked shouting that often accompanied emergence from the yumak slumber. Instead, she looked like one waking from a restful afternoon nap under her favorite pecan tree.

"Am I your captive?" she asked, flashing defiant, luminous hazel-green eyes up at Badu, her strong brown eyebrows arched in a question.

Badu hadn't gotten a good look at her face previously. After the shock of discovering Cor to be a woman and her attack on Faroz, it was a whirlwind. The forward team had covered Corvina's head in a sack and whisked her out of Kursa.

Now, though, Badu found himself staring straight into her striking face, entranced. Her russet hair seemed almost to glow in the afternoon light as it fell in waves to her shoulders, framing a face both delicate and sharp. Yes, sharp was the word. High, defined cheekbones, a thin nose, angled slightly up, and a chiseled chin, with a hint of cleft, gave her the appearance of a fine sculpture awaiting the master's final smoothing pass.

She widened her eyes and shook her head quickly.

So, she does feel it, thought Badu, cataloging and filing the information away as his training had taught him.

"You've drugged me," she stated, rolling her gaze from left to right.

"I... I'm sorry," stammered Badu. "Outsiders aren't allowed to know this place."

She nodded slowly. "This place," she repeated. "Nöz camp."

Salik shot a glance at Badu.

"I... Uh," Badu stumbled, unsure if he should confirm. Still, his gaze remained hopelessly fixed on her despite the rising discomfort.

"I came to join you," she said, shaking her head once more and slowly rising to her feet. "Am I now a prisoner?"

"You're not a prisoner," blurted Salik. "But you should stay here," he added quickly.

"Not to worry," she assured him. "I'm not going anywhere. My name is Corvina Lunari. Or just Cor."

"Oh... Uh, I'm Badu." Badu fumbled over the words, finally dipping his head and tearing his gaze from her. "This is Salik." He threw a hand toward Salik.

Cor looked them over, her eyes roving up and down and finally scanning Badu's face. His stomach twisted. She opened and closed her jaw, then winced, putting a hand on the bruise on her cheek. "The tinmen," she said. "They were going to execute me."

"We arrived just in time, then," said Badu dumbly, searching for something to add. *You fat-tongued fezzi!* he scolded himself.

"Fancy weapon you've got there," Cor said, turning to Salik.

"It's called a dikeni," answered Salik, his shoulders relaxing. "You spin it," he added, with an air of authority now, "like this." He gave the chain an unsteady twirl. Cor raised an eyebrow. "Oh... I'm just learning." He smiled.

"May I try it?" asked Corvina.

Badu shot a reproachful glance at Salik, but the boy appeared equally transfixed. He was already moving toward her, holding the weapon out like a Lotus Temple sacrifice. She accepted the offering.

"It's just a training bulb," said Badu, "but it can still hurt if it hits you." Corvina gripped the chain and slowly started twirling the ball in a tight orbit.

"You want to try to keep it in motion until you're ready to strike. You might try with a simple—"

Even as he spoke, Cor spun the bulb faster and faster, letting out more chain as she went.

Salik stepped back. "Careful with the end."

The dikeni hummed in a blurred circle now. Corvina lunged forward, away from the dumbstruck pair, and whipped the chain around her torso and then back. She stepped left, then sprang back to her right, the bulb flying in a figure eight. Badu and Salik stood frozen, mouths agape as Cor spun and leaped, twirling the dikeni expertly around herself and through the air like an extension of her body.

"There!" came Täs's voice from the direction of the camp, and the sound of rushing feet approached.

Corvina didn't pause her deadly ballet, skillfully wielding the dikeni with moves and stances Badu had never seen. She rolled forward, somehow keeping the ball spinning as the chain passed beneath her. As she rose to a knee, she released her grip, sending the bulb rocketing up toward the canopy of the nearby oak.

She lost it, thought Badu. He had made the mistake before. In the heat of a routine, it was easy to lose grip of the leather handle slick with sweat. A part of him relaxed, grateful for the minor weakness in her otherwise flawless command of the weapon. However, when the chain reached its full length, cracking into a dead tree limb twenty measures up, Corvina ripped it back. She snatched the orb out of midair and froze in a breathless combat stance, back to the crowd.

The assembled group of Nöz stood silently, staring. The dead limb fell and crashed to the ground. Cor was motionless except for the rising and falling of her shoulders from the exertion.

"She's awake?" Efe called out, breaking the spell as he shuffled up to the clearing with Eldiven hobbling in tow. "Has she—oh, I see."

Cor turned to face the group, her defiant face glistening with perspiration in the afternoon light.

No one spoke. Badu noted that many of the men had weapons drawn.

"It's a fine tool," said Cor finally, coiling the dikeni and offering it to Badu. He hurried forward and retrieved the weapon, catching disapproving glares from a few nözan.

"Welcome to the Skyrt," said Garris.

"Quite a welcome it was," quipped Cor with a short laugh. Her eyes jumped from one Nöz member to the next as if taking inventory. "If this is how you treat your guests, I'd not want to be an enemy." Salik laughed a bit too loudly.

"There was a... misunderstanding," said Garris, his stance relaxing slightly. "You see, when we got word of a recruit from Shuuv, we understood... We believed that..."

"We thought you were a man," Faroz cut in.

Cor snapped her eyes over to him. "How's the neck?" she asked. He scowled.

"I don't know how it became so confused, but we do not, cannot, have women in the Nöz."

"I can fight," said Cor. "I want to kill the Farish."

Badu raised his head. *Yes!*

"We've seen you can fight—"

"Like a tingi leopard," cut in Kafa, smiling.

"But I'm afraid there can be no exceptions," continued

Garris. "Please, eat with us, and we'll escort you back to the city."

~

"Is that necessary, Badu?" Corvina asked, with the tone of an exasperated friend, as Badu secured the leather straps to the saddle's pommel.

"I'm sorry," he offered, focusing intently on the saddle to avoid her hypnotic gaze. Every time he caught her eyes, his stomach somersaulted. "We blindfold you for your own safety. It's just for a couple of cliqs. The straps will keep you from falling."

"My own safety?" she asked with a bemused snort and offered her hands like a surrendering prisoner. As he took her delicate wrists in his grip, something in his stomach flipped. He secured her to the pommel.

"That okay?" he asked, finally looking up.

"I'll survive," she replied with a mischievous half smile.

"Enough chirping, yeeli," barked Faroz. "Bag her. We ride."

Faroz, Ferat, and Heffel waited on horseback. The nözan preferred horses over the faster, more exotic choluk when riding to Epis Kopol to avoid drawing unnecessary attention.

"I don't think he cares much for me," she whispered to Badu.

Badu sprang up onto his mount, daring to meet her eyes again. She held his gaze with an unwavering look that seemed to pierce him, causing his chest to thunder.

"He's like that even if you don't flatten him in front of his men." Badu smiled and lifted the black felt bag, offering an apologetic shrug.

"Go on," she said with a sigh. He pulled the bag over her head, gently cinching the drawstring. Salik handed Badu the reins to her horse, giving an exaggerated wink and thumbs up. Badu rolled his eyes.

"Directly to Epis Kopol, then," said Garris. "Take the forest road."

"Yes, Ussa." Badu and the other men saluted.

Faroz spurred his horse ahead. The four nözan and their captive rode single file, slithering out of camp like sand vipers.

9

THE RETURN

"It's been hours," came Cor's muffled voice from the back of the group. "Surely, it must be safe to remove this thing." She shook her head as if it might free her from the hood.

"It won't be long now," answered Faroz from the front of the string of riders. The ride to Epis Kopol from camp could be made in an hour and a half at a hard gallop—half of that on a choluk—however, this party was neither running at a gallop nor riding straight across the meadland plains to the city. They followed a carefully planned route.

While outsiders in the Nöz camp were exceedingly rare, occasionally an intrepid explorer, wayward traveler, or other intermeddler would encroach on the land surrounding the Skyrt, requiring an escort back to the city. The unlucky nözan who drew the short straw always returned the intruder to Epis Kopol via this long, circuitous route, approaching the city from the nost through the thick Blackwood Forest that carpeted the Kambun Foothills running from the plains all the way to the edge of the Tszox Range.

Once back in the city, the intruder, dosed with a cocktail of yumak and a dash of chiproot to erase recent memory, would be deposited in the Saffron Crescent, splashed with strong bandi or sprinkled with ferikökü powder, and planted with evidence of some unmentionable misdeed. When combined with a well-placed witness or two, these clues, plus the lack of any recollection, all but guaranteed the intruder would never speak of the day again.

Despite his declaration that the Nöz was no place for Cor, Garris had agreed to spare her such shame. She would simply be returned to the city, where she could gather information for the group.

"Sevin said to be wary of delving into the Blackwood," Badu heard Heffel say softly to Faroz. "Said he saw something last night."

"Bah," replied Faroz. "Sevin and his dreams. Always chasing ghosts. Remember the blood-moon squall? How we spent two days readying the camp for a storm that never came? Or the monster from the sea who would swallow us all?" The group rode tightly now, and the sound carried easily.

"Sevin says these events usually do happen, just doesn't know when," offered Ferat from the back of the procession.

"You, too, brother?" Faroz glanced over his shoulder and shook his head. "I predict a war," he said loudly, waving a hand for dramatic effect. "I can't tell you when or where, but it will come. This century or the next."

Ferat grunted.

"We've all seen how he's kept us from harm," added Badu. Why did Faroz do this? He knew there was truth in Sevin's night visions.

"Behold! Yeeli has spoken," Faroz said without turning around. Badu tightened his grip on his reins. "Whatever Sevin's superstitions, Garris wants her far from the road when she's uncovered," Faroz added.

Badu dropped back. "I'll take rear," he told Ferat. "You can go listen to your brother's mindless bohk."

Ferat only shrugged and spurred his horse past Cor.

"What's a yeeli?" asked the hooded Cor.

"Not much around here." Badu scoffed.

"Why does he treat you like that?"

Badu opened his mouth to reply but decided to hold his tongue.

"You have one with the gift of niz göru?" asked Cor, changing the subject.

"You know of the night sight?" asked Badu.

"There was a man in our town who claimed to have it," she replied. "He saw it all coming..." Her voice trailed off.

"Sevin's mother had the gift," answered Badu. "His visions are... less reliable."

"And what did he say about today?" she pressed.

Badu was quiet. His faith in the Midlander's visions was inconsistent, to say the least. At times, it seemed that the dreams were just dreams, a result of an active imagination, and their accuracy, a coincidence. There were exceptions, though.

Sevin would sometimes freeze, swearing he had seen the exact same place in his dream, down to every detail. When this happened, everyone listened. The nözan had avoided catastrophe more than once thanks to his insight; he once navigated them around a nest of wild boar after seeing a vision of Garris gored and trampled. Yet, other dreams were less defined. When one followed such visions blindly and was made to look a fool, as Faroz had done, those were hard memories to forget.

"This will do." Faroz's voice offered a welcome reprieve. "We'll break here." He waved over to the trickle of water running down the rock face to the left. "You can remove the captive's hood."

"Looks like you get to see again," said Badu, removing the hood and untying the lashing on Cor's wrists.

"I was expecting a few minutes in that thing," said Cor, rubbing her wrists and squinting in the light.

"Sorry, we have to be careful." Badu offered Cor a waterskin. "It's better treatment than most get."

"I'm sure I can make my way alone from here," she said, glancing around to study the clearing.

"Garris was clear: we are to ride all the way to the city with you. You're an ally now. Besides, we can't spare a horse." Badu smiled.

"Gallant," she quipped.

"We continue in five," said Faroz, who stooped beside the spring to fill a waterskin. Ferat stretched and fiddled with something in his pack. Heffel wandered off the path to relieve himself.

"Eat something, Cor," Ferat said, holding out a torn half round of flattened stone bread and some dried jerky. She eyed him warily for a moment but then snatched the food and ate hungrily.

"It's okay, we're on the same side," he assured her. Ferat's gentle countenance and kind eyes made him instantly likable and hard not to trust. *"A fish in the trees,"* was how Eldiven the poet once described him among the nözan. Badu often wondered why Ferat chose to live this life of battle and conflict among the Nöz, but the answer was clear. He was here for his brother.

"Prep to move in two," Faroz barked.

"Where will you go when you return to the city?" Badu asked Cor.

"Me? Oh... I, uh, I suppose back to my aunt's."

"Where does she live?" Faroz approached, an edge of challenge in his voice.

"She slowly turned to face him. "An ally, am I?" she asked.

"Answer," Faroz pressed.

"Behind the fishmonger stalls in the Red Quarter." She met his eyes. "A faded blue house with a crooked porch."

"Take it easy," said Badu. "She's not a prisoner."

"And your vision is clouded by desire, yeeli," snapped Faroz. Heat flashed through Badu, his cheeks reddening.

"It's fine," cut in Cor. "I know you have to be careful. But if I'm to provide the Nöz with information from within the city, we will need to trust one another."

"Uh, Faroz," came Heffel's unsteady voice from the woods behind Badu. Something was off. The voice carried a warning. Badu spun around to see Heffel emerging slowly from the trees, escorted by two ragged men, one holding a dagger to his neck and the other carrying a sword. The group snapped to attention.

The man holding Heffel was tall, gaunt, and unkempt with a scraggly beard and darting eyes. He pressed the knife against Heffel's throat. "Give us your purses!"

"And your woman," added the shorter companion with a potbelly and a mop of black hair tied in a dingy kerchief. He held Heffel's arm and brandished a short sword, but his hungry eyes roved over Cor. He flashed a smile full of rotten, stained teeth.

"Yes, your purse *and* your woman!" echoed the tall one enthusiastically.

"I'm sorry!" grunted Heffel. Badu saw he carried no weapons. *Foolish!*

"This is a mistake," said Faroz. "But if you let our companion go, no harm will come to you."

"Harm to us?" the short man scoffed, his face reddening. But Badu could see it. Faroz misjudged these two. The edge of the short man's dingy sword was perfectly straight and polished, no chip or rust: *carefully sharpened and regularly used.* The tall man moved with a steady and sure pace, and his eyes flicked from one nözan to the next: *trained. Mercenary or military.* Heffel must have sensed it too, or he would have already made a move. Badu knew the type. These two would not be intimidated or negotiate. They'd slit a throat just to make a point.

"We take what we want out here," he nearly yelled. "Kill him," he ordered his companion dryly, now devoid of emotion. Something screamed silently in Badu's mind.

"Wait!" Cor cried, stepping forward. "Nobody needs to die."

"Well, they gonna if ya keep up the threats," snarled the captor.

"I'll go," said Cor, flashing a look at Faroz.

"What?" demanded Badu.

"No teary goodbyes," the short man said, seeing the glance. Cor looked back at Badu, breathed deeply, and approached the pair slowly, her hands lifted in surrender. "You've saved your friends, at least," the short man added.

When Cor was within a few strides, the tall vagabond shoved Heffel away, his eyes dancing over Cor's athletic frame.

"Come to papa," he said, reaching for her.

Rage crackled inside Badu and his hand dropped to the dikeni. Cor tentatively took the man's outstretched hand. His eyes lit up. Then she twisted it hard with a crack and lunged forward, head-butting the man in the face. As he staggered backward, she ripped the knife from his other hand and, with lightning speed, slammed it into the breast of the short man before he could even register what was happening.

"Cor!" shouted Faroz in reproof as the short man fell, pawing at his chest. *Yes!* Something bloomed in Badu at the swift and brutal justice.

Cor spun on the tall man, who staggered, covering his broken nose, trying to stop the gushing blood. He fell backward. She approached slowly, stepping over his fallen frame until she straddled his torso.

"You want me to come to papa?" she asked, fire burning in her eyes as she squatted. Dark anticipation rose in Badu. *Yes! Do it!* He glanced at Ferat, who likewise stood transfixed.

"N-no! I don't," blathered the man, panic smeared across his face.

"Well, it's too late for that," she retorted, lifting the dagger high and bringing it down.

"Stop!" Faroz's hand clamped on her arm, arresting the blow. She spun on him.

"It's not our way. It's not the Code."

"You can suck your herfing code dry!" she growled, wild.

"Please." Heffel joined the plea. "He's no threat now."

"No threat? Do you know what this slagging pislik wanted to do to me?"

"I won't hurt nobody," came the man's pathetic whimper.

"Shut up!" snapped Faroz. "Please, Cor," he implored, his voice softer now. "You've smashed his face, and I doubt he'll be able to use that wrist again."

She ripped her arm from Faroz's grip and sheathed her knife. "You're a fool. The lot of you are." She shook her head. "You dress up like men to play your games in the woods, but you're foolish boys. A feedling skupp has more sense. If this pinch doesn't deserve the blade, who does?" She spat at the man, turned, and walked off.

"He'll get it sooner or later," replied Heffel. "A man like that always does."

"Besides, he won't go running off anywhere soon." Faroz drew a red feather-tipped needle from his cloak.

"And when he wakes, he'll have a headache he won't forget," Heffel added. Cor only shook her head as Faroz stooped low and quickly jabbed the man.

"No!" His eyes widened, and then his head fell back.

"Shivv!" Ferat's cry jerked their attention. "Look at this one!" He crouched beside the dead short man, his face white.

"What is it?" Faroz hurried over. The others drew close, huddling around Ferat.

Ferat rolled the corpse onto its back. Badu gasped, a

shocking chill ripping through him. There, in the middle of the dead man's chest, encircling the dagger, was a black sandy hole the size of a melon and growing wider by the second.

"No blood!" exclaimed Heffel.

"Yuz, cover!" Faroz gasped.

"Scat," swore Cor. "Fully tainted that one. More margoul than man."

"What does it mean?" asked Badu. He'd never seen anything like it. As they watched, the man's features began to erode. His nose crumbled like a sandcastle in the rising tide.

"A goblin friend," answered Cor. "This one's been turned for a while. Means there are margoul nearby."

"If he's got no blood, then what about the sleeping dart..." Ferat's voice trailed, and he jerked his head around. "Oh, no!" Badu followed his gaze. The fallen man with the broken nose was gone.

"Shivv!" Faroz spat. "We need to move."

"He can't have gone far," objected Cor. "We should find him and cut him down. Surely your Code allows that."

"There's no code against killing margoul," said Faroz. "But part man, part margoul?"

Cor groaned. "You're a pack of schoolchildren!" She removed the short sword from the dissolving corpse.

"We don't use swords—" began Faroz, but Cor shot him a defiant glare and brushed past him.

"We move!" commanded Faroz, struggling to regain his composure and apparently sensing the futility of opposing her.

"We should track him," objected Cor.

"There's no debate," barked Faroz. Cor kicked the dirt, turned, and mounted her horse. The group moved with nervous haste. As they spurred the horses forward, Badu stole a glance back at the tainted man. The corpse was unrecognizable now, a fleshy sand sculpture stuffed into a man's clothing that continued to dissolve even as he watched. He shuddered and kicked his horse.

The black packed dirt of the forest path turned to rocky dust and rubble as it wound out of the dense wood, rising to an exposed sun-drenched ridge littered with massive boulders and a rocky outcropping. Badu had been this way before and recalled the impressive view from the opening along the spine of the ridge.

The cart path ran a short distance along the ridge before plunging back into the forest. A half cliq down, at the foot of the slope, it opened beside a canyon that cut through the otherwise flat, featureless plateau speckled with trees fanning out in every direction. Across the vast plateau, the river split and split again, carving the plateau into a hundred slivers of land as it rushed toward the sea, creating the rocky Kenar Delta, home of the greatest city in all of Yiduiijn: Epis Kopol.

Badu squinted. Ahead, hard white light poured into the forest, marking the edge of the trees.

"The view ahead is worth the wait," he said, looking up at Cor.

"Do you smell that?" she asked, seeming not to hear him. The odor of rot hung in the air.

"Something must've died nearby," Badu offered.

"We should stop!" Cor called ahead. "Something's not right."

"We push on," retorted Faroz over his shoulder. "We'll be down on the flats in under an hour."

Badu hoped the stench would abate once they left the forest, but as the group passed from forest to ridgeline, the thick odor of death only grew until all in the company rode with cloth or kerchief over their faces.

Badu barely noticed the sweeping view that unfurled down to his right, his head swimming from the reek. Rounding a boulder that split the path, Faroz halted. Badu rode up beside him.

"There," Faroz called, pointing. In the path lay a pair of horses and a shattered wagon. Heffel tossed a stick he had been chewing on, sending a black cloud of flies swirling. Something small and dark scurried from the corpse into a fissure at the base of a towering pile of white boulders off to the left of the path.

"Ugh," groaned Ferat, dry heaving. "Let's push ahead quickly. It will be better once we enter the far woods."

As they skirted the wreckage, giving as wide a berth as the narrow path and steep drop to the right would allow, Badu beheld the gruesome scene. One of the horse's heads was facing backwards, and its throat was missing.

"I don't like it," Cor hissed, her eyes roving.

"What could do that?" asked Badu. "A bear?"

"A gorgol could," offered Heffel.

"There aren't any gorgol mead of the Tszox Range," said Faroz. Someone murmured in agreement. As soon as they were clear of the carcasses, the group's pace quickened to an urgent trot. The loose single-file formation had bunched into a close knot.

"Leaving so soon?" came a deep voice, echoing off the rock walls. Badu spun, searching, but couldn't immediately locate its owner. "We have some... unfinished business."

"There!" Heffel pointed up to three figures crouching on the rock outcropping above them. Badu's stomach dropped. The tall figure was unmistakable. Dried blood still caked his face from the bloodied nose, and his left hand was tucked into his shirt awkwardly like a folded wing.

10

AMBUSHED

"Did you miss me?" The tall man blew Cor a kiss with his good hand and flashed a broken smile. His two ragged companions laughed.

"You want another round?" barked Cor.

The man snorted. "Sounds lovely," he rasped, then gave a sharp whistle.

A roar split the air and then another. All around them, bulky gray shapes materialized, seeming to grow out of the very rocks. As the bodies rose, figures took shape, birthed from the bleached landscape. Broad, muscled shoulders sloped up to undersized heads featuring distinctive pointed ears protruding from either side of the skull. Horns of various shapes and sizes either grew out of or were attached to their bony heads.

"Orcs!" shouted Corvina. The word punched through Badu like a shard of ice through his chest. The horses required no further explanation. They whinnied in terror as half a dozen snarling orcs rose from their hiding spots among the rocks, their massive bodies clouded in powdery white stone dust. Badu searched for escape, but to the right, the path fell away in a steep incline of crumbled stone before reaching a sheer cliff that dropped a hundred measures or more.

Orcs! The name boomed through his head like a thunderclap. Badu had heard stories of these monsters but had never seen one or even spoken to someone who had. Their oversized, muscled frames reminded him of the hulking Tszox warriors that he had once spotted in the mountains nost of Epis Kopol, but these creatures were distinctly less human.

Their facial features seemed bunched up near the top of their heads. A gaping mouth stretched across their grotesque faces, featuring a pair of lower fangs thrusting up from a prominent underbite. Despite their feral appearance, orcs were not wild animals; they were warriors. Standing upright and brandishing swords, clubs, and other weapons, each of the muscle-bound monsters donned rudimentary armor and furs over their muddy blue-gray hides. Badu counted five stocky shapes standing like deadly sentries on the rocky bank. The tall man whistled again, and the orcs exploded into action, charging at the group.

"Run!" Faroz kicked his horse, streaking across the stretch of open ridgeline, aiming for the mouth of the forest a hundred measures ahead. Ferat's terrified horse was slower to follow. As it lurched timidly ahead, fixated on the attackers, an orc seized the bridle. Ferat snapped his long, slender fighting staff, the parumak, slamming the wooden bulb into the creature's head. The blow might have cracked a man's skull, yet it only managed to knock the beast off balance momentarily. The orc held the bridle fast.

Ahead, in a dark blur, a colossal orc roared as it flew down the embankment and slammed a shoulder into Faroz's horse. The horse screamed, and something cracked. The thrashing animal took two awkward steps to the side, trying to keep its balance before crashing to the ground. Faroz cried out as he thudded to the rocky ground, a leg pinned beneath the frantic horse. The huge orc, the largest of all, wearing a string of bones draped around its neck and a topknot of black hair tied off in a scarlet knot, leaped onto Faroz, war hammer raised.

Something roared at Badu's side. With the coiled dikeni still lashed to his belt, he had time only to draw one of the dagnek at his waist. The small wooden paddle felt like a toy as he met the black beady eyes of an orc warrior bearing down on him, a dull blade the width of a child's waist raised over its head. Lifting the pathetic dagnek, Badu braced for glory as the orc swiped down, but the whirring blade skimmed past his face, lopping off his horse's head in one powerful stroke. Badu was suddenly falling.

He dove from the crumpling horse and landed hard on his shoulder, managing to roll to the side as he did. Ahead, Heffel cried out as a meaty pair of orc hands ripped him from his saddle.

A deep bellow sounded behind Badu. He spun toward the back of the procession to see an orc fist dangling from the bridle of Corvina's horse, liberated from the stump of an arm now cradled by the screaming orc. Her eyes blazed, and when the dazed and wounded orc approached again, she lashed out again, this time slicing through the beast's neck. The orc pawed at its wound, hot green liquid spilling from the gash and dissolving the monster's skin on contact. It stumbled backward and fell.

"Stop!" came a screech from up on a rock outcropping. The birdlike cry from the lanky brigand somehow froze the entire group, orc and nözan alike. Beside the tall man, his two companions each held crossbows aimed at Cor. She stared back defiantly.

"I would hate to cut short our time together," added the man. "But I won't be tricked again." Cor trembled slightly, and Badu now recognized the look of hate burning in her eyes. *Don't put it down!* he silently urged. *Fight! They'll kill you!*

But Cor's eyes swept down the path, where the decimated Nöz company lay scattered and broken, and she slowly lowered and then dropped the blade.

"Good," called the man.

Rough orc hands grabbed Badu and dragged him to his feet. Another orc pulled the struggling Cor from her horse.

"No!" Ferat's primal scream somehow eclipsed and exceeded the savagery all around them. "What have you done?" he roared wildly, smashing his forehead into the face of his captor and breaking away. Before he had taken two steps, an orc club slammed into the side of his head, and down he went. Badu looked past the scrum and saw it. His blood went cold.

The orc captain bellowed a victorious cry as he pounded his chest and trudged up the path toward the others. Behind him, held by the ankle, he dragged Faroz's lifeless body.

Badu's stomach turned. *We are all dead men.*

"What will you do with us?" Cor demanded of the tall man, who stood with his crossbow-wielding companions. Badu didn't balk at how Cor spoke for the group. None did. The orcs had herded the men together and now encircled Badu, Heffel, who's right arm hung limply to his side, and the broken Ferat, now awake, though he had slipped into listless, stunned detachment. His eyes were fixed on his dead brother, lying off to the side.

"Kovug here,"—the tall man nodded at the orc chief—"has requested we leave your friends alive for now. Something about being fresher that way." He sneered. Heffel groaned, his face a sickly white. "But I'm no monster. Already I commanded him not to eat your dead companion. Not yet. Cooperate and we'll… let them go."

Kovug growled and drew himself up to his full height in challenge.

"Calm," said the man, patting the air. He hissed something to the orc in a foreign tongue. Kovug grunted but relaxed.

Corvina looked over the group with a disgusted sneer. The men with the crossbow moved in, never dropping their weapons.

"Like I said, no tricks this time," said the tall man. "Keep them pointed at her," he ordered the thick, hunched man beside him. "She's a fighter." He smiled.

"I like a fighter," said the thick companion with a gurgled chuckle.

"We're dead men, Cor!" shouted Badu urgently. "Don't give these pislik anything!" A squat orc with a sprout of green hair cuffed him hard on the head, sending a blast of white shapes dancing across his vision.

Badu watched helplessly as the three men marched Corvina off behind a cluster of boulders. His head swam, and the pungent reek from the orcs threatened to overwhelm him. They spoke to each other in a garbled hiss.

"Get off!" yelled Heffel, yanking his arm away from a nearby orc who squeezed it gently and spoke something to a companion. It reminded Badu of one testing a cut of meat at the market, and bile rose in his throat. The stories of orcs were the stuff of nightmares. Badu had dismissed the wild tales of their barbarism as fabrications, exaggerations, but even now, he sensed it. He read the signs: a whisper, a restless shuffling, licked lips, a stolen glance between the captors. Anticipation mounted among the orcs like a surging squall. The savages were preparing to feast.

A shriek burst the silence from behind the boulders. The chief orc rumbled with a dark laugh. A pang spasmed in Badu's chest. *No! Cor!* His mind spun. What had he done? What more could he do?

The tall man wandered out from behind the rocks.

"Now is time?" bellowed Kovug, standing. But he was cut short as the man emerged from shadow into the harsh light, a crossbow bolt protruding from an eye socket. The man staggered and fell. Kovug grunted in confusion even as something whistled and streaked through the air, a second bolt lodging in one of the orc captor's necks. Corvina emerged, tossing the crossbow aside, and drew the sword one of the dirty companions had been wearing moments before. Badu's heart jumped.

Kovug boomed a command, and the orcs sprang into action, charging at Cor. The short, green-haired orc remained with the prisoners, staring in bewilderment. Badu ripped the oversized blade from the grip of the fallen orc, whose body had already begun deflating like a windsock, its muscles liquifying as the margoul corpse melted from flesh to steaming, dark-green ooze. He spun, swinging the great blade at the stocky guard with a scream. The guard dropped under the bite of the hungry blade.

The orcs moved in on Corvina as Badu sprinted after them. Kovug lunged at her, swinging at her head with his huge war hammer. She ducked and twirled, chopping at the leg of a stout orc flanking the chief. The orc cried and fell, clutching its leg.

A third orc tossed aside its club and charged Corvina. The massive beast outweighed her by three or four times. Badu winced as she went down beneath the charging monster. His stomach twisted. Then the creature's body was somersaulting over her, a blade planted in its chest. Cor was back on her feet to the cheers from Heffel and Ferat, who now ran to join the fray.

When he was in range, Badu lunged at the chief orc's back, swinging the great blade at its legs. But the oversized sword was heavy and slow in his hands. Kovug leaped over the blade, slamming Badu with a backhand that snapped his head backward. Badu staggered and fell, dropping the blade and landing hard as exploding lights again filled his vision.

Kovug pounced, raising his colossal hammer just as he had done with Faroz. Badu cringed. The orc chief jerked and froze as the tip of a spear burst through his chest. Black eyes froze on

Badu, then drifted up to Heffel and Ferat, who raced up beside Badu. Kovug staggered and dropped to his knees.

Ferat approached the kneeling orc chief with measured steps, dragging the orc blade. For a silent moment, the two just beheld each other, eyes locked in an unspoken contest. Then Ferat turned away. With a feral scream, he spun, heaving the great blade, and sheared Kovug's head from his body.

11

A NÖZ REMADE

*T*wo years later

THE WAGON BOBBED in the inky night like a vessel at sea, the soft glow of the torchstone betraying its approach through the ravine. *Herfing fezzi!* thought Badu. *A couple of sightstones and the fool wouldn't announce his travel to anyone within a cliq.* An owl cry came from the other side of the ravine. Badu answered with the same call from his rocky perch at the gorge's edge. *Go time.* A spark of dark excitement crackled within.

Dropping down the cliff like a mountain cat, he pounced from ledge to boulder, pausing in a crouch on a large rock just above the canyon floor. A fluttering sound rose followed by a scraping thud as a dark shape landed next to him.

"Target approaches," Badu whispered to Ferat, who crouched at his side. To the left, the glow of the wagon steadily crept toward them from the wide edge of the ravine into the narrows of the canyon. The well-lit procession threw long shadows onto the cliff walls that bowed and danced in silent revelry. On rolled the wagon, straight into the trap.

"Two on horseback," said Ferat, peering through a small spyglass. A puff of steam escaped his mouth. "They look tired. And cold." The night's biting edge might have kept the old Nöz home, but in recent months, every one of the nözan had completed the limits training in excessive cold up in the mountains. This weather was tame.

"And bored," Badu added.

"Not for long." Ferat's voice was dark. There was a time when Ferat smuggled a warm smile or a kind word into nearly everything he said. That time was gone. That man was dead. Ferat pocketed the spyglass and dropped the last ten measures to the canyon's sandy floor. Badu mindlessly pulled the daggers on either side of his belt out an inch from their sheaths and then pushed them back in again, unconsciously repeating the lesson from limits training to avoid the sticking of a frosted blade. He unclipped the dikeni from his belt, the razor pyramid at the end of the chain glinting in the cold moonlight as it fell.

Four stately black horses drew the elaborate coach with a two-wheeled wagon in tow. An armed guard rode ahead and one behind. *Road hypnosis,* thought Badu, noting the first guard's absent gaze fixed on the ground ahead as his head bobbed with the rhythm of his horse. Had it not been for the cold of the night, the man might have dozed off and fallen from his saddle.

As the caravan approached, Badu stood and began spinning the dikeni. The soft humming of the spinning chain broke the guard's trance, his head jerking up as he searched the darkness for the source of the sound. He might as well have been blindfolded, his night vision corrupted by the steady wash of torch-stone light.

"Whah..." He grunted, peering into the dark. "What's that?" he called out to no one. The screech of a mountain cat from the other side of the canyon shattered the night. The guard turned from Badu, now drawing his sword. Badu leaped into the air. Midflight, he let fly the dikeni. The man had no chance. The sleek, heavy iron dart screamed through the air and struck the guard, knocking him from his mount and leaving a gaping hole in his chest.

"Hiya—" yelled the coachman, slapping the reins when a crossbow bolt to the neck cut his cry short. Kafa's lumbering frame emerged from the dark. He swiftly grabbed the two lead cart horses by the bridle and whispered something to the agitated animals. Salik burst from the darkness on the far side of the canyon, leaping into the driver's seat and knocking the dying coachman from the perch. Boyhood had left him, and after a season's growth since his gecit, his hair could just now be tied back.

If the rear guard ever knew they were under attack, the realization was short-lived. Ferat sprang from the shadows. His long, springy parumak staff, now boasting a metal spike in the hardwood bulb, crunched into the side of the guard's head. The lifeless body fell from the horse.

Badu fastened the dikeni cord and slowly approached the side of the coach. No sound came from within.

"Open it," a voice commanded from behind. He glanced back at Corvina, who emerged from the canyon shadows, spear in hand.

He gave a sharp nod. "Yes, Sefa." Drawing his small crossbow, Badu jerked the coach door open. A cloud of ferikökü smoke billowed out, awash in soft blue torchstone. Cor waved the air as she moved close.

"How dare you stop us!" came a husky man's voice, dragging over the vowels. "If you're looking for money, you'll get much worse than—" *Snap!* The small crossbow in Badu's hand fired, silencing the voice. The little snake had struck.

"N-n-no!" stammered a deeper voice. Cor looked to Badu

and nodded toward the man. Pocketing the small crossbow, Badu leaned in and ripped the man from the coach. Festooned in white and blue fox furs, the portly figure tumbled the short distance to the ground, collapsing in a pathetic heap. His wailing and groveling rose.

"I... I can pay!" He knelt before Cor, hands on her boots, raising his round mustachioed face.

"Oh, you will," said Cor, backhanding him, sending the man sprawling on the sandy ground.

"Do you know who you're stealing from!" slurred the man, indignant anger having replaced his fear for the moment. He spun, seeking a new audience. His wild eyes landed on Badu. "Don't be a fool! If this load doesn't reach Kaliim in Epis Kopol, you're all dead."

"Our safety is not your greatest concern," quipped Cor. She nodded at Badu. Without pause, Badu dropped to a knee before the man, placing a hand on the thick shoulder, his fingers sinking into the plush fur, and thrust a blade into the man's chest, just below the rib cage, angled up to the heart. The man's expression froze, confused. It was a common response: indignant dismay at the inconceivable end of one's own immortality. A familiar dark wave rolled through Badu. *Due payment for a life of sins. Ultimate justice.*

THE BLACK NIGHT finally relented to dawn's crisp blossom. Pink feathery clouds bubbled up from the horizon like soap suds against the cool morning sky as the team trotted into Nöz camp. The exhilaration of the mission had long since worn off. Badu lead his choluk to the stables with heavy steps, the image of collapsing into the furs of his sleeping pad his only thought.

"You did well tonight," said Cor, suddenly in his path and meeting his gaze. He straightened, shaking off the daze.

"Want to talk about it in your tent?" Badu bandied.

"Not that well." She gave a playful smile. "But, in truth, you acted decisively; you didn't falter. You make a strong katana." The way she looked at him stoked something within. He pushed it back, forced it away as he always did. He was her katana. Nothing more.

The title still pricked something else in his mind. He had tried to escape the haunting image of that monster dragging Faroz's limp body. The vision had returned many times in his nightmares. It wasn't how he was supposed to earn the katana title. It wasn't the primal challenge of strength and cunning to capture the rank that he had imagined so many times. He had dreamed of upending his rival in front of all the Nöz. Now Faroz was just suddenly gone, his head crushed by an orc war hammer.

"Until morning, Sefa," said Ferat, having passed off the reins of his choluk to the waiting Täs.

"Well done," said Cor, turning to Ferat and lightly punching her open palm. "Stand together."

"Stand and fight," answered Ferat, in a flat but resolute voice, anchored by fatigue. He made the same fist-in-hand gesture and bumped his hands against hers, giving a very slight bow. With that, he wandered off in the direction of the tents.

A man undone, thought Badu, watching him go. Something had snapped in Ferat on the ridge with the orcs that day. The affable, gentle companion could scarcely be found in him now. His once warm brown eyes with the indomitable sparkle were now as flat and dead as a sand shark's. The only time any light returned was when Ferat was on a mission, exacting revenge.

"I've got him, uyesi," said Salik, taking the reins of Badu's choluk.

"Are you all right?" asked Badu. Salik gave a questioning look. Some of the young man's dark hair had escaped his small ponytail, and a scraggly smear of a mustache and chin hair now adorned his face.

"I remember my first raids," continued Badu. "Not always easy to sleep. And back then we never... Things have changed."

"I'm good," answered Salik with a confidence Badu wasn't sure he felt. Badu would never disgrace Salik by mentioning it, but he had heard the young man crying softly in his tent deep into the night after his first raid, where Cor ordered him to shoot an unarmed soldier.

"That man faced justice," added Badu.

"Yes, I know. A slaver, right?" Salik asked eagerly, some of the hard edge melting from his voice.

"One of the top lieutenants for that pislik filth Kaliim who runs half the brothels and slave trade in the Red Quarter. They say Kaliim tortured and killed an entire family last mooncycle because of three days' wages owed by the drunkard father." Salik listened eagerly, drinking the justification like a parched man at a stream. "That overstuffed henchman had ruthlessly killed hundreds."

"Why not take the big man down?"

"Oh, Kaliim isn't safe for long," said Badu, though he had wondered the same thing. "And when we deliver the message and he learns what's happened, he'll see shadows everywhere he looks. Cor may want those shadows to haunt him for a while." Salik breathed deeply, a weight visibly lifting. He extended his hand. Badu gripped the forearm and patted Salik's jaw with his free hand. "Get some sleep."

"Yes, Katana. As soon as the choluk are settled."

A dull ache permeated Badu's whole body from the intensity of the attack and the long ride. He stretched his back as he returned to camp. Deciding without deciding, Badu strayed into the colonnade, seeking a deep breath or two of cold, salty sea air and a glimpse of stars before turning in.

"A hard night?" came the voice from the dark.

Badu spun and peered into the shadows, but he knew the voice. "Garris, what has you up so early? It's freezing."

Garris sat on a stump, wearing his heavy furs, a pipe in his mouth. "Up early? I'm out late." He smiled. "A crisp night is good for the soul. I worry more for you."

Here we go, thought Badu. "You seem to do a lot of that these days."

Garris nodded slowly. "It's true. I mourn for what's become of the Nöz."

"Yes, I know the new way is... different from how you preferred things."

"Preferred things." Garris gave a bitter chuckle. "Killing in cold blood marks more than a preference. What of the Code?"

"The Code failed us," snapped Badu. "If it weren't for Cor breaking it, half of the Nöz would be dead." They had debated the point a hundred times.

"The Code is what makes us nözan." Garris's reply sounded automatic, resigned.

"Not anymore," Badu said dismissively. "The fist has become a blade. A blade for justice."

Garris had fought to keep the balance in the fractured Nöz, but when the week of grief and mourning for Faroz had ended, most of the nözan had voted for Cor to join the group. Following a hastily conducted gecit marking ceremony earlier in the week, Badu's vote was finally counted among the men.

Garris, Sevin the seer, Eldiven the poet, and Efe the elder were the only members who voted against Cor's joining. Sevin warned of dark storm clouds that haunted his dreams, but without any crisp image of demise, he only managed to convince Eldiven. And just like that, a crack appeared in the rock that was the Nöz. The fissure grew to a chasm in a matter of days. As soon as the vote went through, before anyone could stop her, Cor challenged Garris to nishpat omak.

"This new brand of justice only feeds your hate, son," said Garris.

"If you speak of the Farish, then yes, it prepares us, me, for that day. A day Cor says will soon come."

"Oh?" Garris raised his eyebrows. "Now the Nöz will assault the Far Seer Priest castle?"

"No, nothing like that," said Badu, remembering Cor's recent charge to tell Garris only what he must, which wasn't much since Garris refused to join most new missions. "But she says we'll have an... opportunity."

Garris pursed his lips and nodded, looking off. "I continue to ask Yuz, the ruler of peace, that your burning anger might yet find rest." The men had nearly revolted when Cor carefully proposed turning Garris out of the Nöz, so she didn't bring it up again.

"I will find peace when the Farish is dead." An uncomfortable silence followed.

"It's fear, you know." A puff of steam from Garris' mouth caught the moonlight.

"What do you mean?"

"Your rage. Beneath anger there always lurks something else."

"Garris, you don't—"

"The little boy inside you is terrified that you'll open yourself again, that you'll let in the danger that shattered his world so many season ago. He screams in your head."

Badu shook his head. "Will you join us in Epis Kopol tomorrow, Garris?" he asked, changing the subject. The nözan would ride to the city to deliver the message—the ring finger of Kaliim's trade lord wrapped in a note. It wasn't an assassination, so perhaps Garris *would* join, and besides, Cor was giving the men a night off in the city.

Garris snorted softly. "There is a great man inside you, Badu. For many years, I have felt it, seen it. Yet that vision grows dim." Badu looked away. "Still, I will continue to petition on your behalf. For a life of truth and true joy, a respite from all this."

Badu caught the look in Garris's eye. "Are you going somewhere, Ussa?" Badu hadn't called him that for seasons and didn't mean to now. Ever since Cor took the seat of the Sefa, the man had become simply "Garris." Badu silently swore not to make the mistake again.

"The night fades," replied Garris, "and this old man grows weary." He rose slowly, embracing Badu. The two walked in silence back to camp. With a nod goodnight, Badu trudged to his hut and collapsed on his sleeping mat. As he lay beneath the furs, awaiting the warmth his shivering body would bring and the approaching fog of sleep, his mind wandered back to the shift in the Nöz.

Scarcely two months after being added to the Nöz, Cor issued the challenge. Nobody quite expected it, yet it somehow felt like an inevitability. The cracks in Garris's leadership were impossible to ignore. Efe went man to man, pleading for them to stop it. The Code didn't allow an outsider, much less a woman, to issue nishpat omak. Efe managed to convince Eldiven and the yeeli, but the old allegiances had been replaced.

"She should lead us!" Badu remembered the epiphany whispered by Heffel on the ride back to camp after the orc attack. Badu had been shocked. He remembered swiveling in his saddle to look back at Heffel, noticing the thin line of black smoke from burning orc bodies still visible above the tree line. Yet that little comment had flashed like lightning in his head. *Yes! Her power! Her swift justice!* Under Cor, the Nöz could be something so much greater.

"She's earned my loyalty anyway, my life debt," Heffel had said. Badu glanced ahead where Cor led the line of men back down the path, Ferat at her side as a guide. *When did she take the first position?* He couldn't recall any discussion or debate. Cor's leadership had swept in like night after a long golden afternoon, an unspoken inevitability. "I stared death in the face today!" Heffel had said. "We all did. We all owe her a life debt!"

Cold crept over Badu as he recalled the scene for the hundredth time: the thorough devastation of total defeat, the impotence in the face of those savage, bloodthirsty orcs, the pathetic Nöz weapons like toys in the hands of babes. He felt the chill of that moment of pregnant silence on the rocky pass as those brigands ushered Cor away and the unsupervised orcs eyed their catch hungrily.

"What would it be like to be eaten by orcs?" Heffel had asked the question that chilled him to the core.

Badu shook off the memory and shivered despite the warmth of the furs and fell into the pit of sleep.

12

———

EPIS KOPOL

The nözan always entered Epis Kopol from the sea. Dozens of cart paths trickled into the city, joining like capillaries into the few primary arterial roads that flowed into the great golden city. A handful of priestguard soldiers loosely monitored these large roads, conducting ad hoc checkpoint inspections that could result in confiscated goods, beatings, or worse. However, the sprawling layout of the city made avoiding the checkpoints easy for a rider on horseback.

The nözan followed a river path, one of many that dropped into a canyon that snaked and split as its crooked fingers wound through the broken rocks of the delta, ever reaching for the sea. As long as the water hadn't overrun the banks, the men could follow the narrow dirt path that flanked the river, beneath the many arching bridges of the city until they reached the coast. There, dozens of footpaths and roads climbed back up into the heart of the city. To the slag, city buildings and streets tumbled down the rocks to the sprawling Fisherman's Quarter where rocks turned to sandy beach within the protected cove.

Badu enjoyed the ride. In warmer weather, children played

117

on the rocky riverbanks. The line of nözan on their horses always earned stares from the bathers and hunched figures washing clothes. Badu knew that look of instinctual wariness. It was the same one he got from the bluebirds in the colonnade as they inspected him, quickly assessing the danger, ever ready to flee.

Here, the look was usually reserved for the tinmen. Every Kopolian commoner knew to keep a wide berth from the roving priestguard soldiers. They operated with impunity and often were no safer than the brigands on the forest roads.

"Badu," Sevin called urgently from the back of the line. Badu slowed his horse as Sevin pulled up beside him.

"I woke last night with a dream," said Sevin in a whisper. Badu glanced up at Cor, but she was far ahead out of earshot. She had forbidden Sevin to talk of niz göru, his night sight, months ago after he wrongly predicted an assassination attempt, resulting in a full Nöz attack on a wagon carrying a pike melon farmer and his family.

"I stood before a great copper cauldron of blood." Sevin's voice quavered with the retelling. "Each of the nözan dipped their hands in the blood and smeared it across their faces."

"You know these are to be kept to yourself now," Badu said, shifting uncomfortably in his saddle. A gaunt-faced old woman looked up from a pile of sodden clothes at the men as they passed. Badu nodded.

"There's more," said Sevin, wearing a pained look. "About you. This one means something. I can feel it."

"The visions are unreliable. They're for you and you alone," Badu said with finality. "Yes, there is blood. We are the blade, but it's the blade of justice."

"But it's not just that," Sevin objected. "In the cauldron. I saw—"

Badu held up a hand, silencing him. "Better to not speak of the visions again, brother." Sevin opened his mouth again, but

Badu spurred his horse forward. Ahead, Cor glanced back, meeting Badu's eyes. He sighed. She would later press him about this conversation, he knew. The last time Sevin had spoken of his visions, she exploded, threatening to expel the seer from the Nöz permanently.

~

"KEEP THEM FOR US UNTIL TOMORROW," said Cor, dropping a few coins onto a makeshift counter at the front of the stables. The men removed a few things from their saddlebags as flitting attendants checked the horses, loosened straps, and led the animals away.

"In twos and threes," said Cor when they had stepped into the wide road in the Coastal Quarter at the edge of the city. "Kaliim's messenger meets us at the Saffron Crescent in three hours. After we deliver the message, your evenings are your own."

The men acknowledged the command in a wave of grunts and nods. Without anything more, Cor turned and slipped off, heading alone up the cobblestone street. Badu watched her go with a pang of disappointment that she hadn't asked him to join her, even if only to discuss Nöz business.

Beyond Cor, his eyes drifted up to the massive city of Epis Kopol. The late morning sun sparked across the dozens of yellow domes of city buildings, each lifted to varying heights by the city's varied topography and surrounded by the choppy sea of roofs, pierced by the proud golden spires of the seven temples. He looked back to the road, but Cor was gone. It was what she did whenever they came to the city. Where she went, he didn't know. She never offered the information, and he never pressed. *Perhaps her aunt's home in the Red Quarter?* Badu sighed.

"Why not go after her?" said Ferat quietly. "It's clear how she captivates you, uyesi."

Badu drew back. "What? She's our Sefa," he replied, trying to sound indignant. Badu had worked hard to treat Cor only as a superior officer.

"To me, yes. But to you, I think she's more than that," Ferat answered with a knowing smile. "Today is the day for deeds. Tomorrow is not promised."

"No more proverbs. I'm hungry," Kafa broke in.

"Well, that only means it's daytime," teased Sevin.

"Or night," added Salik. The men laughed. Badu noticed Salik's proud satisfaction at the reaction, a slight curl at the corners of his lips. Badu remembered being newly initiated and the constant struggle to be one of the men while never betraying any effort to do so. He also spied Täs staring with admiration at his brother, who had left his fellow yeeli to become one of the men.

"How about we treat you boys to a real Midland meal?" said Sevin. "Finnur and I found a chubbing roastery that even serves pepperfruit and sparkish cider!"

Finnur's blue eyes lit up. "Yes!"

"Bah," said Heffel. "You Midlanders can keep your oversized naked birds and bubble water. Now, some grilled goat wrapped in warm elmek with chimi sauce..." His voice drifted off.

"Oooh. Goat," agreed Kafa, licking his lips. Badu's stomach growled imagining the warm goat in paper-thin, flaky elmek dough, a favorite in the city.

"Or charred bowfish?" offered Täs. The group was silent for a moment and then burst into laughter. Täs's cheeks went red.

"Don't you get enough fish at camp?" asked Heffel.

Salik patted Täs on the shoulder, offering the solidarity of another fisherman's son. The brothers would never tire of seafood.

"Sounds like the lines have been drawn," said Badu,

assuming his rank. As close as the group might be, the splintering was inevitable when it came to a topic as sacred as food. "Go, eat. We meet at the Crescent in three." Finnur shrugged with a resigned glance to the group as he and Sevin left for the Midland district in the Green Quarter upcity. It was one of the few places where the pair, with their light hair and blue eyes, would be among the majority.

"You and Täs will be okay?" asked Badu.

"Yes, Father," quipped Salik, rolling his eyes.

"Just know we're marked," Badu cautioned. "All in the Nöz are. Cover your heads if tinmen are near." Salik closed his eyes, nodding dismissively, and he and Täs set off. Both boys had grown in stature and in standing in the group. Salik wore the eagerness of a newly marked nözan just as Badu had not long ago, and Täs counted the days until his gecit testing with small notches carved on the wooden post beside his sleeping mat.

"We're going for stone bowls," said Eldiven, nodding toward Ferat.

The pairing was no surprise. The two had become very close since Faroz's death. Eldiven, the introspective scribe and poet of the group, had lost a brother at a young age and seemed to know exactly what to say to Ferat, and perhaps more important, when not to speak. Badu had watched the two grow closer, even as his bond with Ferat dissipated. He and Ferat were joined more than ever in mission, in dispensing the Nöz's new brand of justice, and in hate for the Farish, but the camaraderie and banter they once shared had all but vanished.

Goat it was, then. As an extra precaution, Badu split up from Kafa and Heffel and agreed to meet them in the Market Quarter. There were spies everywhere in the city, and even groups of three men could draw attention. Badu walked down by the seawall skirting the Fisherman's Quarter on his circuitous route back up to market.

Here, the wide cobbled street sloped down from the heart

of the city to the Fisherman's Quarter. He could see the great bay from here and the line of reef out at sea. Badu wondered how many thousands of people over hundreds of seasons had passed where he now walked, equally captivated by the vast, glittering ocean.

"Jug of bandi?" called a street vendor from the shadows of a booth festooned with loud-colored fabrics and a pyramid of brown and green glass bottles.

"Thank you, no," replied Badu, a glowing bottle catching his eye. Even as he slowed to glance up at the bottle, Badu knew his mistake. The man rushed out of his tent, drawing close to Badu.

"You like the uzum?" The man pulled back a bit, turning his one good eye to Badu, his face filled with unspoken glee.

"No, thank you," repeated Badu. *Shivv!* he thought. *I've done it again.* Having not lived in the city since boyhood, he still hadn't mastered the Kopolian street customs. *Never acknowledge a street seller with so much as a greeting or even a glance. Saying no in anything other than an angry bark might as well be shouting you want to trade.* Heffel's coaching came back to him, but it was too late.

"I see," said the man with the silkworm eyebrows and weathered face. "One daagü and it's yours."

"A daagü?" Badu scrunched up his face. "Twenty shalip for a single jar?" He batted the air and kept walking.

"Too expensive?" the man added quickly, "Well, today I can give you two for the price of one." The man cradled the glowing jar as if it were a baby. Badu finally slowed and looked down at the prize. Even through the cloudy glass, he could see the clear, gelatinous liquid and the marble-sized balls glowing a brilliant green within.

"Caught two nights past," said the man, holding the jar close. "Pre-hatchlings, you know." His face winked and smiled and twitched a bit all at once. "Quite a ride…"

Something within Badu had already conceded defeat. He was in the dance now and he knew a purchase was the quickest way to end the affair.

The first time he had drunk uzum, it hadn't gone well, and he swore never to return. After getting past the idea of swallowing the glowing eggs carried on the back of a mother uzum skate—swallowing, not chewing, he had learned—the world had spun, and explosions of color filled his vision. He barely remembered anything the following day except Kafa laughing and scolding him for swallowing three eggs instead of just one as prescribed for the uninitiated.

"I have also vials of the finest ferikökü," added the man in a conspiratorial whisper, leaning close.

"*That* I definitely don't need," said Badu sternly. The man held up his hands deferentially. Ferikökü powder was technically outlawed within city limits, but few cared. Priestguard and pauper alike could be found floating off in feathery fingers of the fairy cloud, as it was called. At the dinner parties of the zengin, those rich elite handpicked by the Farish, it was rumored that servants passed around gilded pinch pots of the dust on silver platters to guests lounging on sofas in the open air after feasting on some delicate meal that cost more than a month of commoner wages. Yet possession and consumption of the stuff remained illegal, primarily so the Farish had yet another hook to execute his sham justice.

Badu fished an agü, worth ten shalip, out of his pocket and pressed it into the dealer's hand. He took the jar and gave a nod. It was half the daagü the man had requested.

"Wait! That wasn't the offer," objected the vendor, his voice rising. "I said two, for a daagü." But Badu knew the deal was done. He saw how the man had relaxed his grip on the jar as Badu pulled, and the vendor's eye twitched slightly, as it had twice during their interaction, each after gaining ground on Badu in their conversation. The hawker slid the agü note into his pocket, even as he continued his surprised and distressed theatrics. Badu twisted his closed fist in the air, thumb turned up, in the common goodbye gesture, turned his back on the vendor, and walked away.

The city always filled Badu with anticipation and excitement. The constant hum of people and activity pulsed with an energy that dredged up scraps of memory from childhood. Unlike so many others, these were fond memories. He recalled market day on the Bishmat holiday, the exhilaration, tinged with fear, as he gripped the maroon braided cord his mother had fashioned that tethered him to the twins ahead and Ildemala behind as they snaked through the pulsing crowd.

Yes, that cord, he mused, recalling it for the first time in years. It was the anchor line securing him in the rough seas of bodies and shouts, keeping him close enough to see his mother's glowing face looking back. He could see it now, the mischievous smile both reassuring and daring them to abandon fear and soak up the pounding rhythms of Bishmat ceremonial drums and the thick fragrances and sounds of the market. That was Damla's way, rushing boldly into life's currents.

"Please, no." A woman's urgent voice snapped Badu back to the moment. He found the owner of the voice. A priestguard grasped the wrist of a young woman, his large frame pinning her against the low seawall. The countless reminders of the Liar and his rotten reign had again shattered the city's tranquil façade.

The priestguard soldiers were imposing by design. By decree, each soldier was required to wear full armor at all times. Removing armor in public was punishable, but especially the black facemask. If a soldier ever revealed his face before commoners, he could be executed. Maroon chainmail with flame-red edges draped each soldier, the cold matte black greaves, vambraces, and gauntlets providing far more protection than necessary for the typical scuffles with common street rass.

"A thief!" declared the soldier, lifting the woman to her feet and inspecting her figure. Badu's stomach dropped. The declaration carried the full weight of the Farish.

"I'm no thief!" insisted the woman. "I am selling coral fruit with my father." She dropped a round blue fruit to the ground, and it rolled away. Badu spotted an older man hobbling out from behind a fruit stand.

"Take your hands off of her!" the man shouted, waving a cane. "She's no thief. She's my daughter!"

"You'll have to come with me for questioning," said the soldier, ignoring the approaching man. Badu's stomach turned again as the woman's two crimes became crystal clear: she was poor, and she was beautiful.

"You'll not take my Henna anywhere!" The old man hurried beside the girl, taking a feeble swing at the soldier with his cane as he did. The thin wood cane skittered off the heavy armor harmlessly.

"You attack me!" roared the priestguard as he pushed the old man with his off hand. A surprised cry escaped the man as he lurched backward. The man's balance was off. He stumbled, and when he hit the low seawall, his legs caught, causing him to flip awkwardly over the edge. In a sudden flurry, he was gone. The woman's shriek followed her father down the precipitous cliff to the rocks below. Someone nearby screamed.

"Herfing street soz," proclaimed the soldier. Badu froze midstep, a cold blast ripping through him, his white knuckles clenched on the dagger handle beneath his cloak.

"Monster!" the woman bellowed, turning back from the scene with wild eyes as she pounded on the guard's chest plate.

The guard pulled her close. "I'd stop that hitting if you don't want to join him!" he hissed. He marched the woman away against her struggling and loud protestations.

A pair of onlookers raced to the wall and looked over. The closest one, a man, drew back slightly, color drained from his face.

Badu still stood in the middle of the street, knife in hand, his glare boring into the back of the guard, who stopped briefly to inspect fruit on a cart as he escorted the catatonic woman away.

In a flurry, he rushed up behind the guard, stabbing him beneath the armor. As the guard reeled and staggered, Badu slammed him in the face and then grabbed him by the back of the collar, dragging him to the ledge. Roaring with rage, Badu hurled the man over the wall to join the girl's father on the jagged rocks a hundred measures below.

The imaginary vision vanished even as the guard continued down the street, disappearing among the busy seafood vendors with his prize. The soft sobs of the shaken woman nearby filled Badu's ears. Hate saturated him.

BADU HAD LOST HIS APPETITE. Instead of joining Kafa and Heffel for mutton, he wandered Epis Kopol, his mind swirling with the image of the old man falling and hateful flickers of memory of the brutal tinmen from his own childhood. An hour later, he passed through the Golden Row, a line of great manors that housed the zengin, priests and other elite devoted to the Farish. He made note of Kaliim's opulent mansion with its carved statues and gilded doors. *How is that filth still living in luxury?*

Finally, Badu found himself at the slag end of the city, facing the massive black gate on the bridge leading from the city edge to the Farish's great black castle. Whether he had come by design or accident, he couldn't say. The gate usually remained open, but no fewer than six priestguard soldiers manned the entrance at all times.

Flanking the gate on either side stood what looked like small stone fountains, providing faithful Kopolians a place to pray for their leader. Precariously stacked coin offerings adorned the fountains, untouched by even the poorest visitors who would lose a hand for removing a single copper pimika. The stone bowls at each station were permanently stained a dark maroon from the blood sacrifices of some unfortunate bird or small mammal slain in the name of the Farish's health and prosperity.

Beyond the gate, a delicate bridge stretched over a deep gulch to the Farish's castle. Except on Byran Hanu, the feast day that occurred twice a season, no Kopolians were permitted to pass through the gate except on official business. On Byran Hanu, the gates were flung open and all Kopolians were invited to cross over to the sprawling plaza at the foot of the Farish's castle. From a balcony a hundred measures above, the Far Seer Priest would grace his subjects with an address met by frenzied cheers, encouraged by the ferikökü roots, or shims, generously distributed to the citygoers.

Badu knelt before one of the stone offering stations, his eyes locked on the black monolith across the ravine. The dark castle stood in stark contrast to the whitewashed, sparkling city with its golden domes and low-slung buildings that bowed at its feet. Black spires jutted up from every side, rising hundreds of measures into the sky. From here, the towering façade dominated the view. Somewhere up there, beyond the gates, tucked against the far cliff, lay the courtyard beside the sea called the Altar. All Kopolians knew that the Farish's enemies were facing death when blue smoke billowed from the Altar.

"The day is not far off when we will meet within those black

walls, my *Farish*," said Badu quietly. "That day will be mine."
He felt the wandering eyes of the guards on him. Lifting his
right hand to his forehead, he knelt and dropped forward in a
short bow. As he did, he scooped a pile of coins into his pocket
with his other hand, rose, and left.

THE INFORMANT

Sitting in shadows, Badu pretended to be invested in the bread and cheese resting on his lap as he monitored the faded yellow façade of the Saffron Crescent across the street. He had spotted Kafa and Heffel doing the same a stone's throw up the street at the shoe and hat stall. Nothing looked out of order. Badu rose, took one last bite of bread, and tossed it and the chese on the ground. As he crossed the busy road, movement above caught his eye. An attractive young woman draped in purple, with a shoulder exposed, leaned out over one of the many private balconies that studded the façade of the Crescent. She blew him a kiss.

Not today. Badu lowered his eyes and pressed ahead. He nodded at one of the two well-armed thugs at the door, earning a nod in return, and passed through the tall wooden doors into the dark interior. It took a moment for his eyes to adjust from the sun-bleached streets to the pink glow of the tavern. The smell of ferikökü pipe smoke, bodies, and the signature saffron incense brought a wave of memories. Patrons packed a long bar on the left of the room and filled the tables and the booths lined up along the right wall, beneath the giant mounted buyuk skull. Business was good.

"Hello, soldier," a voice cooed from beside him. Badu didn't need to look to match the voice with the woman from the balcony, but he did anyway.

"Hello, Arva."

"Have you come to visit with me?" She touched his cheek.

"Here for a meeting," he replied levelly.

Her painted face dropped into an exaggerated pout. "Well, come find me when it's over." She flashed an alluring smile.

No, not today, Badu repeated. He returned the smile, gave a short nod, and moved across the room to one of three beaded archways in the far wall. Beyond the hanging beads, he entered a small, dimly lit room with a large table surrounded on three sides by benches adorned with navy-blue and mustard-yellow cushions. The incense was so thick it burned his eyes.

"Welcome," said Cor, seated at the head of the table. Their eyes met and held for a moment. Badu looked away. Salik and Täs had already arrived, as had the Midlanders, Sevin and Finnur. "No trouble today, I trust?" asked Cor.

He paused for a moment, the shout of the falling man registering in his mind. "Nothing out of character for this soulless city," he replied, sitting beside her. "Kafa and Heffel are outside. They'll be along shortly."

"Excellent," she replied.

"You skipped a great meal," said Finnur, a wide smile on his face. "Chubbing and pepperfruit!"

"They even had fresh cloudbread," Sevin added. Yes, if only he had joined the pair instead of walking down by the seawall.

"Did we miss anything?" Kafa and Heffel ducked into the room. Even when trying to use his inside voice, Kafa boomed.

"The last are just behind us," Heffel said to Cor, reporting with the formality of a trained guard as he removed his cape and sat.

"Very good. We'll start when they arrive." She poured herself a cup of water from a clay pitcher.

Kafa dropped a jug of glug on the table and squeezed into a bench.

"Aha," said Finnur, rubbing his hands together.

"Well, if I had known it would be that kind of meeting..." said Badu, withdrawing the uzum jar and setting it beside the jug. The glowing green orbs swirled and sloshed within. The men murmured.

"We have business." Cor eyed him with reproach. Badu held up his hands in deference.

"And you, Sefa? Where'd you go?" Salik asked. Badu shifted uncomfortably as Cor's face hardened.

"I had business elsewhere in the city," she retorted. Salik glanced at Badu for a clue as to what line he had crossed to earn such a cold reply. Badu gave a subtle shake of his head. Salik hadn't been on the earlier trip when Cor snapped at Ferat for a similar inquiry.

"Time to start," said Kafa, breaking the awkward quiet as Ferat and Eldiven entered. Eldiven still walked with the hint of a limp from the ankle broken seasons ago that had never healed quite right. The hindrance kept him from some of the most rigorous excursions, but he never missed a chance to carouse in the city. His eyes lit up when he saw the uzum. Badu gave him a wink.

"Ferat, the package?" asked Cor. Ferat fished a wooden box from his bag and set it on the table.

"Is the note inside?" asked Cor. Ferat nodded. "Very good. Kaliim's messenger should be by shortly. He'll slip the package into a crate of yasbandi wine to be delivered to Kaliim this evening."

"Kaliim will be furious," said Eldiven.

"He'll learn his lesson," answered Kafa.

"And he'll see there's more to fear in this city than just the

Farish," said Cor with a hint of a smile. "If he crosses us again, the next body part in a box will be his." Murmurs of agreement rose.

"Why do we let him live?" Ferat cut in.

"What?" Cor asked.

"Why do we let that abuser, that scourge of the city, breathe a moment longer than necessary?"

"His time will come," she replied flatly, a steely look in her eye.

"May Kaliim choke on his pudding!" Kafa raised a glass, and the group toasted with water.

"That's it?" asked Salik, glancing around. "Business is done?"

Was I so impetuous? wondered Badu. *Indeed, you were,* answered a silent voice.

"No, not entirely." Cor's voice hardened. Badu looked up, brow furrowed. "Something has... come up," she added.

"What something?" A cold feeling skittered across Badu's skin like a spider. He ignored it.

"There's an urgent... engagement."

Badu stared at her searchingly. He and Cor always discussed the details of any mission at length before it had materialized into a plan, and certainly before the Nöz struck.

"Someone has discovered our camp," she said plainly. Ferat sucked air through his teeth, and Kafa grunted in confusion. "And they're bringing that information to the Adder."

"You learned this?" asked Badu, his voice more accusing than he intended. "From where?"

"I just received the message from a... source of mine. A reliable one. We have a short window to intercept the informant before the information reaches the Adder. I only need two."

The Adder. Mention of the name recalled the picture permanently burned in Badu's mind: the dead-black silhouette of the man, drenched in morning sun, framed by the narrow alley bringing a sword down on his mother as Garris dragged him away. The Adder had replaced the Butcher as the Farish's general. The Butcher was cold, but it was said the Adder's skill with the blade was only outmatched by his savagery. Some claimed he couldn't be killed. Badu hoped to prove that wrong someday, too.

The spy network confirmed that, with the Nöz attacks growing more brazen over months, the Adder had developed an obsession with finding and destroying the group. Badu had tried brushing away the notion with his usual bravado, but the idea of the crazed murderer relentlessly hunting them was impossible to dismiss. This information could not be allowed to reach him.

"I'll go," blurted Ferat. "The Skyrt must remain hidden."

"And me," Badu quickly added.

"Very good," Cor said. "We leave in twenty minutes."

"You need only two?" asked Eldiven, though Badu knew he wouldn't be included even if she needed five. Cor nodded sharply.

Badu glanced up to see Sevin staring at him intently. *Ahh yes, the dream,* thought Badu. *What did he see?*

"I'll be right here when you get back," said Heffel. "Babysitting your uzum." He winked at Badu.

"I would come," Kafa said, raising his hands, "but I can't leave Heffel alone." His eyes smiled.

"If the information is good, it will be quick," said Cor. "A lethal graveseeker strike."

Badu looked up at her. "A graveseeker? You have a zehi?" How could this be? The incredibly deadly, venomous zehi that dragged its massive, tentacled body along the bottom of the deep ocean floor was rarely encountered.

Cor glanced knowingly around the table as she removed a small bundle wrapped in black cloth and set it before them. The men exchanged glances.

"A hatchling?" asked Heffel. "How'd you find it?"

"My sources," she replied, peeling back the layers of cloth. "And I can get more." Badu stared transfixed as Cor unwrapped the deadly prize. He felt himself drawing back from the table and noticed the others doing the same.

Before them rested one of the deadliest creatures in Yidui-ijn, in miniature. No bigger than a meat pie, the object could have been mistaken for a rounded hunk of quartz. The surface was a cloudy pink color and hollow as something moved inside. Cor tapped the outside of the pod, and immediately a dark object within darted at her finger, sucking to the side of what Badu could now see was no stone but rather an inflated bladder.

"Heard a zehi can kill a man in three minutes flat," said Eldiven.

"Faster for a hatchling," said Cor. "Can't regulate its venom."

"How do you control it?" asked Ferat.

"You can't," came Salik's voice. Surprised eyes turned to the young man. "I've seen it. A fisherman, a friend of my father, caught one in his deepwater nets. I was young but remember it like yesterday. The pod cracked open with a pop when he jabbed it with his knife. Something flew out. The man was dead before we could even get to him."

"There is a way," said Cor. "If the umbilical sack, the cherry, is removed"—she pointed to what looked like a scarlet berry affixed to the outside of the pod by purple filaments—"the hatchling follows it like a hound. Don't want to be nearby when it reaches the cherry, though."

Badu swallowed. "Couldn't we use a more... traditional method?"

"This sends a message that a blade cannot," Cor said. "The Adder needs to know we're not to be trifled with."

Badu had to give her credit. She had style. *The Nöz will become known and feared.*

"Could be him next," said Ferat darkly.

"Exactly." Corvina smiled and upended her water glass.

"How committed are you to the Nöz?" Cor whispered. She crouched beside Badu high in the limbs of a great oak tree beside the cart path a cliq outside the city. Dusk was here, the mountains off to the nost already standing black against a plum sky, gashes of pink and red streaking over the sea behind the city.

"Committed?" Badu almost laughed. "Why do you ask that? You know I'm more devoted than any. The Nöz is everything to me."

"The Nöz is family," she agreed. "United by mission."

"To kill the Farish."

"Yes. And anything that stands in the way of that mission—"

"We destroy," Badu cut in. "I *will* have his blood." His jaw clenched.

"Yes. Good. You'll have your chance. Sooner than you know."

A mourning dove call rang through the open forest.

"He's coming," Cor said, removing the bundle from her pack. A shape below darted from tree to tree across the road. Again, a single dove call. The muffled clinking sound of a horse wagon echoed through the trees.

"You sure you can do this?" she asked, placing the bundle in his hands.

Not at all, he thought. "Yes. You know I can." The plan was simple: Ferat would confirm the target—a crow call meant it was the wrong wagon, but a warbler cry meant they were on. Cor would drop down, close enough to toss the cherry inside the cart, and Badu would crack open the zehi pod. How he earned the job of handling the deadly creature still wasn't entirely clear. What if it didn't seek the cherry? What if it just attacked the first person it saw? The sound of the wagon grew louder.

Part of him wished for the crow call. *No! That would be far worse. We must destroy the informant,* he reminded himself. His heart raced. A warbler cry rang out loud and clear. Looking up, his eyes met Cor's. She gave a tight smile and a shallow nod. Something felt off. Her thumb fidgeted. *What's behind her smile? Worry? Concern?* He searched her face, mentally flipping over the shard of fear. *Does she truly know how the creature works? No,* he quickly concluded. *She wouldn't recklessly endanger him, would she?* He pushed the thought away and returned the smile.

Cor took a deep breath, ripped the cherry off, and thrust the pod into his arms. She dropped silently through the branches. The zehi pod felt hollow and too light for its size, like cloudbread in his trembling hands. As soon as Cor had removed the cherry, the hatchling began flailing wildly within. It would survive only a couple of minutes without the umbilical pod. Badu lay on his stomach on the large branch and carefully removed a knife.

Below, the smudged shape of a tall brown horse appeared through the leaves. A single coachman sat on the mahogany driver's bench of the wagon. *Strange the Adder hadn't bothered to dispatch a priestguard to escort this prize,* Badu mused. *All the better.* Corvina crouched at the base of an adjacent tree. As the cart passed, she popped up, tossed something into the coach's open window, and disappeared into the brush.

Badu drew back and jabbed the pod with the knife. The surface was harder than he expected, and the blade skittered off the side. The pod lurched to the side, popping out of his grip. As it rolled off his leg, Badu's hand shot out faster than his mind, catching the pod just before it fell away. He jerked to the side and collapsed on the limb, nearly falling off himself. The zehi thrashed and ricocheted against the walls of its prison. He steadied himself, heart racing, drew back, and slammed the knife into the pod.

Pop! The sound of a bursting wineskin startled Badu, and he almost dropped the bundle again. He carefully twisted the blade, releasing a hiss. As soon as his knife had created an opening in the pod, a black shape shot out. For a moment, the miniature squid-like hatchling just hung in the air. A half dozen tiny serpentine tentacles covered in small pouches that inflated like windsocks caught a breeze Badu hadn't even felt and held the creature suspended before his face. *Is it looking at me?* Badu held his breath.

Suddenly the creature retracted its tentacles, collapsing the pouches, and dropped like a stone straight down through the canopy toward the approaching wagon. Badu sat frozen with equal parts horror and fascination. In midair, the creature inflated again, sending it floating lazily through the air like a dandelion seed, over the head of the oblivious driver onto the roof of the carriage, where it collapsed again, landing with a soft splat. With the speed of a wolf spider, the hatchling darted across the carriage and disappeared through the open window. Badu let his breath out.

A cry from the carriage pierced the quiet woods, and the coachman jerked up. He wrenched the reins pulling the horse to a skidding stop.

The coachman stood, an alarmed look on his face as he peered over his shoulder. "Sir, are you—" A whizz and thud cut him off as Ferat's crossbow bolt struck him in the chest. He tumbled from the bench.

Badu landed softly on the dirt, thankful to be on solid ground again.

"Confirm the traitor is dead," Cor ordered. Badu nodded, drawing his dagger. A closed coach could contain nearly anything. Ferat had reloaded and covered him from behind. Badu flung the door open and quickly surveyed.

"Just one," he called. The slumped figure appeared not to be moving. Badu ducked in, his eyes taking a moment to adjust. Then his breath caught, and freezing ice lanced through his veins.

There, slumped against the bench, sucking in thin, ragged breaths, his eyes wide and searching, lay Garris. On his neck, as if permanently affixed, clung the small, lifeless body of the zehi hatchling, tentacles splayed. Badu couldn't breathe. He lurched backward, hitting his head on the frame of the coach. *What... what's this? Where is the informant?*

When Garris's wild gaze landed on Badu, he suddenly relaxed, as if finding a lost friend. "I... I see." Garris's voice scraped.

"They said you were a traitor," stammered Badu. "Delivering Nöz secrets to the Farish..."

Garris only offered a half smile as he blinked slowly. "Badu, death comes for me. I can feel its breath. But... first..."

"No. I... I..." Badu couldn't find the words. A thousand emotions tore through him: fear, panic, shame, and confusion exploded in his whirling mind.

"Your soul. Your heart." Garris coughed, and blood trickled from the corner of his mouth. "They grow cold. It's Cor... She's not..." He closed his eyes again.

Badu spotted the bags on the bench across from Garris, and the tempest of emotion quieted, focusing on a single thought. "Wait... You're leaving? Running away?" In an instant, his shock and sorrow had hardened. *Garris is deserting the Nöz. He is a traitor,* the accusing voice sounded in his head. In an instant, the fear and shame flashed to anger.

"Beware... the killing." Garris now struggled even to breathe. His eyes stayed closed.

"I know," snapped Badu, surprising himself with the edge

on his voice. "It's not your way. It's not your Code. But things have changed. We are stronger than we've ever been. You kept the Nöz weak. Faroz died because of it. And now, you leave?" It was the first time he'd given words to the torrent of anger and betrayal he felt.

"Find your center. Find the light." The voice was just a whisper. "And do... not trust... Cor."

A familiar wave of defiance rose. Badu had argued this point with Garris a hundred times. "She leads us boldly. She leads well," Badu replied. "She will bring me before the Farish. To face him. To kill him."

"So be it." Garris's breath was barely perceptible. Badu swallowed hard. Suddenly the man spasmed, and his eyes flashed open. "Wait! I... left... in your tent."

"What?" Badu leaned close.

"I left... a gift for you... in your trunk." He shuddered, grabbing Badu's arm.

"A gift?"

"Istak tevin," said Garris, and with a sharp gasp, he jerked and was still.

For a long moment, Badu didn't move, paralyzed in the thick air of the coach, gazing at his dead mentor. His Ussa. The storm within him shifted again, winds of sorrow rushing in with howling accusations. *What have you done? You have killed my Ussa!* As the horror of those words swelled within him and his eyes burned with hot tears, he felt a hand rest on his back. Somehow, at the touch, the rising tide within him immediately stopped, and the waves of sorrow vanished.

"It had to be done," came Cor's voice. "He was deserting us."

"He abandoned the family," came Ferat's voice as well.

So, he knew. "There was no informant," Badu stated rather than asked.

"The old man knew everything," Cor replied coolly. "Can you imagine what would happen to him, when the Adder found him? What would happen to us? This was the way. I needed you here for this."

"You lied to me." Badu slowly turned on her. "*You* killed him!"

"Yes. I did—we did what had to be done. You had to be here. To be strengthened by this." She leveled her eyes on Badu. A flicker of unconscious thought informed him that Ferat's crossbow was trained on him. "The old man's time had passed. He was deserting us. His Code would have gotten us all killed." Cor rested a hand on Badu's arm.

The rage bubbling up inside him receded. He closed his eyes. "Yes," Badu finally said, nodding. "Yes. The fist has become a blade." Cor motioned to Ferat.

"A blade for justice," answered Ferat, lowering the crossbow.

14

FERIKÖKÜ

Silence swallowed the small back room of the Crescent, shrinking it to the size of a coffin as the news of the strike settled. Täs looked wildly from one man to another, tears pooling in his eyes.

"Garris led us well," said Heffel finally, raising a cup of glug from the nearly empty jug. "But he held us back."

"When a Guti chief can no longer lead, he picks another, and they fight to the death," rumbled Kafa.

Badu looked up and found himself locked in Sevin's gaze. The Midlander's blue eyes glistened, and he looked profoundly troubled and sad. Badu knew Sevin had foreseen the event. *What would I have done if he had warned me?*

"He deserted us," added Ferat. "And his Code killed Faroz."

The mention of Faroz had a strange effect. It acted like an elixir, instantly uniting the nözan, many of whom were still haunted by fitful nightmares that brought orcs back into their tents at night. They remembered why they had chosen Cor. Everyone at the table drank, even Cor and the young brothers.

After two more jugs and more toasts, Salik stumbled out,

lugging the semiconscious Täs off to find somewhere soft to collapse.

"We saved it for you, Bizhak." Kafa smiled at Badu, holding up the uzum jar, mischief in his eyes.

"That's my cue," said Cor, rising.

"You won't stay?" Badu asked, locking eyes with her and speaking freely.

"No. But walk with me?"

Badu rose obediently, the room tilting just a bit as he stood. Cor led him through the haze of ferikökü smoke out into the street and the warm night air. The street was far emptier than during midday but still had plenty of activity. The moon was strong, and two days of workfast began tomorrow, drawing the revelers out in droves.

Cor led them a block from the Crescent to the archway of a bathhouse and stopped.

"Are you okay?" She turned to him, resting a hand on his arm. Her tone was different. For the first time he could remember, she didn't speak with the voice of a superior officer, a resistance leader. The question held an earnestness behind the words as she gazed up at him. Badu started at the intimacy of the stare. *She is beautiful.* His slackened thoughts slipped past his usual defenses.

"I asked a lot of you today," she continued. "But I believe you can handle it."

Badu rested a hand on hers. "I... I think I understand it," he finally replied. "Like the Guti custom. I know why it had to be done." Even as he said it, silent splinters of regret and remorse assailed Badu, but he had long since mastered the art of segregating and locking away the avalanche of emotions that might overwhelm a common man. It was the only way to take the life of another.

"I've never spoken to you of my past. When I was a girl of eleven seasons, my town, Ghiesa, was attacked." Cor looked up at him with a foreign unsteadiness behind her eyes, as if weighing each word before she spoke it. Badu leaned closer.

"For weeks, we had watched the ever-growing Kopolian camp creep into the valley that separated us from the rest of the world. They flew a foreign banner. Red and black." She looked down, nodding slightly, lost in a memory. "My father was a great warrior. He wanted to take up arms, to rally our neighboring villages to strengthen our defenses and expel the invaders from the valley, but the alderman argued for a delegation to negotiate patience and peace. He swayed the council." Her eyes swept back up at him. Were they glistening? "I still remember the vacant stare of the alderman's head on a pole two nights later as our town burned. The flag planted in the town square flew the blood-red and black colors of the Far Seer Priest."

"Shivv!" Badu seethed. "And your parents?"

"Killed," Cor replied flatly.

"And what about you? How'd you ecape?" But even as the question left his lips, he saw her stiffen. The deep sorrow in her eyes vanished, and again, she was strong, hard.

"Garris would always have stood in our way," Cor said, slamming closed the door to her past. "If not in the flesh, then in your minds. The old way had to pass."

Badu nodded, still feeling the embers of rage stoked by Cor's story. "He would have kept me from killing the Farish," Badu replied simply, the thought jumping to his mind with startling clarity.

"Yes, it was not his way. Not his Code." She flipped strands of tawny hair from her face. "But I will have you standing before that imposter as promised." Her flitting gaze locked on his own. His pulse raced. "Badu..." Her voice faltered. "There's something I need to tell you."

"Anything," he replied quickly.

"I... I..." Her eyes darted from one of his to the other, and her mouth moved to form words, but nothing came. He had never seen her like this.

Without thinking, he put a hand on her waist. Time froze as each searched the other's face. *What are you doing? She's the Sefa!* But instead of pushing him away, Cor raised a hand to his cheek. Their faces moved slowly toward one another, her green eyes sparking in the moonlight. He was sure she could feel his thundering heartbeat. Just inches from him, she stopped.

"The morning will not be your friend," she finally said, patting his cheek and shattering the trance as she pulled away. He opened his mouth to object but found nothing. She dropped her hand and turned to go. Stealing one last long look over her shoulder, she locked eyes with him, the look bursting with the unsaid, the undone. Then, just like that, she turned away and was gone. Badu stood alone in the dark street, steadying himself on the stone archway.

"Pour it!" bellowed Badu, bursting through the shower of beads to rejoin Kafa, Ferat, and Heffel, the sole remnant still holding down the back room. The others had wisely dispersed to their quarters in the Crescent or next door at the Lotus.

Heffel's eyes lit up as he snatched up the jar of uzum. Like an alchemist, he carefully deposited exactly two glowing beads in each of the three cups. His face glowed emerald with greedy delight as he watched the brilliant, luminescent marbles tumble from the jar. When they left the thick liquid and touched air, the beads flared with a bright green intensity.

"To my brothers!" Ferat said, lifting his cup, no hint of irony on his face.

"To the Nöz," answered the others as they threw back the drink.

For a few moments, nothing happened. Then, as a man

losing his footing in a strong current above a waterfall, Badu fell into the uzum swirl, carrying him over the edge, into the rushing night.

～

A LARGE BIRD screamed just inches from Badu's pounding head as the hateful sun lit a red fire behind his eyelids. Without opening his eyes, he tried to find himself. The first clues were his splitting headache and how his mouth tasted like a bogmarsh. Shouts rose from somewhere below him.

Badu squinted a puffy eye open, trying to fill the black canvas with memory to determine where he was and what had happened. Epis Kopol. Something jabbed him in the back. As he slowly sat up, the world heaved to the side and swayed. He quickly lay back down but moved from the pile of broken baskets and discarded fishnets that he now dully recalled seemed like a perfect place to collapse the night before. He was on the open-air roof patio of a low building littered with supplies and encircled by a short wall. The sounds of the waking city surrounded him. He lay flat on the roof tile, his eyes squeezed shut against the already bright sky. *Never again,* he promised himself.

As the pounding blacksmith within his head flattened his will to move, he tried to piece together the blur of the very long night, working to distinguish reality from fantasy. He waded through the tangled thicket of his muddy thoughts, plucking scraps of memory like weeds that he examined in the light. *Garris.* The thought stabbed a hole in his gut. *Not a nightmare. Cor, by the bathhouse: also real.*

He remembered singing loudly with his brothers. Then the fight. He touched his lip, and the bruise on his cheek twinged. The street thugs had picked the wrong drunkard. *Did I kill one? No. Kafa stopped me. Ugh, the stranger with the ferikökü pipe. Why had I been alone?* The cloud of memories then faded into a dream. *Was the woman real? Arva?* He recalled pulling back from a kiss and seeing Cor's face. Calling her name. Then a slap. *Nope, not Cor.*

And the battle. He had dueled with the Farish! *No, not possible. A ferikökü hallucination.* Yes, *that* was what had him finally thrown out of the Crescent.

"*Are you mad?*" He recalled the hissing voice of the door guard as he shoved Badu out. "*Screaming about killing the Farish is a dead man's game!*"

A small crowd cheered as Badu staggered out of the Crescent and into the street. "*Traitor!*" He dimly recalled the birdlike man with hollow cheeks and the maroon cloak who had spit at him.

Fear lanced through Badu now as he recalled his shouting threats to kill the god who ruled the city. *You fool!* Spies were everywhere. "*Your hate makes you reckless.*" He recalled Garris's warning. *Garris.* A wave of nausea. Everything burned a raging red against the relentless morning sun. He slipped in and out of consciousness.

"Come!" a shout pierced the din from the street below, jerking him awake. He could make out the distinct shuffle of boots on stone, more urgent and closer than the general street traffic. Badu crawled to the wall and peered over, squinting through puffy eyes.

"Up there!" shouted a man in a maroon cloak, pointing. It was the very same man who had spit at him the night before. He now stood with a patrol of eight priestguard. "Come to kill the Farish, he said." Badu dropped out of sight. *Shivv!* Two stories below, soldiers pounded on a door, demanding entry. Adrenaline jolted through him, quickening his thoughts and clearing the haze in his mind.

He scrambled across the roof on unsteady legs to the far side and peered over. A guard stood stationed below, watching the back entrance and dark, narrow alley. There would be one, maybe two guards at the front as well. Badu glanced around frantically as rushing feet entered the building and thundered up the stairs.

Gripping a fishing net draped over the edge of the roofline, he groaned as he lowered himself a few measures and then, with a deep breath, dropped directly on top of the priestguard below. Badu let his full weight crash into the man with a heavy crunch. The stunned guard wriggled like a worm on the dirt as Badu forced himself to his feet. He ripped the guard's helmet off and slammed the man in the head with it twice, knocking him unconscious. He glanced up to see if anyone had spotted the commotion, but they were alone in the shadows.

Against the protest of every muscle in his body and fighting the angry sea that sloshed in his stomach, Badu heaved the guard in through the doorway and quickly slit the knot holding his maroon cape. Pushing the helmet on and tossing the cape over his shoulders, Badu stepped back out through the doorway just as a half dozen soldiers burst out onto the roof above. Boots scraped on the sandy tile as the soldiers fanned out. Crates were upended and boxes overturned.

"Nothing!" called a guard, peering over the edge down at Badu.

"I swear he was here," came the whiny voice of the man with the maroon cloak.

"Waste of time," someone grumbled. Badu stepped inside, releasing the breath he didn't know he'd been holding as he tossed the helmet and cloak on the guard, who moaned and stirred. He knew he should go, run, yet even as he looked at the priestguard, Badu's vision flickered to his family sitting room in his childhood home: the door bursting open with a crash. The Adder slamming his father in the face. The priestguard soldier dragging his sister by her hair. The sword falling on his mother.

The semiconscious guard spasmed as Badu drove the man's

own blade into his chest, dark rage coursing through him like a furnace fire. Footsteps sounded on the stairs. Badu spat on the dead guard and then turned and stumbled from the house. Shouts sounded from behind as he slipped down an alley and disappeared into the thin crowd of early marketgoers.

15

THE RITUAL

Bathed in the light of a hundred candles, a bony, trembling hand reached for the sleeve of the ceremonial robe.

"You've waited too long this time, Tahvil," barked the Far Seer Priest, his voice quavering like an old man's.

"Forgive me, Master," groveled the frail priest as he held out a golden chalice. Tahvil wore a long blood-red robe with a towering collar rising past his semitranslucent ears. Like all priests in the castle, a dozen thin scars disfigured Tahvil's face. The Farish snatched the goblet with shaky hands, splashing a bit of the thick purple liquid on the floor before reaching his lips. He drank greedily.

Tahvil retched slightly from the vile odor of the healer's potion. "We held the ritual two mooncycles ago like we always do, Your Grace—"

"You've miscounted your days," snapped the Farish, even as he tipped the chalice to suck the final drops of the potion.

"Yes, my lord," Tahvil offered. The Farish could feel the chief priest longing to steal a glance at his master's face, with the golden mask raised and resting on his forehead. The Farish's pale and shriveled skin, splotched with age marks and streaked with ancient purple scars, looked like wet paper. The Far Seer Priest pulled his mask down, pausing to wipe his lips with a silkeen table napkin before fully lowering the golden veil into position. The nasty potion was utterly undrinkable when the healers had first presented it to the Farish, causing him to retch the stuff back up, and costing one of the healers his life. It took weeks for him to hold down even a thimbleful. Now, he drank it eagerly. The foul potion filled him with a warm, invigorating rush of energy.

"I'm sure I have erred," answered Tahvil deferentially, his eyes on his own feet now, his voice trembling slightly. He was alone with the Farish, of course. No other servant was trusted to be present in the cavernous dining chamber when the Farish removed his mask. Nor was any other permitted in the ruler's sleeping chamber. Despite Tahvil's special position of trust, the Farish had made it exceedingly clear that if he caught anyone, Tahvil included, looking at his uncovered face, that man's blood would be the next sacrifice for the dragons.

"Or perhaps the power of the shard wanes," Tahvil offered.

"Ha!" the Farish croaked. "Its power is greater than ever and growing. Bring it!" he commanded. The Farish's voice already sounded stronger, yet behind those words, his mind swirled.

"Of course, Great One." Tahvil bowed, palm to forehead. "You will be pleased with today's offering."

The elixir had already begun its work, bringing the Farish a renewed vigor but also ushering flickering pictures of the unseen into the edges of his vision. Through the blurry clouds brought by the potion, a voice tugged at him to leave the confines of the throne room. *I am coming,* he answered silently.

Tahvil stooped and unlatched the clasps on the wooden box resting on the table beside the Farish. His hands trembled slightly as he lifted the lid. A sliver of blue, glowing light escaped the box as he did, sending fluttering through his chest.

Tahvil took a sharp breath, as he always did when he beheld the relic.

The heavy, intricate gold lattice adorning the pectoral bib could have made a man rich for years, but the precious metal was scat compared to the prize cradled at its center. Suspended in a canopy of shimmering gold hung a long navy-blue crystal, wider at the top near the neck and tapering at the bottom. A thin black shroud covered the jewel, a soft blue glow escaping through the fabric. Tahvil's hands shot out, seemingly unbidden, to caress the glassy surface. Even through the cloth, the moment Tahvil's hand touched the hard surface, his entire body shuddered.

"Tahvil!" commanded the Farish. He knew all too well the painful, wrenching feeling of being ripped away from the stone, like a knife severing the hundred invisible tendrils that had already begun lodging in his very soul. Tahvil was suddenly himself again. He turned sheepishly to the Far Seer Priest, who said nothing but only gave him a permissive nod. A new, strong light had returned behind the old ruler's eyes, yet his outstretched hand was as old and frail as it had been.

Tahvil gently lifted the ornament from the box, careful to touch only the gold chain. With the precision of a master tinkerer, he draped the artifact on Farish's chest and secured it behind his neck. Now it was the Farish who shuddered. He caught the wince of jealousy that passed over Tahvil's face. *He knows of the power,* thought the Farish. *He knows only of its shadow. The true power would surely destroy this worm.*

"I go to..." The Farish jolted, and his eyes fluttered. "To commune with Kilzhet." His quavering voice trailed off as the tremor shook him, first from his core and then throughout his body. His long, bony hand shot to the crystal beneath the shroud, causing his entire body to jolt and his back to arch as his head flew back. Tahvil stepped back.

Yes! screamed the Farish silently as his vision flickered and the stone pulled him in, down. Falling, no it felt more like flying, flying down. A bat plunging into a deep mining shaft. When he finally came to rest, he was in darkness, like always. Everything was black except the massive stone bowl on the floor before him, the glassy surface of the liquid glowing a hot red. He sank to his knees.

Be renewed, came a voice, or the idea of a voice, in his mind. *Renewed to serve.*

"Yes, Master," spoke the Farish, bowing low and crawling on all fours toward the bowl. Kneeling, he placed his hands on the edge of the bowl and rested his forehead on the black stone. He wore no mask in this place. Hot, thick liquid splashed on his head and back, running down his neck and into his face and eyes. The relic around his neck pulsed and surged, sending jolts of energy through him even as the red syrupy liquid enveloping him burned. He braced for what was coming.

Like one struck by lightning, the Far Seer Priest suddenly reared up, blinding energy ripping through him. His hands clenched into tight balls, and every muscle went taut as he threw his head back and screamed. The agony and ecstasy of the moment owned him. His cry was quickly muffled by more hot liquid that filled his mouth and lungs.

More than a hundred seasons earlier, he was first called to this deep, dark place. His rule had come to an end, his old and shriveled body failing. Death was days away, if not hours. In a silent revolt, the lords of the city had already placed a successor on the seat of power as they quietly waited for him to die.

As he slipped in and out of consciousness, he heard it: a raking whisper in the night. A command to unearth the treasure buried in a forgotten stone tomb deep in the vault. His loyal servants brought the dusty wooden box they had recovered at his direction, opening it to reveal that dull blue glow, and everything changed. For a hundred seasons since, the voice behind the stone had drawn him here, ravaging his soul and renewing his body.

Slowly the darkness subsided, and the light returned. The Farish found himself rushed back up and into the throne room like a man atop a geyser. As he reentered his body, he surged to his feet, filled with buzzing energy and fire. Like one awakening from an active dream, he whirled about, ready for any threat as recognition gradually returned. *What cursed wretch is this before me?* His hand groped for a blade on his belt.

"Welcome back, Master," said Tahvil quickly. "Your servant, Tahvil, is here. Here to serve." Tahvil dipped his head, repeating the practiced words. The Farish's transformation had occurred before his very eyes. The god had returned.

The Farish stood before him, a tall and strong man, his feet planted like a tree and his chest full. Again, the Far Seer Priest wore the unmistakable defiant self-possession of a king. He looked at the backs of his hands as he clenched his fists, no longer the papery and wrinkled skin of an old man but strong and firm. He felt his complete renewal, accompanied by the familiar rushing urge to destroy. Even now, his eyes roved, resting on Tahvil, and the desire to kill surged. In the past, the Farish had lost servants to this dark compulsion, and he no longer wore his sword for the renewing. Tahvil backed slowly away from the Farish.

The Far Seer Priest, however, had learned to master this craving, or at least forestall the desire. He walked briskly in a tight orbit around his throne, sucking air and centering himself. After four passes, he breathed deeply and resumed his seat.

"Very good," he said breathing deeply. "Is she here?" he finally asked.

"Yes, sire," answered Tahvil, releasing a breath. "I will show her in." Gathering the chalice and box from the ceremony, Tahvil nearly ran from the room. The Farish smiled to himself, covering his pectoral with robes and picking up his scepter as he took his throne.

Beware of this one, came a voice in his head. Long ago he grew accustomed to hearing his master's voice while he wore the relic. *She keeps something from you.* The Farish nodded imperceptibly. *Yes, Master.*

Tahvil squeezed through the sliver of an opening in the large double doors and slipped out. The opening grew as two Tszoi warriors flung the doors wide and entered the throne room. Each Tszoi took his place beside the throne, messy, flowing hair draped over their massive shoulders, ever adorned in white furs. One planted a huge axe handle loudly on the stone floor as the other did the same with a spear.

Two priestguard entered, taking up position on either side of the double doors. The soldier on the right looked lost. He followed the left guard before turning awkwardly one way and then the other before scurrying into position on the right. *Why do they send me incompetent sarsmak?* growled the Farish inwardly. He made a mental note to have the man removed from the detail and lashed. The priest handler, too. *These fools underestimate the old man who hobbled into this room,* he thought with rising anger.

A bald priest whose bright pink facial scars had not yet fully healed bowed low before the Farish.

"Speak," boomed the Farish.

"I present Lady Corvina Lunari," announced the priest.

Lady! scoffed the Farish. *Rat.*

Cor strode into the cavernous room and bent a knee on the maroon carpet before the Farish. "May you live for a thousand years," she offered.

"Rise, Corvina," said the Farish. "Speak to me of the Nöz." He said the name as if it were a bitter herb on his tongue.

"You have nothing to fear, my liege. The leader is dead. I

control the Nöz now. Already we have begun to do your bidding."

"Kaliim's betrayer?" The inscrutable stare of that golden face fixed Cor.

"Yes, my lord. We dispatched the traitor who plotted against Kaliim." She opened her mouth to speak, then closed it.

"You wonder why I use your band of boys for these tasks." He quietly relished the satisfaction of reading the mind of another.

Cor hesitated. All knew that speaking openly to the Farish had cost many their lives.

"Speak," he coaxed.

"It would be easy," she said. "You could send the orcs again. Or simply the priestguard."

"I do not stay my hand because of the difficulty of the task," croaked the Farish. "But Kaliim cannot feel too comfortable. The pislik is part of the city's fragile... equilibrium," he continued. "An important counterbalance to the perceived power of the zengin lords. If an ally can infiltrate his men, so can a foe."

"Yes, Your Highness. Very wise." She dipped her head.

"And what of the young man?" She looked up. "Don't be so surprised, child. I see much." The Farish absently touched his chest, his bony hands pressing against the contours of the pectoral necklace beneath. "They say his skill exceeds even your own." He had her off balance.

"He... he is under control," she replied.

"Under your control?" pressed the Farish.

"He will be."

"Go, bring him to me," demanded the Farish. "I will break him this very night."

"No," retorted Cor too quickly. "I mean, I cannot, my lord. For he is no longer in the city," she added. "But I will turn him to you. Just give me time."

"Will he come willingly?" *You know he will not,* answered the voice.

"Yes, my lord. He will become one of our strongest allies." Cor spoke with confidence now. "But he is not yet ready. I will turn him, though."

"You must," snapped the Farish. "And quickly. Time is short."

"He will be ours by the end of the second harvest."

"No! I have waited years for that which has begun. You have until moonrise in three days," retorted the Farish. Her eyes widened. "If you cannot convince him, I will bring him by force. I will break him. He will join me, as the Adder joined me. If not, I will destroy him and the rest in the club you babysit."

"He will be ours," she stated. "He burns with hate already."

Hate for me, he thought. *She knows this, yet she conceals it.* "Excellent. I have plans for him and his... skills." Cor cocked her head and raised an eyebrow. "We will begin our assault on the Guilds after harvest."

"The Guilds in Wyntis Mis?" asked Cor.

"Wyntis Mis is the key to the Fahyzen Kingdom, home to great power. When we topple the Tinkerer's Guild, the Family, the city will turn on itself. We will have our foothold."

"You risk a war that awakens the dwarves," Cor blurted without thinking. The Farish stood. Cor immediately dropped her head in deference. She had spoken too freely.

"I will take care of the dwarves," he roared. He slowly returned to his seat. "Still, you question," he goaded.

"Forgive me," she added.

"Speak."

"My lord, an attack on the Fahyzen Kingdom could be seen as a substantial challenge to the Midlands."

The Farish laughed. "You see very little. This is not the beginning. We are in the final act, child. Kilzhet is on the move. His power grows like a towering wave. The Narsk blade is nearly remade." He was on his feet again. "It is he, not I, who will crash over the world of men. Kilzhet will not challenge the Midlands; he will decimate it." He rapped his scepter on the stone floor, and his tone told her the conversation was over.

"May you live forever," she said, bowing, palm to forehead. He could see the bewildered expression on her face. *Good.*

"Dismissed." The Farish sat as she backed away from his throne and then turned to go. He placed a hand under his robe, letting his fingers rest against the cool blue crystal.

Her allegiance cracks, came a voice. *She was once yours, but her loyalty shifts, fractured by her feelings.*

"Yes, my lord. I see it," the Farish answered aloud.

16

THE DARK CASTLE

H*ours earlier*

STILL WADING through a haze from the long night, Badu staggered through the streets. After a series of quick turns down neighboring alleys, he had disappeared, leaving the tinmen buzzing in futile circles around the building. He heard the urgent horn blast in the distance, signaling their discovery of the dead guard. None kill a priestguard. The intensity of their search would surely multiply many times over.

Straining to focus on the blurry sign swinging above him, he read: "Opulus Salamander—Bathhouse." *This will do.* He ducked in. Blinking heavily to stay awake, he paid three shalip and followed the attractive assistant with the sandy blonde hair wordlessly up a winding set of faded limestone steps to an open room with a series of small privacy huts beside the salt pools.

"You would like to rest before you soak?" she asked. He nodded dumbly and stumbled into one of the huts, collapsing hard on the thin pad atop the wooden slats of the squat

158

sleeping platform. The thick aroma of lavender and cypress shavings filled the hut, and a melancholy pinging rose from a mushroom-shaped copper dome as drops of heavy liquid struck it again and again. Before the assistant had even tied closed the heavy linen curtains covering the hut's entryway, Badu was asleep.

❧

STANDING atop a massive spike of ice just wide enough for both feet, Badu knew he was trapped. The spire rose hundreds of measures through a blanket of fog where it brushed the clouds. He couldn't see it but somehow he knew dark, frothy water roiled beneath the cloud layer. The wind whipped, and a deep cold penetrated him.

"Come to me," a rumbling voice echoed from beneath the clouds. "Bend a knee before me and you will know power. You will have your dreams."

"To kill the Farish?" asked Badu, though his lips didn't move.

"So much more. I will lead you from your tent in the woods into wealth beyond your imaginings. And power. Power to kill and crush any who oppose you."

"The Adder?" asked Badu. A delicious, dark feeling spread over him.

"These are petty men. I can satisfy all of your desire. And so much more. Kingdoms will bow before you." Badu had never considered anything beyond the day he faced the Farish, a day he wasn't sure he would survive. "Come. Step off." Badu looked down and the clouds now swirled a hypnotic blue like disturbed water reflecting the night sky. The blue darkness called to him, urged him forward. *What else do I have?* he thought in defeat, stepping forward into the nothingness.

"Stop," came a new voice. "You know it's not the only way."

This new voice rose not from the swirl below but from over-head, which now burned golden white.

"Garris?" How had he missed the slender, translucent bridge leading away from his spire and the figure silhouetted against the bright clouds?

"Falling is the easy path. Abandon your hate. Join me." *No. Not Garris.*

"Father?"

"Your anger does not own you. Step away from those shackles into life." There it was again, the prick of hope that he kept locked away. Hope that there could be more for him. More than revenge. Badu stepped out onto the narrow bridge, barely wider than his foot.

The wind whipped ferociously, and lightning flashed angrily all around him.

"He is weak," rumbled the thunderous voice below. "He betrayed you. He betrays you now. Ask him," the voice prompted.

Badu felt the truth in the challenge. He looked up at the figure. "Will you help me? Help me avenge you first?" The wind suddenly died.

"No. Vengeance will not fill you," spoke the figure. "Leave the anger of your youth. Walk to me."

Laughing rose below. "I told you." The voice reverberated up through the clouds as another figure materialized. Badu's breath caught. Floating up through the tempest came the unmistakable shape of none other than the Farish himself.

"Ignore this pathetic ghost of a wasted past. Killing him, killing all of them was... exquisite. Divine." The Farish lifted a bony finger to the frozen golden smile as if recalling a fine meal, even as the clouds behind him morphed into the image of the bright alley from Badu's childhood. It was just as he remembered it: the Adder raising the sword over his kneeling mother, but something was new. The shiny black carriage. He could now somehow see inside. There sat a slender figure in a golden mask, looking on approvingly.

Badu felt the sword grip in his hand before he looked down. He didn't hesitate. With a scream, he hurled himself from the bridge onto the monster behind the smug golden smile, swinging his blade with all the power he could muster. An explosion crashed like lightning striking a raging sea, and everything went dark. *Good.*

Badu jerked awake, panting.

"Sir, are you all right?" asked a quiet voice belonging to the fair but blurry face peeking into the private cabana beside the healing baths.

"Uh... Yes. Sorry." Badu fumbled, rubbing his eyes as he sat up in the lounge.

A beautiful young woman stepped into the cabana, draped in a short lavender silkeen robe tied around her waist by a thick magenta sash. Her eyes were painted like a sunset; dark-purple eyeshadow on her lids blended into brilliant red, then orange, and then yellow that faded down over her cheeks. An array of thin wooden spikes fanned out from the back of her head, woven together with magenta thread. She carried a tray. "Would you like some tea?"

"Tea?" Badu blinked, still working to collect himself.

"Yes, toasted peppercorn blossom." She smiled, extending the tray, her delicate porcelain hands and arms outstretched. "Or perhaps something stronger? Yasbandi? Ferikökü?"

"No!" blurted Badu. "I mean, no, thank you." He brushed his black hair from his face and took the wooden saucer and porcelain cup. "Tea would be fine. What hour is it?"

"Nearly nightfall, sir." The day had slipped by in a smear of semi-consciousness as he soaked in the salt pools and slept in the small privacy hut, recovering from the night before.

She poured the steaming tea into a delicate cup adorned with blue brillflowers. "Would you like another muscle treatment or soothing candle?"

"No, no. This is perfect." The woman smiled but didn't leave. "Oh, yes. Of course." He leaned over and fished an agü note from his pack.

"Oh, very generous," she remarked. "Please let me know if you require anything else." She smiled again, locking his eyes with startling intensity behind the waterfall of color. "Anything at all," she cooed, meeting his eyes.

This herfing city, thought Badu. "Thank you very much. This is all I need," he replied quickly, taking the teacup. The young woman bowed slightly and swept from the room, letting the flap close behind her. Badu let out a sigh.

The floral tea with the hint of aromatic spice enlivened him. He breathed deeply, trying to reset, but he couldn't escape the image from his dreams—the golden jeering face and swirling darkness that had stirred his sea of rage. The more he tried to push it away, the more agigated he became.

Perhaps an errand before leaving the city. The thought materialized on its own in his head. His pulse raced as he weighed the idea, though he already knew he would try it.

BADU CROUCHED among a stack of crates a short distance from the prayer platform and bridge that spanned the deep ravine separating the city from the Far Seer Priest's castle. Had it only been a day earlier that he knelt beside the prayer fountain? It felt like weeks. The torches beside the bridge blazed brilliantly, nearly white, in the orange daylight afforded to Badu by the sightstones he had swallowed before departing the bathhouse. The rest of the world saw the darkness brought by a cloudy night two hours past sunset.

As he shuffled to the side to get a better view of the small caravan leaving the castle, his foot hit the body of the disrobed priestguard soldier at his feet. Badu now wore the sentry's helmet, robes, and boots. Other than pledging fealty to the fraud on the throne, the man's only mistake was fitting Badu's size almost exactly. That and wandering over to Badu's hiding spot in the empty supply building to relieve himself. Badu ambled out into the street in the priestguard armor as a merchant caravan crossed the last span of bridge and rumbled by. He dipped his head and raised his spear in salute as he had watched the guards do a dozen times since he had taken up his post.

Crossing the bridge proved easier than he feared. The well-timed flare pod ignition that engulfed a prayer station in flame served as a sufficient distraction, and then he simply walked through the open gates and across the bridge, moving the way he thought a guard might. In all the commotion, nobody seemed to notice him.

Once across the bridge, Badu considered whether to simply walk into the castle, but the gate was closed and there would certainly be protocol for entrance. Instead, he crossed the open square, moving past a grand fountain toward the left edge of the castle where the outer wall met the craggy cliffs climbing almost as high as the castle spires. On a night like this, the severe shadows of the rock served as the perfect cover to creep up and over the outer wall.

Badu longed to shed the loud and stiff priestguard armor in favor of his nightwrap, the tightly wrapped black cloth garment that had become his second skin since he had it commissioned two seasons earlier. However, he knew the disguise might still have its use.

From the shadows of a rock overhang beside the lower castle wall, Badu observed the black behemoth structure before him. *What are you doing here?* a voice inside accused. In truth, he had no good answer. Cor had promised to bring him to the Farish, so why venture out alone? Something from his dream had drawn him here. A renewed sense of mission burned within him. He needed to see this place with his own eyes.

After climbing up the cliff for forty measures, Badu leaped from the stone outcropping to the top of the wall, clanging loudly in his armor. He pulled his heavy frame over the outer wall and onto the rampart. Straightening himself, he quickly took up guard in case the noise drew attention, but no sentry arrived. He took a deep breath and assessed the dark castle. It was like a labyrinth. Footbridges and walkways crossed like cobwebs from tower to spire to rampart, with the hulking mass of the building ever rising higher.

"You're no guard!" came a voice from behind him. Badu whirled on the sound, knife drawn. Hanging from the edge of the outer wall was a metal enclosure, like a giant birdcage. It had looked empty from below. Now Badu saw the half-naked man with the long beard stuffed inside the small space. *Will he sound the alarm to earn his freedom?*

"Save a soul?" pleaded the frail man with the blackened teeth. "Yuz rewards the merciful. I'll keep your secrets. Carry them to the Downs." Badu didn't move. "I don't know why you're here, and I don't care," continued the man, sensing Badu's hesitancy. His voice was urgent. "But if you release me, I will be forever in your debt."

I don't have time for this, Badu thought. He turned to go.

"An enemy of your enemy, an ally makes," said the man.

Badu froze, the nözan motto ringing like a bell in his head. He spun, now sure he recognized the stranger's hoarse voice. "No," he stammered. "Could it be?" Badu rushed to the cage and stared in wonder at the gaunt, bedraggled man behind a snarled beard who flashed a broad, gap-toothed smile. "Oster?"

Oster could barely contain himself as Badu quickly hooked

the cage using the metal climbing claw attached to his dikeni and swung it back over the wall. He picked the lock with trembling hands, and Oster tumbled out.

"You're alive! I'm without words!" Badu exclaimed, crouching down over Oster's thin, crumpled frame.

Oster stretched, moaning in pain. "Most of me." He held up a bandaged hand, missing a finger.

Badu shook his head in disgust. "Can you walk?"

Oster nodded wordlessly, wiping tears of joy and struggling to his feet, as he hugged Badu again.

"We have to get you out."

"Why are you here, brother?" Oster asked.

"Scouting," offered Badu. He wasn't sure what else to say.

"You're as crazy as ever!" Oster laughed and clapped Badu on the back. "We'll both be dead if they find us here."

"If I escort you out, we can walk straight across the bridge. They won't stop a tinman."

Oster shook his head. "It won't work, uyesi. I'm afraid I have been too... vocal a guest here."

"Of course you have, you goat," said Badu, slipping back into their regular banter.

"They will surely recognize me. Besides, the Farish always requires pairs of guards for moving prisoners." Oster peered over the castle wall to the thin strip of ground with the wall on one side and a gorge on the other that ended in the cliff face. "If you can lower me down, I will drop to the river and simply float out. I've imagined as much ever since they locked me in that cage."

Badu's mind whirred. Could he make it out on his own? He met Oster's eager face nodding in encouragement.

"We've tarried too long as it is," urged Oster.

"All right, uyesi. I will see you in camp." The two embraced again.

Using the dikeni cord, Badu slowly lowered Oster down the steep wall. To his surprise, the man had retained much of his strength and climbed catlike down the final stretch of rock. Then his shadowy figure hobbled over the lip of the gorge and was gone.

Badu hesitated, considering leaving, meeting Oster at the river mouth, and joining him in his celebratory return to the Skyrt, but something within urged him on. *You are inside the Farish's castle in a priestguard uniform! You may not have this opportunity again.* He pushed away the thoughts of the Skyrt and ascended to the next layer of the castle wall, slipping from shadow to shadow, avoiding detection from the sentry.

There were priestguard soldiers throughout the castle, but most seemed to be sleepwalking. The decades of the Farish's tyrannical fearmongering and the foolish belief in his deity left the guards within the castle feeling far too safe. *Fools!*

After an hour of creeping and climbing, Badu found himself on the far side of the castle, now hundreds of measures above the courtyard where he began. The black glittering ocean spread out across the landscape, awash in the unnatural orange light.

Heavy footfalls rose up a flight of stairs to his left. Before he could move, a guard appeared in the doorway.

"What are you doing up here? This is my track," came the voice as the guard approached.

"Just following orders," called Badu, turning slowly away from the guard. Still, the man approached.

"Did Cap tell you to—" The guard froze two paces away, his eyes fixed on Badu's shoulder. He didn't need to look down to know his mistake. As a strict rule, the guards kept their hair shaved close to the head, but Badu's long black hair had come untied and snaked down over his shoulder. The guard cocked his head in confusion and then cried out, reaching for his sword. Like lightning, Badu leaped forward, jamming the guard's sword back into the hilt and slamming his helmet into the guard's face. The guard staggered, swinging a backhand at Badu's head. Badu ducked under the blow and, in a practiced, fluid motion, snatched a dart from his cloak and planted it in the guard's neck. The guard's hand jerked frantically up to the foreign object lodged in his neck, and he spasmed. Badu planted his feet and slammed both palms into the guard, ramstrike, sending the man's seizing body flipping over the outer wall.

You should leave, the voice inside urged as his heart thumped. He quickly removed the helmet, tucked his long hair up and out of sight, and pushed it back on. The voice was right, of course. Badu had a long ride ahead of him to reach camp tonight, and deep into the castle, near the rear of the sprawling compound he had already seen much of this forbidden place. He beheld the final structure within the castle grounds. The massive stronghold adorned with burning torches. It had to be the Farish's inner keep. It called to him. *No, time to go. But I will return,* he promised himself.

"Ho! Gan." Badu froze at the voice from behind. He carefully picked up his spear and turned slowly. "Why are you off patrol?" asked the priestguard in the tower doorway.

"Uh... Sorry." Badu guffawed, giving his best impression of the fallen guard. "Had to take a leak," he added.

"You're a blum pinch!" hissed the man, gesturing for Badu to come over. "You know protocol! The Adder'd have your head on a post if he saw you pissing off the castle wall in view of the Altar." Badu lowered his head in deference and hurried over. "Probably split me open for fun, too," the man added, cuffing Badu's helmet with a metal gauntlet as he drew near. "You sloshed?"

"No, just had to go," said Badu quickly in a muffled voice. "Sorry."

"Do it again, and I'll throw you off myself. Now, let's go.

We're late!" The guard turned and marched down a set of spiral stairs into the tower.

Run! screamed a voice inside. *No! That will only raise the alarm,* he argued with himself. *Besides, there's nowhere to go but over the edge. I'll slip away once I'm inside.* Though it did limit his vision, the full-faced helmet with a slit for eyes offered an excellent disguise. It made it hard to tell the priestguard apart. Badu thought he could blend well enough as long as his hair didn't come untied again. Down the steps he followed the priestguard.

"Should'a heard Alif rambling," called the guard over his shoulder as they went. "Swears he saw the Farish hobble into the throne room like an old man. I think he's lost his mind. A god don't get old, right?"

"Hmmph," Badu grunted the reply.

"Yeah, I'd say he's full of sheep bohk, too. Like the time he said he beat a Tszoi in a staring contest. I'd sooner eat my own arm than spend a minute locking eyes with one of those humps."

A hurrying soldier rounded the curve in the corridor and nearly collided with the guard escorting Badu. "Sir! There you are. I didn't find him—"

The man's report was cut short as the escorting soldier jabbed a thumb over his shoulder at Badu. "Found him, Nehir. Taking a piss off the wall." Nehir looked up at Badu, his head cocked a bit. Badu just shrugged. Nehir shook his head.

"Let's go. Farish'll spit fire if the doors don't open on his command."

The three men moved briskly through a long, narrow tunnel lined with torches. The passageway was dark even with the aid of the sightstones. It must have been nearly pitch black for the soldiers.

Nehir and the senior guard continued their banter as Badu

scanned for an exit. If he disappeared down a passageway, would they notice? *Wait*, thought Badu. *This tunnel, the slight turn left.* They must be at or near the main tower. A quiet voice inside alerted him that he might draw near to the Farish himself. *Stay ready.*

The cramped passageway opened into a large foyer, met by five other passages. Tall columns burned with torches beside a towering pair of carved wooden doors.

"Where have you been?" snapped a slender, bald priest whose face was crossed with fresh pink scars and who paced on the fine carpet before the entryway. A pair of Tszoi stood guard, one before each door. Badu swallowed hard.

"Sorry, Your Holy One," said the senior guard. "We had a"—he glanced back at Badu—"a slight incident."

"We'll address that later," growled the priest. "Prepare to enter."

"Gan, you're on the left." The senior guard jerked his head to the side, obviously annoyed. Badu became an observer. He absorbed every detail of the room: the slight movements of each soldier and the agitated waiting of the priest. A formation, he realized. He saw how the other guard, Nehir, took position in front of the right door, staring straight ahead over the shoulder of the Tszoi. Badu mirrored Nehir's position and posture on the left side. He fought the urge to shift his gaze a measure to the side to the hollow steel-gray eyes of the Tszoi.

"They approach!" hissed the priest. Badu heard the shuffling of a half dozen feet approaching down the hallway behind him, but he dared not look back from the door. His heart raced. *Sezlik merkaz; calm the center,* he commanded himself. *You will find a way out.* The assuring words helped, even if he doubted their veracity. Marching feet stopped just behind him.

The massive door on the left groaned, opening inward only a measure or two. A pale-faced old priest with a ridiculously tall collar carrying some sort of package slithered through, taking a deep breath of relief as he did.

"No missteps," the elder priest spat the command.

"Yes, Lord Tahvil," replied the young priest with the pink scars. "Enter!" he commanded. The pair of Tszoi pushed the doors wide-open with little effort and strode into what Badu now saw to be a cavernous and exquisite throne room.

A sea of polished black marble on the floor danced with burning red flame reflected from a dozen short columns. The opulent golden throne adorned with blood-red crystals looked like a lampstand for the towering flame that rose twenty measures into the air behind it. A massive dome circled in glass crowned the vaulted ceiling, supporting the impressive gold-and-red crystal chandelier that hung over the throne. Glittering gold torch posts stood like sentries beside rows of expertly carved maroon marble columns lining the entry. There on the throne sat none other than the golden-faced Farish himself. Badu's stomach leaped.

The Tszoi marched straight ahead and took up position beside the throne. Entranced by the scene, Badu failed to watch Nehir for a moment. He jerked into lockstep and hurried to enter the throne room just behind Nehir, taking up post beside the man on the right side. Nehir shot a look at Badu, and he immediately recognized his error. He was to mirror Nehir, not follow him. Badu scurried back to the left side of the entryway. He could hear the infuriated, muffled wail from the corridor, even as the young priest with the fluttering robes hurried in.

The young priest shot a deathly glare at Badu before scurrying ahead and bowing low before the Farish.

"Speak!" boomed the Farish.

"I present Lady Corvina Lunari," announced the priest. For a moment, Badu was frozen, dumbstruck by those impossible words. Then Cor's familiar figure with the burning amber hair strode past him and knelt before the Farish. The edges of

Badu's vision flickered black, and sparkles danced before his eyes. He was short of breath, a sharp twisting in his gut. Everything was wrong. His mind warred with itself to make sense of the scene.

"Rise, Corvina," said the Farish.

Badu's world vaporized.

17

CONFRONTATION

The moon was low in the sky when Badu stumbled into camp. Twice, he had nearly fallen from his saddle with exhaustion, but he had pushed hard to make it. Quickly counting saddles, he noted that all of the nözan had returned safely and now slept in the Skyrt. All but Cor. *And Garris,* the voice added. He brushed the thought away. No, she wouldn't have made it back sooner than Badu.

In the castle, abandoning his disguise, Badu had slipped off down a dark side passage, even as the young priest escorted him to something called the rectification room to answer for his poor discipline. He discarded the priestguard robes and armor in favor of his nightwrap, and, clinging to the shadows, he flew from that fortress of lies.

"Bizhak! You made it back." Kafa startled Badu, clapping him on the shoulder as he ambled from the shadows. "After your dance with the uzum, I wasn't sure." Kafa beamed a knowing smile. "When you didn't show last night, we started to worry."

Badu only snorted.

"Where were you?" asked Heffel, who must have been on

172

night shift with Kafa.

"I... I went into..." he took a breath. "I crept into..." Their faces waited for the update. "A bathhouse. The Salamander," he finally blurted. "Recovering from the night with you sarsmak," he added. "Slept through the day." Something inside kept him from telling them about the castle. About Cor.

"Have some nice *company* in the bathhouse?" Heffel winked at him. "Have some beautiful birds there."

"They do," Badu replied flatly; the face of the cabana girl flickered through his head. "But the gorgol stampede in my head was company enough." He rubbed his temples.

Lying on his mat back in his tent, Badu's mind spun at the events of the night. *How could Cor have been there? She spoke to the Farish like a servant or at least an ally.* He lay awake, listening and thinking. *Will she come back? What of the nözan? Should I tell them? Yes!* He would have to. He would confront her. He would destroy her. What choice did he have? She was an enemy of the Nöz. Something pricked in the back of his mind. *Why did she lie to the Farish? Why did she claim he was no longer in the city when she knew he was? Could she have been helping? Protecting me? No! Everything had been a lie!* Killing Kaliim's messenger was only protecting the pislik. *She knew about the orcs! She can't be trusted.*

The battle swirled inside him. *"Find your center. Find the light."* Garris's final words echoed in his mind. The hours crept by until sleep finally wrestled him away from his thoughts. When dawn arrived, cold as clay, he reluctantly returned to the world. Before opening his eyes, he just listened. There was activity. He could feel the urgency. A shout pricked the morning. Badu jumped up.

"Stranger in the Skyrt!" came Eldiven's panicked shout from the lookout ridge high over the camp.

Badu leaped to his feet, an icy surge of adrenaline filling him. He snatched his blade and ran out, joining a half dozen nözan rushing to meet the intruder.

"Top of the chute!" called Eldiven. The men took up position at the mouth of the tunnel, the Skyrt's primary entrance. Intruders almost never discovered the chute, and none had made it this far before. A hunched figure on horseback emerged slowly from the dark passage. Badu gripped his knife and crouched, readying himself to attack.

"Old man," shouted Ferat. "How did you find—"

"Oster!" cried Badu in sudden recognition. He abandoned his defenses and rushed forward. Confused murmurs rose from behind.

The reunion was epic. The nözan flocked to Oster with the enthusiasm of schoolchildren welcoming back a forgotten classmate. Before long, they were plying him with food and drink around the morning fire as he regaled them with an endless stream of tales of the horrors within the walls of the black castle.

"You forgot this part of your story!" Kafa said, turning attention back on Badu after Oster told of his escape. Badu offered a half-truth account of his impetuous decision to enter the castle in disguise. He told the men he had followed Oster out shortly after.

The reunion continued late into the morning when Oster finally excused himself to his long-empty sleeping tent. After eating his fill and beyond, for the first time in months, Oster's fatigue caught up with him, and he could barely keep his eyes open. The mood in the camp was positively giddy at Oster's return from the dead, filled with a joyful brotherhood that had long been absent. *Garris should be here for this.* Badu quashed the thought the moment it entered his mind.

As the day wore on, Badu became more and more restless. He attacked the sparring course with ferocity, seeking to sate his buzzing agitation, but it was no use. By midmeal there was still no sign of Cor. He felt like his soul might rend in two.

At two past midmeal, hoofbeats sounded as Finnur rode

into camp from his scouting loop.

"Any sign of Cor?" asked Sevin. Badu perked up.

"None. But I did see evidence of margoul to the slag," he said, sliding from his horse.

"Margoul?" asked Ferat, standing.

"Probably just a couple of halfies." Finnur took a long swig of water from his skin as Täs untied his saddlebags.

"Goblins?" said Täs, his eyes wide.

"Came across a family traveling up to Helmun. All pretty shaken. Claimed to have outrun a 'swarm of monsters,'" Finnur said in an exaggerated voice, tossing the bridle to Täs. "But you know how valley folk can be."

"How close?" asked Heffel, assuming his guard's captain role. "Should we investigate?" He was ever eager to secure the Skyrt perimeter and gather actionable information.

"Let those pinches beat each other silly," said Eldiven, leaning back against a tree stump. "Sooner or later, the goblin scat will pick a fight with someone who knows how to swing a sword and end up a pile of sand."

"I'll go," Badu blurted, standing. All eyes turned to him. "To go check it out, I mean." He had to do something; letting off some steam on a clap of halfies would feel good.

"I can come, too," said Salik.

"No," Badu cut in quickly. "I'm... I'm fine alone. A ride to clear my head of the city would be good."

"Bizhak took a beating from the uzum, huh?" Kafa chuckled. Badu offered a wan half smile in return.

"Well, if it looks like anything more than a handful of goblins, come on back," said Heffel.

"Everything okay?" asked Ferat quietly, helping Badu saddle his choluk.

"I... I saw something I wish I hadn't," answered Badu. "Just need to clear my head. Think about it."

"By going out and chasing margoul?" Ferat pressed.

"Remember the orcs. There could be other things besides goblins out there."

"I know. I'll be fine."

Ferat raised an eyebrow.

❧

THE SUN HAD BEGUN its slide into the ocean under a stained sky when Badu came trudging back into camp atop his choluk. After a day of chores, upkeep, and hunting, the men had returned to recline by the fire, rejoined by Oster, who was telling stories again.

Täs dutifully jumped up to grab the reins of Badu's choluk. "Finally back, eh? We started to wonder—what in the downs!" Täs cried out and stumbled back as Badu drew close.

"What's this?" Heffel stood followed by the other nözan. Badu's choluk thumped with heavy, exhausted steps into the clearing. Splattered mud and dried blood covered both bird and rider. Badu wore an emotionless expression.

"You found the halfies, then?" asked Finnur.

"Found more than that!" exclaimed Sevin. "Look at him."

Without a word, Badu threw a bundle down on the grass before the half circle of men. Then tossed a second bag that thudded hard, its contents clinking like heavy pottery.

"Cor back?" Badu asked lifelessly.

"No. We haven't seen her," answered Ferat. "But what's all this?"

"We should look for her in the morning," added Heffel.

"Herf me!" cried Salik, inspecting the bundle on the ground. "It's goblin hoods." He rifled through the pile of hoods strung together by cord. "There's... twenty-two of 'em!"

"Twenty-two!" Now Kafa was on his feet. The clinking of stone on stone drew all eyes to Täs, who had upended the heavy sack. There on the ground beside the goblin hoods, in a broken pile, were eight stone hands. Troll hands. All from the right arm.

"What'd you get into?" asked Ferat.

Badu didn't answer. He just slid from his saddle, landing unsteadily as if he might fall over. He picked up one of the men's discarded wineskins, took a long draught, and stumbled to his tent.

As the men spoke in low tones behind him, Badu threw open his tent flap, and without removing his riding cloak or muddy shoes, he collapsed in his bed, utterly spent.

Hours later, Badu awoke from a deep sleep to a commotion. Shouts rose in camp from the dark night. A horse whinnied, and a woman's voice sounded.

"Cor's back!" Täs's head poked into Badu's tent. "She's coming to see you. Seems mad."

"What hour is it?" asked Badu.

"Don't know," replied Täs. "Maybe two till dawn?" Badu nodded and Täs slipped out.

His muscles yelling in protest, Badu pushed himself into a seated position on his cot and shook his head clear. Quick footsteps approached. Badu removed the long knife from his hanging belt and thrust his hand under a blanket just as Cor appeared in the doorway.

"You're filthy!" she snapped. He only glared up at her. "What the downs are you trying to prove? That was foolish, taking on a whole herfing margoul knot yourself." She stepped into the tent. "Heffel said you killed twenty halfies and a knot of trolls?" He only continued staring up at her. "You should have returned to camp when you discovered so many. We have bigger plans." She rested a hand on his shoulder, her tone softening. "Get cleaned up, we have much to discuss in the morning—"

Before she could finish, Badu grabbed her wrist and spun, flinging her down hard on his cot as he swept her legs. She fell with a short cry as he brought the knife to her throat. Pinning her down with his weight, he pressed the blade to her neck.

"What the—"

"Shut up!" he hissed ferociously. "I saw you."

"I don't know what the downs you think you're doing—" she blurted angrily.

"I saw you," he seethed, cutting her off.

"What are you talking about? You better put that herfing blade away!" her voice threatening.

"In the Farish's throne room," he answered.

"Too much ferikökü powder?" she snapped, an edge in her voice. "Get off of me—"

"I was there, Cor. I was in the room." Fire blazed behind his eyes. "I heard it all. How you've been using us. The orcs. How you plan to give him the Nöz. Give him me!"

"Wha... Impossible." Color had drained from her face.

"You have three counts to tell me everything, or you don't take another breath." Badu could barely hear her shallow breathing over the cacophonous pumping of blood in his ears. *Do it!* wailed the voice. *Don't wait!*

"I... It's true," she suddenly blurted, tears filling her eyes. "I have been his for years."

"Shivv!"

"But... It's not what you think." She choked back a sob.

"Not what I think?" His voice was low, dangerous.

"I hate him as much as you. More, maybe."

"You are his puppet!"

"No. I once was. But no more." Her eyes screamed up at him. "I have held much from you," she said. "The story I told you. Of when I was a girl—"

"That was a lie too?"

"No. No, it wasn't. But there's more. The Farish didn't kill my parents." Badu snorted mirthlessly. "Not right away, I mean. He took them prisoner. Even as a young girl, my father trained me to fight. When the Farish's army stormed camp, I fought. I killed a priestguard, my first kill. Word got to the Farish that a girl of eleven seasons had killed a guard. I was terrified. I thought he would torture and kill me. Instead, he was sickly fascinated. He took me as his property, devoted to turning me into his weapon."

"Well, he succeeded." Badu pressed the blade down.

"He had my parents in a cage." She swallowed again, the motion lifting the blade slightly, like a boat rolling over a wave. "Whenever I didn't obey him, I was beaten ruthlessly."

"How do I know any of this is true? I never heard of the Far Seer Priest raising some sort of daughter."

"I was never his daughter. Let me show you something." Cor lifted her free hand and slowly moved down to the hem of her shirt. She pulled it up a few inches, and Badu sucked in his breath. Her stomach was crisscrossed with thin, old scars. "He broke me. And when I was still a girl, he had me do something awful. To prove my loyalty." Now, streams flowed down her cheeks.

"Your parents," said Badu softly, nodding, the answer suddenly obvious. "He made you kill them." Cor nodded silently and shut her eyes tight. A tremor shook her, and her chin quivered. Badu had never seen even a hint of weakness or flash of vulnerability in the rock of a woman before.

"I've never told a soul about that," she finally said. "He sent me off to an outpost in the badlands to train and learn to kill. Whatever shred of my heart I still had died in that place." She closed her eyes. He slowly lifted the blade.

"But why the Nöz?" Badu pressed.

Cor took a deep breath, raising her hand to wipe the tears. Badu didn't stop her. "As soon as the Adder learned of the group, he started looking for a way to stamp out the Nöz. But the Farish had another idea."

"To use us," said Badu. Cor nodded, the terror gone from

her eyes. "What of the missions you led us on? The dozens we killed."

"The targets were his... enemies. His opponents."

"Herf me!"

"But that's over now. I've changed," she pleaded. "You've changed me, the Nöz has. I cannot expect you to believe it, but right there in his throne room, I put to death the last shred of my loyalty. I vowed to kill him, whatever it cost. If you were in that room, then you know I lied to him!" she said, her eyes suddenly begging. "To save you. I could have delivered you into his hands a hundred times over. The Adder begged that I do just that."

His gaze bored into her own, his sharp breath hissing through his teeth. He knew, without pausing to catalog the subtle clues in her face and body that, despite all the lies, she was finally telling the truth.

"You made me kill Garris." The accusation was quiet, resigned.

"It was the Adder. He needed proof of your loyalty to stay his hand against you. The Farish agreed. If I couldn't bring proof of your allegiance, they would come for you. The Adder wants your blood. They both do. But I've been delaying, protecting you... for months."

"The Farish wants something else from me," said Badu, recalling the conversation in the throne room. *"We could use him."*

"Yes, he wants to convert you into one of his champions, as he did the Adder. But he's not going to." Cor sounded defiant. "I won't let it happen. You must believe me. I promised to give you a chance to kill the Farish, and I will. My hate for him burns as strong as yours. That herfing fraud will still fall at our hands."

"Our hands? How can I possibly trust you?" He tried to sound incensed, but his wall had begun to crumble. Badu finally named the seed of hate he had recognized in her months ago. *The monster ruined her, just like he did you. Worse.* Anger rushed through him but it burned not for Cor but for the masked tyrant whose dark will had corrupted them both.

He searched her eyes, his thoughts jumping between the growing hope that she was telling the truth and the dark voice calling for him to finish the work of the blade at her throat. Deep inside, he longed for it to be true, begged that it was. Cor had crowded his thoughts for months. What had begun as admiration had bloomed into affection and more. He had analyzed hundreds of tiny clues, desperate to discover if she shared his growing feelings for her. She had remained a mystery, yet every minute he spent with her felt like drinking from a cool mountain stream.

"Maybe you don't want to trust me," she answered, swallowing hard. "Or feel as though you can't... But you should." Her eyes changed again, another look replacing the desperation. *Was it fear?*

"Why?" he demanded, feeling the knife's handle still in his hand. "Give me one reason why I should trust you!"

"Because..." Her gaze suddenly penetrated his own. "Because I love you, Baduh'oan Chrintzu." The words froze the air around him and shattered the night. Badu's sharp senses felt it all: her arm wrapped around him, the slight trembling in her body beneath his, her quickened breathing, dilated pupils. *What? Is it possible? Can it be?*

He felt at a loss. His eyes flicked back and forth across hers, desperately searching for a hint of truth or deception. She gently pushed the blade away. He found himself allowing her to. Then her slender hand reached up and touched his neck. The hypnotic trance of her green searching gaze and the infinity beyond pulled him in. She kissed him, and Badu crumbled into her embrace, drowning in the torrent of the unspoken. A rushing river swept away the fear and rage of betrayal and filled him with surging relief and desire.

18

THE PLOT

"She did what?" demanded Ferat, rising to his feet, dropping his knife and the half-eaten buzzardfruit as he did.

"It's not what it sounds like," answered Badu. "I mean, that's how it started, but she has become one of us. The Farish corrupted her. She lied to him to protect me. She's been protecting us all for months."

"How can you know that?" Ferat paced before him.

"I know. It sounds crazy. But I can sense it," replied Badu. "I just know."

"She was in the castle?" Ferat shook his head picking up the knife and fruit. "Badu, she was feeding the Farish information about the Nöz!" Ferat put a hand to his face, squeezing his eyes.

"She wants him dead, like you. Like me."

"Even if we let ourselves believe that she has turned on the Farish, this plan of walking into the castle is madness." Ferat tossed a peel of buzzardfruit off the cliff's edge and returned to his seat, cutting a chunk of the speckled pink fruit and handing it to Badu.

"It will be carefully planned." Badu took a large bite. "She has been misleading the Farish, yet he believes her to be one of his most faithful. He believes she's under his control. We can use that to our advantage."

Ferat just shook his head as he gazed over the ocean, glowing like molten glass in the red sunset. "All on your hunch?"

"It will be dangerous," Badu confessed. "But I finally have a chance to face down the Farish. How can I not take it?"

"Do you ever wonder what would have happened if she hadn't come to us?"

Badu looked up. "Most of us would have been dead at the hands of those orcs, for one thing," he answered too quickly. Badu tried to avoid bringing up the day Ferat lost his brother.

"We wouldn't have even been there if it weren't for Cor," Ferat answered wistfully.

"The Code held us back. Garris did." Badu used the very words Ferat had spoken a dozen times over the last two seasons. But even as he did, he had trouble believing them. Badu recalled sitting in this exact place with Garris, two seasons before, looking over the sea. It felt like a lifetime ago. As always, Badu pushed the thought of Garris from his mind.

Ferat tossed the rest of the buzzardfruit core over the cliff's edge. "I don't want to lose another brother because of Cor."

"You won't." Badu spoke with confidence he didn't feel. If he succeeded in the impossible—in killing the Far Seer Priest— escape from that place would not be easy. "But imagine the Farish dead. It's what we've trained for, lived for."

"Maybe we have," said Ferat. "But I'm not sure. Not sure it will solve anything."

"Not solve anything?! How can you say that? It would change *everything*. Besides, you're not one of the Temple Odalik in his harem or a pauper taxed to starvation in the Red Quarter. He's a monster."

"True," replied Ferat listlessly. "But isn't there a power-hungry ruler at the center of every city? Is his evil worse than the corrupted powerful scattered throughout the land?"

"Yes. Much worse. It's dark, twisted. He calls on Kilzhet. With plans to enslave the Midlands." Badu put a hand on Ferat's arm. "He would bend us all to his will." Ferat sighed and shook his head. "You sound as though your fire for that pislik has died," Badu pressed.

"Perhaps it has. Perhaps my fire for all of this has died," Ferat answered, sweeping a hand off toward the city. "What's it for?"

"When he's dead, everything will change." Badu stood. "When we show the people that he's no god, that he bleeds like any other man, they'll tear down his kingdom of lies. Trust me, brother."

"I've seen that look," said Ferat with a smile. "You're resolved." He stood and rested a hand on Badu's shoulder. "I won't try to stop you. I couldn't, anyway."

Ferat looked off to the sea, both men lost in the glory of the sprawling color. "You have senses that most of us could only dream of. If you truly believe that Cor speaks the truth, then I suppose there's a chance. If anyone can do it, it's you. You've become twice the warrior I am."

"I don't know about twice—"

"Who in camp can best you?" interrupted Ferat. "I watched you disarm Heffel and Kafa together after harvest sun. Even Cor can't match you." With a short nod, Ferat stepped away, pausing to steal one last glance over the sea.

"Ferat," called Badu, reaching for his friend's shoulder. Ferat paused, his black wavy hair blowing in the wind. "Promise me you won't tell the others about the throne room, the deception. I will tell them myself when I return." Ferat met Badu's eyes, patted the hand on his shoulder, and turned and walked back toward the Skyrt.

Badu watched until Ferat had disappeared down the path,

then looked down at his palms, calloused by thousands of hours of training. *It is possible,* he told himself. *It has to be.*

~

"MAKE SURE THE RELEASE WORKS," said Cor, snapping the iron shackles on Badu's wrists. He touched his wrists together and twisted, engaging the secret release latch, and the right shackle sprang open with a snap.

"What about the other one?" he asked, lifting his left arm, the metal cuff dangling from his wrist.

"It only comes off with the key, but I have an extra." She pressed a key into his waiting palm. He slipped it into the hidden pocket under his collar. The pair stood off to the side of the cobblestone street in a blade of shadow as a guard pod marched by without looking up.

"What if they throw me in the dungeon? Or use their own shackles? Or just kill me on the spot?" With the dark castle filling the view at the end of the street, he felt his resolve beginning to erode.

"The Farish wants you as an ally first," Cor answered. "He will only harm you if he feels he cannot control you. You must make him believe."

"The Adder wants me dead."

Cor held two fingers to her lips as a pair of marketgoers passed, talking loudly.

"He does," she continued. "You're a threat. Perhaps he fears being replaced. But he won't cross the Farish. He's a slave to the stone."

"And you sent the note?"

"Yes. I told the Farish I planned to capture you after a long night dancing with the ferikökü. He'll expect you to be waking from the haze."

"I know what that feels like," said Badu dryly.

"Head back," Cor instructed, dripping two drops of dark-purple liquid into each eye. Badu winced as the burning dye spread over his cornea. "The plum root will give you the look of the haze." Cor had already punched and struck him on the face half a dozen times early in the day to produce convincing bruises and swelling.

"And the hatchling zehi?" Badu asked.

"I was able to secure another. It will be in place. My faithful priestess, Mona, was part of Temple Odalik once. She is only too glad to deliver that gift if needed."

"I hate those things." Badu shivered, remembering how the zehi darted from its egg sack and swam through the air like a relentless tracking hornet until it found Garris. "Just put a sword in my hand. I'll do the rest. I'll drive it through him myself."

"I know you will. Your spikes?" she asked. Badu reached up to the rat's nest that his hair had become and located the three rigid ends of the poison-tipped needles. It had taken hours to roll and knot his long hair into thick, tangled locks to conceal the spikes.

"Remember, no matter how strong the urge, do not look into the blue crystal on his necklace," she warned.

"I'm not scared of his parlor tricks."

"He may not be a god, but there is power in that stone. I've seen it. Felt it." She shuddered.

"I'll shatter it, then."

"Then do it with your eyes closed." She smiled. "And don't forget this." She carefully untied a cloth pouch and dropped what looked like two brown rabbit-dropping pellets on his hand.

He slipped them into another hidden pouch, this one in his waist. "Right. The wavesbreath."

It was Sevin who showed Badu and Cor how to shuck the

dozens of violet seaberries to remove their tiny orange seeds, and when the seeds were crushed and mixed into a paste with bluefire squid ink, how to measure, form, and dry the paste into pellets, into wavesbreath. Sevin told them wavesbreath was a secret of the sea-dwelling Eiklin people for centuries. It granted them their legendary ability to breathe underwater for up to twenty minutes at a time. How he had learned the secret, Sevin wouldn't say.

If they succeeded in the mission, their final escape would be over the seawall. Once beneath the roiling sea, they would simply walk along the seafloor using wavesbreath.

"Remember, just take one," she cautioned. "Too much can explode your heart." She caught his wide-eyed gaze and smiled, piercing him with her own green gaze. She wrapped an arm around his waist and leaned in close. He cupped her neck, sliding his fingers up through the thick copper-red hair at the back of her head, and kissed her deeply. Their eyes met.

"What are we doing?" He asked the question without thinking, without filtering.

She cocked her head to the side. "Don't lose your focus now," she snapped.

"I could take you away. We could leave this cursed city tonight. We could have a new life, a new start."

"Stop it!" she scolded him, her voice stern and her eyes glistening. "What we do now, we do for the thousands of souls he has slain. For our parents and friends. For Yiduiijn."

Of course, she was right. He had rehearsed this day in his head hundreds of times. They were too close to turn back. He nodded resolutely.

Her countenance softened. "When he's dead, when we are free, we can leave this place together. I have dreamed many times of leaving all of this and returning to the quiet rolling hills blanketed in blue brillflower fields in Ghiesa, where I roamed as a child. When I was free. But these dreams are scat while the Farish yet breathes."

"Okay," said Badu with a deep breath, finding his dark anchor and turning his gaze to the castle. "Let's go."

19

ASSAULT

"Special prisoner for the Farish," said Cor with an air of authority to the pair of guards at the edge of the bridge. Badu let his gaze wander up to the sky and batted at some invisible creature.

"He's high as a cloud," snorted the guard on the right.

"And be glad he is," Cor answered. "This is the one who broke into the castle fortnight past." The guard stiffened. The other guard snorted in understanding, laced with fury. He pulled a short club from his belt and advanced.

"He's not to be touched until he reaches the Farish," snapped Cor.

"Like downs he isn't! Earned me a dozen lashings this one did." The guard continued approaching.

"At your post!" boomed a voice from the bridge. The guard stopped midstride. Giving one last glare at Badu, he hurried back to his spot. Badu's stomach sank as he found the owner of the voice. There in the middle of the bridge, atop a black stallion and flanked by four Tszoi, was the Adder. The plan was for Cor to walk Badu straight into the throne room herself. *This could complicate things.* Cor pulled him forward roughly past the guards.

"This is him?" croaked the Adder as they drew close. As always, the Adder was clad in dull black armor layered like reptilian scales over his body. When he moved, the blood-red underside of the scales flashed. His black helmet had a sliver of opening across his eyes met by a slit down the center, in a Y shape, like the tail of a slender whale diving into the depths. Embossed on the black metal above his eyes were two fangs and an intricate design of multiple serpents disappearing under the hood of his cloak, so dark red it looked nearly black. His left hand was missing two fingers. Badu tore his eyes away, pretending to watch something hop across the bridge and off the edge.

"Yes," replied Cor. "I bring him to the Farish as promised—"

The Adder kicked, catching Badu solidly in the face and knocking him on his back. White flashed in his vision, and with his hands bound, he slammed hard into the ground, nearly taking his breath. He started moaning and laughing, pawing furiously at nothing above him.

"Look at him; he's incapacitated," objected Cor. "Mind's gone on fairy cloud. I'm to bring him unharmed to the Farish."

The Adder snapped his head toward Cor and fixed her with a challenging stare. *Don't,* Badu silently pleaded. *Not yet.*

"To the Farish, then." Just the sound of the Adder's gravelly voice triggered a tide of fury in Badu. He could slip the shackles now and take the man who killed his family. The man who held the sword. *No.* Even if he succeeded, he would surely die, and the Farish would be untouched. "Search him," the Adder ordered, nodding. One of the Tszoi and two priestguard approached.

"I have already," offered Cor. Neither the Adder nor the approaching guards paid her any attention. The massive Tszoi draped in white fur with long silver hair reached down, lifting

Badu off his back and depositing him on his feet like he was a child. Again, Badu looked up at the sky trying to mimic the bewilderment of the haze. The two priestguard quickly searched him from neck to feet, removing his boots and tossing them off the bridge.

"Nothing," called a guard.

Again, the Adder shot a piercing look at Cor, who stared back defiantly. "Bring him," the Adder called as he turned his horse back to the castle. The knot of soldiers pushed forward through the maze of the castle.

Cor and Badu had gone over the plan a dozen times. They had even choreographed the escape sequence, using the crumbling pillars in the Skyrt to mark the marble throne room columns. But everything had changed. It was to be Cor, not the Adder, leading him into the belly of the castle. The guard detail marched straight past the hallway Badu recognized leading to the throne room antechamber.

"Am I to present the prisoner to the Farish?" asked Cor.

"Not in there," the Adder shot back. Cor's and Badu's eyes met. Fear flashed on her face. Badu continued his charade, rolling his head in swooping circles and stumbling ahead. Not that it seemed to matter. The Tszoi escort appeared not to care. He could have been unconscious, and the powerful grip of the brutes would have kept him upright.

No throne room? Do they know? For the first time, Badu's driving desire to stand in this place with a chance to kill the Farish, gave way to fear. He probed this new feeling. *Is it the fear of death?* No, he had long since embraced that likely outcome of this mission. It was something else. Failure of losing? Of coming so close to what he had spent his life seeking, only to fall short? The mission's odds of success had always been remote. Failure was never something he allowed himself to consider. No, that wasn't it, either.

Realization blasted him like a cold wind. It was Cor. His

fear was for her. Failure meant more than just his own death. His pulse began to race and his mind whirred.

They climbed a winding staircase and passed through an arched opening that emptied into brilliant sunlight that hurt Badu's eyes. Pungent smoke wafted past. He knew this place. It was the open courtyard with the burning columns he had spotted from the wall. *The Altar.* A raised platform stood at the far end of the courtyard with a block of stone on it. The sea stretched off to the left. The blue smoke from the fires rolled down and seeped across the stone floor.

"What? Get your hands off me!" Cor shrieked as one of the Tszoi grabbed her from behind. Feet scraped on stone as priest-guard soldiers rushed over to her and began removing her weapons. "What is this? I've brought the prisoner to the Farish!" She struggled against the vise grip of the massive Tszoi. Badu's stomach turned.

The Adder's mocking, scraping laugh sent chills through Badu. "You won't need weapons for that," he croaked.

No! This is all wrong. They know! The plan is ruined.

Cor must have thought the same. She suddenly slammed her head backward, cracking into the face of the Tszoi, who staggered. She ducked out of his grip and swept the legs of one of the guards and stepped on his throat. *Shivv!* cursed Badu silently. The Tszoi regained himself, lunged forward, and wrapped his huge arms around her, lifting her into the air with a roar. The fallen priestguard jumped up and struck Cor with a malicious backhand. The blow might have knocked her down, had the Tszoi warrior not held her fast. Badu abandoned the show of mental oblivion, his mind racing. *How had they lost control so quickly?*

The plan had been simple: Cor would drag Badu before the Farish on his throne. Then Badu would slip the shackles, grab Cor's sword, and kill the Far Seer Priest. The poison needles would serve as a backup in case they were escorted by a guard.

Badu's mind raced, searching for a new plan. The rigged manacles still bound his wrists, and the hidden needles hadn't been discovered. If he could get close to the Farish, perhaps he could deliver a fatal blow with one of the darts.

"Bow!" shouted the Adder, and Badu was kicked in the back of the legs, bringing him to his knees. Cor was forced down beside him. For a long moment, nothing happened. Then he heard it: the echoed, muffled wailing that rose from behind as a stream of disciples emerged from the castle and entered the courtyard, singing and beating drums as they took their places along the seawall. It was the sacrifice ceremony.

"Priestesses," whispered Cor. "The one in blue." Badu glanced up at the line of devotees in flowing robes carrying small drums, bells, and dancing scarves. The one wearing blue stood near the front of the line. Badu noted how she moved, like one constrained. Did she have something concealed beneath her flowing blue robes? One by one, the zealots fell to their knees, the wailing continuing. The Adder strode forward, ascending the three shallow steps and taking his place beside the stone block.

A door slid open at the back of the raised platform, revealing a black archway. Badu recognized the slender chief priest. The man scurried through the opening, followed by a stately figure who strode with measured fluidity. *The Farish!*

Standing, he was taller than Badu remembered. He wore the same blood-red and gold robes as he had in the throne room. Badu's pulse quickened. Familiar hate bubbled within, a metallic taste in his mouth. The Farish sat on the stone block, the breeze billowing his robes. His frozen golden gaze fixed on the pair. Moving as if underwater, the Farish slowly raised an arm and gave an almost imperceptible "come" motion with a white bony hand. Rough hands dragged Badu and Cor before him. Badu fixed the Farish with a stony stare.

"Master!" Cor called. "Why am I treated like a prisoner? I have brought him to you as I promised. An offering."

"Have you?" The Farish's voice slithered out, like a serpent inspecting its prey. The Far Seer Priest turned to Badu. "I have waited for you. Great... potential swirls in you, a strong current. I can feel it." Badu felt the seductive lure of those smooth words as they slid over him, curled around him. "You see us as enemies, but there is another way. I will show you." The Farish sat on the block of stone, and an attendant scurried up behind him, arranging his robes. "You have come to settle a petty grudge against me, but true power awaits you."

Badu fought the dark tentacles beneath the Farish's words that encircled him, pulled him in. *Yes, true power.* The thought was his own, yet he had no control over it. "This golden city is nothing compared to what is coming," continued the Farish. "I will rule all of Yiduiijn, with a power you can only imagine. Those at my side will become gods themselves. Those who stand in my way will burn like grass."

"Ignore his lies!" hissed Cor. The warning sparked like flint in the dark, snapping Badu from the seductive blanket that had settled on him. The guard holding Cor slapped her hard.

"How well do you know your companion, Badu?" the Farish continued, saying his name like a bitter wine. "Did you know she's my spy?" Badu sneered. He was ready for this. "Did you know she has been serving me for years? That she was never my captive? Can you remember the day your band of cubs rescued her from Kursa? Or what about the orc encounter?" He cocked his head. "I heard you lost a friend in that skirmish?"

Badu feigned surprise. *Let him think he's won.*

"So, you've kept some secrets, have you, Corvina?" The Farish sounded pleased. "But you've changed. I can feel the deception within you."

"I brought him as I swore I would. The deception was to fulfill my promise!" she insisted.

The Farish doesn't believe it.

"No. No, I don't think so," hissed the Farish. "Perhaps it started that way, when I handed the Nöz to you on a platter, but you've changed. He has changed you." The Far Seer Priest's mask turned to Badu. "Abandon her and join me." The voice was deep like thunder, felt more than heard. The pull was strong.

"What?!" Cor objected. The image of the blade falling on his mother flashed in Badu's mind. "You will never own me."

"Ha!" rasped the Farish. "You may yet find me to be... persuasive. I have lived a dozen lifetimes. For hundreds of years, brave men like you have stood defiantly before me only to be melted like wax. I can see through you, Badu." He hissed. "I know who you are."

"No," Badu retorted, suddenly emboldened. "You do not know who I am." He spat on the ground and met the black eyes behind the golden mask. With the speed of a viper, the Adder's long knife was out of its sheath, and he was lunging forward. Just as quickly, the Farish's arm snapped up, blocking the way. The Adder froze and then reluctantly stepped back, sheathing his knife.

"No? Then tell me," the Farish commanded. Badu could feel the grim smile behind the mask. He was toying with his prey.

Badu lifted his chest, drawing himself up as far as he could from his knees. "I am Baduh'oan Chrintzu, son of Damla Chrintzu, priestess of the Lotus Temple, Tanrila Kisi, marker of the god." The golden mask twitched at the name. Someone among the disciples gasped. *Good.* Badu could feel Cor's eyes on him too. She wasn't the only one with secrets.

"I watched you order the death of my family," Badu continued. He glanced at the Adder. "And I watched *you* kill them." His voice was steady but strong as he addressed the Farish. "If you know all things, then you know I'm here to send you to meet my dead family." The Adder ripped his broadsword from its scabbard, unable to control himself, yet still, the Farish's sinewy arm blocked the way. No gate of iron or wall of flame could have been more effective.

"No," the Farish gasped in a hiss, his voice full of intrigue. "It couldn't be! Could it? The one who escaped?" The hiss turned to a scratchy laugh, like dry leaves crunching underfoot. "And you've been right here under my nose, in this Nöz"—he spat the name—"waiting all this time? Only to die today on my altar like so many others before you." The scratchy laugh turned to a bellow.

"It will be your blood that spills," retorted Cor, abandoning her deception.

"Master!" The Adder couldn't control himself in the face of such threats.

"No!" snapped the Farish, his voice booming even as he lowered his arm. "He will bend his knee." Rage now filled his quavering voice. He nodded, and the Tszoi wrenched Badu to his feet. Nobody had heard the click of Badu's shackles releasing. As he was lifted, Badu swatted at the brute's leg. The priestguard holding Cor yanked her to her feet.

"Bring the helmet to—" The Farish stopped and cocked his head. The mountain of a guard behind Badu had begun shaking so violently that Badu could feel it through his feet. Frothing at the mouth, the Tszoi fought to control his spasming body, still oblivious to the small, feathered needle protruding from his thigh.

The priestguard holding Cor watched with wide eyes even as Badu shot his free hand out, no longer bound by the shackles, burying a second needle in the priestguard's neck. Cor slammed her head back into the guard's face, and Badu grabbed the man's sword. He crumpled.

A second guard leaped at Corvina with blade extended, but she ducked under the swing and caught his legs between her own, slamming him on the ground. She bent his wrist with a crack and plunged the man's sword back into his torso. The Altar erupted with activity.

Feeling the heavy footfalls thundering through the stone, Badu spun just as a hulking Tszoi guard swung a two-handed sword longer than Badu himself. The massive blade would have cleaved him in half, but Badu slipped under the swing, placing his final dart in the brute's flank. Three priestguard pressed in on Badu as the frozen statue of a Tszoi convulsed behind him.

Between two attackers, Badu spotted Cor sprinting toward the seawall. *What's she doing?* Behind her the Adder strode toward her at a measured, deliberate pace. *Has she seen him?*

Badu wanted to yell a warning, but a blade flashed before him. He tore his eyes away in time to parry a guard's sword and dodge another. The priestguard before him paused, glancing up. Something was off. The man hesitated a count too long and Badu felt the danger. He dropped to the ground just as an arrow whistled overhead, barely missing him and lodging into the guard's chest.

Without pause, he swept the legs of the closest guard, sending him crashing to the stone.

The third guard sprang to action, lifting his sword high overhead and swinging down, but Badu was too fast. He dodged, rolling to the side, and ripped a dagger from the belt of the unconscious body beside him. Before the guard could bring the broadsword down again, Badu flicked the knife up, striking the attacker in the throat.

Jumping to his feet, fear lanced through him as he searched for Cor. She bent over the priestess in blue and removed two short swords from the covered bundle, twirling to face the Adder. *Yes!* thought Badu as the dread turned to a flicker of hope. Cor was deadly with a pair of swords.

His eyes darted to the Farish. The man looked lost, standing out in the open glancing around the mayhem that now surrounded him, a step behind the stone block. Their eyes met. Badu smiled inwardly. He snatched up a sword and leaped forward, racing to meet the counterfeit god. *You'll bleed!*

Before he could reach the Farish, something slammed into him, sending Badu flying. A Tszoi standing over him, jabbed down with a long spear. *No!* Badu cried inwardly. *I'm almost there!* Badu batted the spear aside and rolled away, the sharpened tip grazing his shirt and slicing his shoulder. He grabbed the spear's shaft and didn't let go as the mighty Tszoi warrior jerked it backward for another thrust.

The powerful force lifted Badu off the ground into the air. His raised his sword as his body collided with the mountain man, burying the blade to the hilt in the warrior's chest. Again, Badu found the Farish, now backing reluctantly to the arched chamber door at the urgent pleading of his high priest. Badu's eyes narrowed on his prey even as a new pair of Tszoi guards rushed up behind him. But they were too late. Nothing now stood between him and the Farish. He ripped the bloodied sword from the corpse beside him and crouched to leap forward.

A scream from behind froze Badu where he stood. He tore his gaze from the golden mask to find Cor. She had a gash from her cheek down to her arm, and the Adder bore down on her with incredible speed, striking with his long black sword. Her double swords flashed back, but her right arm wasn't moving well. Fresh fear twisted like a knife in Badu's gut. The Adder was a cold and ruthless killer.

Cor parried a swing and snapped one of the blades out, catching the Adder on the calf. He barely reacted, swinging back with amazing speed. Cor dodged, then spun, the blade in her good arm biting into the Adder's side. Now he staggered back. *Yes!* thought Badu. *Finish him.*

The pair squared off again and Cor lunged. Badu spotted it immediately: the overextension. The Adder did too. In a flash, he grabbed her sword arm and smashed his helmet into her face. Cor staggered backward. The Adder leaped at her, striking her with a backhand that sent her sprawling. She struggled back to her feet, bleeding from her mouth, raising a sword in her only good arm. The Adder swung his heavy blade down in a powerful stroke that knocked the sword from her hand and sent it skittering across the stone. He stepped behind her, grabbing her by the hair.

"No!" cried Badu. His insides flipped, and a flash of cold dread washed over him. Her frantic eyes found his and locked on him as the Adder thrust that great black blade through her.

Cor's surprised eyes fell to the blade protruding from her stomach, then back to Badu. "Badu!" she managed to cry with a wince.

"That soz can't save you now," croaked the Adder.

"Catch." She made a weak throwing motion, but the Adder snapped his hand forward, catching her wrist.

"What's this?" he asked, prying her hand open. "Huh?" The Adder raised a black gauntlet to his face, inspecting the small semitranslucent red bulb he held between his fingers. *The cherry.*

Pop! The sound of a bursting wineskin came from the priestess in blue, who held a knife protruding from the large pod cradled in her lap. Badu watched with dark satisfaction as a tiny squid-like shape shot into the air. It floated, suspended for a brief moment before collapsing its parachute tentacles and darting across the stone. It traversed the courtyard with amazing speed, darted up the leg of the Adder, and disappeared under his helmet.

There was a muffled scream. The Adder lurched backward, pulling his blade free from Cor. He spun and flailed for a moment, pawing at his helmet before dropping his sword and falling to the ground. Badu's mind slipped back to the sun-drenched alley, to the Adder's blade falling on his mother. The fire within that had glowed for years flared hungrily. The Adder writhed and squirmed on the ground and then grew still.

20

THE ALTAR

Badu was suddenly aware of the wavesbreath berries pressed in his pocket. *You can still escape.* He eyed the unobstructed path to the seawall. *No! Kill the one you came for! Finish what you started!* But he ignored both voices. Instead, he raced to Cor's crumpled figure. She had slid down to her side, her eyes wide as her blood pooled. He dropped his sword and scooped her up in his arms, oblivious to all else.

On this day, in this place, a moment he had trained for and prepared for his entire life, Badu realized something with startling clarity. He had finally found something—no, someone— he cared about more than revenge. More even than his own life. And only now that he had found her, she slipped away in his arms. He kissed her, staining his lips with her blood.

"I love you," he whispered, lost in her green eyes. For a moment, he was swept away to somewhere else, a quiet and beautiful place where he and Cor had found an escape from death, a place where nobody hunted him, and what woke him each still, quiet morning was simply a desire to love and be loved. In this brief imagining, he had found the center, the quiet his father had once spoken of. He had found it with Cor.

Even as Badu cradled Cor's dying body, something huge slammed into him from behind sending him sprawling. Strong arms pinned him to the ground.

"Bring him!" came the voice of the Farish, frothy and seething.

As the Tzsoi brutes dragged him away, Badu found Cor's eyes one last time. Her head lay on the stone, and her lips mouthed some final word for him. Even as he stared, the green spark behind her eyes went dim.

"No!" he screamed. A shock of lightning ripped through him.

The guards threw Badu to the stone before the stage, and heavy hands crammed some sort of helmet on his head, sending searing pain over his scalp. When they jerked him back to his feet, Badu readied himself to fight to the end but found he couldn't move anything below his neck.

"You have nothing!" shouted the Farish, the quiet, ominous calm gone. "Now you will be mine! Proceed!" He screamed the command, insistent and unhinged, ignoring the motionless body of the Adder just measures away. Resuming his spot on the stone block, the Farish threw back his red cloak. Every guard and priest dropped to a knee, hiding their faces. Deep inside, Badu recalled the whisper of a voice, an urgent warning. Something about a crystal. But as the Farish ripped the black cloth from his necklace, the shred of thought blew away like stone dust. Badu's eyes shot to the resplendent stone hanging on the Far Seer Priest's chest and locked there. Everything that was and ever would be, everything that mattered now or ever, had faded until all that existed was the sparkling midnight-blue stone. It swallowed him—no, it called him into its gaping maw, and he rushed in, offering himself to it.

The helmet on his head heated to the point of burning, but he barely noticed. Wailing and chanting filled the air, but Badu didn't care. All he cared about, all he needed, was that stone.

Even the thoughts of Cor were blown away like fog. The navy blackness of the crystal drew him in. He hungrily drank of the sweet, dark power. But as he surrendered to the stone, the unquenchable lust for more only grew. The dark ecstasy rose until the hungry joy blurred into pain and then agony. The pleasure became fear, then terror.

The euphoria was gone. Horrific visions of demons with stretched black wings, of death and gruesome evils, consumed him, flashing like a lightning storm in his mind. Then, in that nightmare, time stopped. Like a man pinned beneath waves, he knew neither time nor space, only torment. It wasn't the faces of men or monsters that haunted him but rather the essence of dread itself. It came to roost in his bones.

From the blackness, the Farish appeared.

"I told you I would have you." The voice was not that of the man in the robes. It was stronger, wider, deeper. It rumbled and permeated Badu. "This place, this power," continued the Farish. "It is but a taste of what will come, of what you could join."

The words surrounded Badu, closed in on him.

"The Adder was like you once," the Farish continued. "A great warrior from a proud clan. Eiklin. But I called him to so much more. He has spilled a sea of blood for me. But you have killed him. You and your deceptress." A distant flickering memory of Cor pricked his mind like a searing needle. "Not to worry. You will soon be free of those memories, free of all that binds. Simply bend the knee and join me."

Badu was suddenly standing before the Far Seer Priest, who had grown in stature, looming three measures higher than he had moments before.

"Bow to me!" The darkness from the stone crashed over Badu anew, filling him with dread and dark joy again. He fell to his knees, unable to control his body. He found himself holding the Farish's huge bony hand, adorned with a blood-red ring, between both of his own. "Kiss the ring!" He did. "Now utter the Concession, and it will be finished!" commanded the Farish. "It's simple. Speak the words, 'I surrender my body to the Farish. I commend my soul to Kilzhet,' and it will be so."

Badu saw it, felt it. The path felt easy and smooth. A simple utterance and he would be delivered from the burning thicket of pain and sorrow that had been his life. How he knew this, he could not say, but it was truer than any fact he ever swore.

"You have lost everything, you are over. But I offer you life that you could never imagine. Rise to power! We will rule together. We will take all," urged the Farish. "The Concession! Speak it!" His booming voice exploded now like thunder, consuming everything in this black void.

Badu felt the Concession rising in him; his diaphragm tightened as his obedient body prepared to utter the phrase like the slave he was becoming. So simple, so good. As he opened his mouth to speak the recitation, he felt a jolt from deep within.

With sharp clarity, the words were suddenly in his throat. "I..." he began. The Farish smiled greedily. "I am heir to a throne I could never own." The Farish's smile twisted to a confused frown. "I am a warrior, a warrior washed in color and light," continued Badu. "I am a light, a light on a rock above the crashing waves." The proverb came to him in the voice of his father, in the bedtime song of his mother, in the innocent defiance of his sister.

The Farish screamed in furious rage. "Fool! You have failed! You will die!" The voice reverberated through the darkness as the vision of the deity disappeared.

When Badu saw light again, it felt like weeks or months or years. As he opened his eyes, he found himself lying on the cobblestone. Everything remained as it had been before. Voices slowly came to him.

"The prisoner shall die!" screeched the high priest, now undone. The Farish drew a curved, glistening red sickle from his waist, the very same weapon from Badu's visions. Without moving a step, still twenty measures away on the platform, the Farish swiped the sickle forward into an invisible enemy, and Badu lurched with a stab in his stomach.

His hand instinctively shot under his shirt where he touched something sticky and wet. When he drew it back, his hand was covered in blood. *Impossible!*

"Bring them!" screeched the Farish. "Bring death from the sky!" Rough hands ripped the helmet from Badu's head. Lying in the fetal position on the stone of the Altar, sucking air as his blood ran from him, scraps of remnant terror lashed him. *Surely this man* is *a god,* Badu admitted as his life seeped from him.

He is not! came the voice, loud and clear like a trumpet blast in his head. *You must live!* Badu jerked slightly with a painful spasm of what almost resembled a laugh. He had surrendered the idea of leaving here alive long ago. *All is lost. I have failed, and now, I will die.*

Letting his vision drift upward, he spotted the dragons. The familiar shapes high above were circling.

"Come, Kilzhet! Come, death from the sky!" chanted the priests and priestesses as one.

"How dare you oppose me!" accused the Farish. "You could have had everything! The beasts will feast on your flesh!"

The dragons descended quickly. Highland drakes, Badu could see now. *These are his dragons?* The cow-sized reptiles were rarely spotted other than buzzing atop the peaks of the Tenner Range like flies on distant scat. Badu knew the creatures feared humans. Encounters were exceedingly rare. *Another mystery I'll never solve.* Down they came.

Flowing robes billowed in every direction as the priests and priestesses fled from the descending drakes. Even the Farish moved backward into the covered alcove at the back of the stage, his glittering golden mask seeming to hang in the darkness in the archway. A hovering drake folded its wings and dropped fast, crashing into a priestguard soldier who hadn't made it to cover. As the guard struggled to rise, another ripped his helmet off. After a third beast attacked, the guard stopped moving.

Badu looked away as a pair of drakes landed on Cor's body. *This is where I die.* No sooner had he thought the words than a shadow covered him. He glanced up to see the outline of a plummeting drake. His body relaxed, knowing what was coming. All strength was gone, and his mind and soul had been ravaged. It was over.

Fight! Stay alive. The scream of a voice splashed over Badu like icy spring water, jerking him alert. Even as he refocused, his vision was filled with outstretched talons falling on him. With a burst of energy he didn't know he had, Badu dodged to the side, and the empty talons clacked and scraped, hitting nothing but stone.

Without thinking, he dove at the drake, grabbing both of its legs in a bear hug. The drake kicked and jerked, thrashing its tail, but its razor teeth at the end of that long neck couldn't reach far enough to snap him.

Frantic, the drake beat its wings and rose a few measures into the air, trying to dislodge Badu. He held on for all he was worth. Higher the drake rose until they were swooping unsteadily ten measures over the Altar. Badu's grip began to slip as the first arrow whistled by. The castle archers were trying to shoot him from the sky. Fire burned in Badu's side. Still, the beast kicked and shook. Badu hooked an elbow around one of the legs, and with his free hand, he latched the loose shackle hanging from his wrist to the drake's other leg and let go.

Pain shot through Badu's wrist and arm as he dangled from the drake. The wound in his side felt like it would tear him open. The frantic beating of the dragon's wings only increased as more arrows zipped past. They rose out over the seawall, now hundreds of measures over the roaring ocean.

Thud. An arrow slammed into the drake's side and the creature screamed. They jerked wildly; it spun and flapped, veering back toward land as it tried to keep altitude. Another arrow passed through the membrane on its wing and a third grazed its neck. There was nothing Badu could do. He hung helplessly from one arm as the wounded drake struggled to stay aloft over the mouth of the river separating the castle from the city.

Down toward the city they plunged. Shouts rose from terrified fishermen who fled from the street as the drake swerved and dropped, careening into the thatched roof of a hut. Badu scrabbled his foot and fumbled to release the shackle, but the drake surged forward with a scream, taking to the air again. The frantic creature yanked Badu's forward, nearly pulling his arm from its socket. It flew across the street dragging Badu and slammed into the back wall of a barn. Exhausted and bleeding, the creature finally collapsed in the corner of a stall. Badu quickly twisted the manacles, releasing the lock. The drake's eye, a slit of gold and green, fixed him for a moment before it closed.

With every inch of his body on fire, Badu forced himself to his feet and ran.

21

DANCING WITH DEATH

A hand clamped tightly over the wound in his stomach, Badu staggered into the Saffron Crescent. The late afternoon crowd had begun to arrive and already the tables were full.

"Hey, handsome. What brings you—" Arva's greeting cut short. "Gods! You look awful!"

"I need..." Badu winced. "Bed."

Worry streaked Arva's face. "Yes, yes, of course. Shuuv will make space for you." Badu knew the hard old innkeeper to be tough with her patrons and staff, but beneath the gruff exterior, Shuuv was kind and loyal.

"What's the interruption—oh. I see," said Shuuv, rising as Arva dragged Badu through the door into the back room. "Trouble in the street?" She fixed him with a piercing glare. He shook his head no. "Castle trouble, then."

He nodded. "Afraid so." Badu's voice was weak and scratchy.

Shuuv sighed loudly and glanced out the window, calculating. "So be it. Quickly now," she finally said, scurrying to the tall bookshelf in the wall. She pulled a concealed lever, and the bookcase swung away.

"Should have known you weren't a reader." Badu smiled weakly.

"Big surprise," quipped Shuuv. "In here." She helped Arva support Badu as they dragged him over to the bed. "You going to stay with him?"

"Yes. For a while... I mean, if that's all right."

Shuuv sighed again, her lips pursed as she surveyed Badu with a scowl. "Very well. I'll bring a washbasin and some herbs. You'll be wise to lie low until I come for you." With that, the aging innkeeper stepped through the bookcase, pulling it closed behind her. Just before it shut, the false wall stopped and her head reappeared. "If you don't die, you'll owe me a herfing pile of silver!" With that, she was gone, and the bookcase closed with a clang.

Tormented hours turned to days as Badu writhed in the bed in the hidden room. Fever ripped through his racked body, and deep sleep eluded him, his every rest filled with fitful nightmares and terrors. He watched Corvina die a hundred times in that tiny room, each one ripping him open afresh.

Arva plied him with foul-smelling tea and herbs and a heavy dose of whiskey as she sewed the mysterious blade wound in his side. When he was conscious, she tried pressing him for the account of the injury, but she never got much. Badu couldn't understand how the Farish had stabbed him from twenty measures away, so he didn't try to explain.

She lay beside him to comfort him until he finally threw her out. He had woken too many times from a fitful sleep to Cor's bloody corpse beside him. The wound in his side burned like he was being consumed from the inside out; like a firebrand was being pushed back and forth through the stab wound. When his groaning grew to muffled screams of agony, Arva finally brought the ferikökü.

The next three days passed in a haze. Badu wandered in and out of dreams and nightmares. He spoke with his mother, fought the Farish, slew a cave full of ferocious drakes; he even visited the shores of death itself. But death did not claim him. He lost count of how many foul brews of bitter herbs and foaming broths Arva force-fed him. On the sixth day, as he finally began the long, slow climb back to consciousness, the worst had passed. The brewing infection had subsided and the inexplicable jabbing inside his abdomen had faded.

"How do you feel?" Badu woke to a blurry picture of Arva's face.

"Just great. As long as I don't move." He forced a half smile and winced. "Or smile."

"This place has been crawling with tinmen," she said, dabbing his head with a damp towel. "The whole city has. They've been upending the whole slag of the city, going door to door. Whatever happened, you poked a shivving hornet's nest, you did."

Badu listened to her words, waiting for the rising fear that being hunted by the Farish's entire army should bring, but he felt nothing. Everything had dulled—sights, sounds, thoughts. Even recalling the Adder's death brought with it no spike of joy or satisfaction. All the remembering did was summon the flickering image of the black blade piercing Cor's perfect stomach. It ran in a loop through his mind. He threw a pillow over his head, trying to push it all out.

"Come, rise," said the Adder through the blurred darkness. He sat across from Badu at a game table in a smoke-filled room, stacking circular chips. "Why do you hide? Come, wander out of this prison. Find a knot of tinmen and give yourself up. Why not? What else is there for you but death?"

He jerked awake. When had he slipped off again? Badu was alone in the room. He rose, oddly feeling none of his injuries.

The Adder's coaxing rang in his head. *What else is there but death?* He was right. Sliding the hidden door open, Badu stepped quietly from the hidden room into Shuuv's office. A dull ripple of voices rose from the bar area outside the study. Embracing boldness born of indifference, Badu opened the door wide and stepped through. Margoul filled the great dining room. Goblins, trolls, and orcs sat at the bar and filled the tables. None looked up as he entered. A long banquet table filled the center of the room, packed with margoul sitting in chairs on either side. Badu moved to get a better view of the long, ornate dish, adorned with vegetables and garnishments at its center. As he drew closer, he froze. It was no great slab of beef or roast hog; there on the center of the table lay Cor. She turned to him even as the margoul drew up forks and knives.

"Wake up!"

Badu snapped awake, panting hard. The fire in his side and the woozy feeling in his head told him he had escaped the nightmares. The Adder had been a vision, yet his words hung over Badu like a cloud. *What does life hold for me that death does not?* Even if he somehow wasn't captured and killed in this city, he would never get within a cliq of the Farish again. Cor was dead, and the Nöz had begun to crumble. His mind spun these questions over like a silkeen worm spinning its cocoon until sleep pounced on him again. He didn't resist.

When Badu finally awoke from a stretch of hours, maybe a day, it was to Arva blotting his forehead with a damp towel. He felt restless; he had to move. The tiny room was suddenly suffocating. Filled with a thick cloud of incense, it smelled of sweat and the remnants of ferikökü. The walls of the tiny space were closing in, and Badu felt like he couldn't breathe.

"I must... get out," he said, sitting up.

"You're not ready," she objected. "Still hot with fever."

"Just out... out of here." He panted from the effort of sitting and swinging his legs over the edge of the sleeping mat.

"Wait. Let me check for tinmen," urged Arva. Badu grunted his agreement, and she slipped out. He was going nowhere quickly, but he couldn't stay. Rising to shaky legs, a sharp stab jabbed him in the side as he stood. The new muscle and skin growth protested against his rising. He breathed deeply and steadied himself against the wall.

"Okay, no patrols have been here for a while," said Arva, returning. "At least wear this." She thrust a cape and huge, floppy velvet hat into his hands. He threw a skeptical glare at her. "It will keep you from being noticed."

"Don't know that I'll make it past the bar." He smiled, though it held no joy. He wondered absently if he would ever know joy again.

By the time Badu had hobbled the twenty paces to the main room, leaning heavily on Arva, he was winded.

"What hour is it?" he asked Arva.

"Eleven past," she replied. "Eve's Day."

That explains the crowd at almost midnight, he thought. At the far end of the room, he spied an empty booth. "There." He pointed. With the cape and hat pulled low, trying to act natural, he walked arm-in-arm with Arva until he collapsed into the booth.

"Keep to yourself," said Arva. "And absolutely no glug." She flashed a smile and turned to go.

"Wait." Badu reached for her hand, stopping her. "Thank you." Their eyes met. "For everything. You have... saved me." She held his gaze with a wistful look and offered a tight smile. Then she turned and walked off.

As soon as Arva was out of sight, Badu ordered a tankard of glug. When it arrived, he sat back, losing himself in the receding surface of the drink for the better part of an hour. After his second, he felt terrible and was ready to leave. Just as he slid to the edge of the bench and pushed himself up to go, a man dropped heavily into the booth on the other side.

"Mind if I join?" The slender man with a heavy cloak spoke with a slaggish twang, not the pure tongue of a native Kopolian. He slid into the bench without awaiting a reply and dropped two tankards of ale on the table.

"I was leaving," replied Badu.

"Sit, friend," he insisted. Badu hesitated. There was something familiar about the man, whose face was hidden within the shadow of the cowl, but Badu couldn't place what it was. His feeble mind spun, trying to catch the elusive shred of familiarity. He longed for the bed in the quiet little room, but the thought of the extraordinary effort it would take to get there kept him planted.

"Toast to a good Eve's Day to you, my friend," said the man, raising a goblet. Badu didn't move. "Bad luck not to meet the eyes, you know," the man taunted playfully.

"Mine's run out," Badu replied without thinking. *Why even engage?* he wondered.

"I must've stolen your portion, then." *Wait.* Badu knew that voice. He glanced up as the man threw back his hood.

"Herf me! Oster!" Badu nearly shouted. Oster beamed his irresistible, goofy smile, albeit from a strangely clean-shaven face.

Oster gave a fully belly laugh. "We've been out looking for you everywhere! Ferat said something about returning to the castle, and then the city turned upside down! We thought for sure you'd been killed."

"It's a bit of a story," exclaimed Badu. The men clasped forearms.

"Shaved my beard and cut my hair so they wouldn't recognize me in the city," said Oster grinning and showing off his new look. "But it makes no blummin' difference. Whatever happened in the castle, the tinmen only care about finding you. I could walk out and throw myself at the feet of a guard troop right now, confessing everything, and I doubt they'd even look at me."

"Cor's dead," said Badu. "Took the Adder with her."

"Herf me!" Oster whistled. "No wonder!" He raised his tankard but caught himself. "I'm sorry about Cor. Ferat says she meant much to you."

Badu only nodded, reaching inside for stabbing grief only to find hollowness. "By the Color, I made it out, somehow. I've been hiding out here recuperating."

Oster shook his head. "Well, I'm delighted to find you. The men will be thrilled."

"I failed, Oster," Badu said, dropping his head. "Cor brought me to the feet of the Liar. I had him." He closed his eyes and shook his head. "Now she's dead. Gone. We'll never get close to the Farish again." Badu took a drink.

"We'll get another chance—"

"He knows about the Nöz, Oster. He knows everything. It's just a matter of time until he finds the Skyrt. I've failed," he said again. The last of his words came out a bit blurry, and he noted that it was time to end the night. A silence fell on the men. Badu silently hoped Oster wouldn't try to console him or offer a platitude.

"Maybe there's still hope," Oster said at last. Badu laughed bitterly. "Do you remember my story of Uzgül?"

"Of course," Badu replied. "You captivated me as a boy with those stories. I used to imagine the monster taking to the air from the bottom of the sea and swallowing an army."

"Or a castle." Oster's smile faded, and he fixed Badu with a hard gaze.

Badu snorted. "Or that." He threw his glass back, finishing the glug. When he lowered the glass, Badu started, finding Oster still staring, now more intently.

"It's true, you know," hissed Oster. "All of it."

"Ha. You've had more to drink than I, my friend," answered Badu jovially.

Oster rolled up his sleeve as he spoke. "I know you all have doubted." There on his arm was a scene tattooed in great detail. It was a tattoo Badu had seen many times and even studied as a boy. A small figure stood before the horizon, a great creature rising from the water. Oster had it done years ago.

"It must be you," Oster said after another pause, his eyes glittering as if with a secret. "I saw it in a dream. I had almost forgotten the whole thing. He told me to share it with you."

"What? What are you talking about? Told? Told what? By who?" Badu's head spun.

"Yuz, of course." Oster laughed off the question.

"You? A main of faith?" Badu gave him a hard sidelong stare.

"I lost much in that dark castle but gained much, too. Why you, I can't say, but none of this is an accident, I think. You are bound together with this tale, uyesi."

"What tale? Of Uzgül?" Badu strained to follow. "What are you saying?"

"I have a plan. Born of a dream and a legend." Oster straightened, his eyes bright. "It's the same one I shared years ago. Simple. And impossible." He flashed his winsome smile. "You must find the sleeping Uzgül and wake him." Oster took a swallow from his mug.

"Ha! You saw this in a dream?"

"You have waited your whole life to kill the Farish, have you not?" Oster pressed.

"Yes," Badu replied quietly. "And I've failed."

"Your story isn't yet written." Again, Oster glanced around furtively. "There is still time. I was also told to bring this tonight. I don't know why, I truly don't," he said, reaching into his cloak. "Do you remember it?" Oster drew a yellowed leather scroll from a deep pocket. He unrolled it before them. It was the faded ink drawing of Uzgül.

Badu reached for the scroll, turned it back over, and studied the ink drawing again. "And Yuz told you to bring this to me tonight?" he asked doubtfully. Oster nodded eagerly. "You truly believe, don't you? That this monster sleeps on the seafloor in the bay?"

"I do." Oster smiled wide. "I tried to convince Garris seasons ago." Something in Badu wanted to believe, like Oster.

"And if this fantasy were true, if I could somehow find and wake Uzgül, then what?" Badu couldn't believe he was indulging this lunacy.

Oster's eyes flashed with excitement. "Simple! I will set stacks of yellowflare grass around the castle. If you can find Uzgül and wake him, he will rise into the sky once more. After he has flown out over the ocean and gained his strength, Uzgül will be back and will be hungry. The yellowflare fires will draw him like a moth. We can kill the Farish, brother!"

"Why don't *I* light the fires, and you go swim around the bottom of the bay searching for a monster?" Badu winked.

"I would." Oster grinned. "But it was you in my dream. Besides, you know I can't swim."

Badu shook his head and smiled, recalling Oster thrashing around a waist-deep bathing pool while the nözan all looked on, rolling with laughter.

"I'm sorry," said Badu as he rose to leave. "I will see you back in the Skyrt in a day or two. Goodnight, old friend." He clapped Oster on the shoulder and turned to cross the sea of revelers back to his cave.

"Remember the blue brillflower fields of Ghiesa," Oster blurted to Badu's back as he walked away.

"What?" Badu spun. "What did you just say?" A stab of pain and rage rippled through him.

Oster's hands shot up in surrender. "The words mean

nothing to me, uyesi. They only just flickered in my mind as if written on a wall. But I now heed such things. And it sounds like they might mean something to you."

For a long moment, Badu stood silently, his eyes fixed on Oster. *What do you have left?* asked the voice inside. *You'll be hunted now more than ever. Better to die chasing an impossible dream to kill that tyrant than at his hand as a slave.*

"Tomorrow night, then," Badu heard his words before he could stop himself. "We'll see if your fairytale monster exists and can kill a fake god. But for now, I'm going to bed."

Oster rose, a disbelieving twinkle in his eyes. "Trimidious! Give me a day to make arragements and gather the yellowflare. I will send word tomorrow with instructions." He positively beamed, his gap-toothed smile flashing. The men embraced and Badu hobbled back to bed.

22

THE LAGOON

"Go out? You mustn't!" scolded Avra. "They're everywhere. And they search for you!"

Badu winced from the pain in his gut where the Farish's invisible blade had pierced him, and he nursed a hundred bruises and a cracked rib from the crash landing with the wounded drake.

"Arva, you are a pearl among the rocks. Thank you." Patting her arm, he offered an apologetic smile. He kissed her on the cheek and staggered out of the Crescent.

After sleeping most of the day away, after his long night with Oster, Badu rose to a knock at the door. Nobody was there when he opened it, but a simple note on the floor read, *"Make ready."*

At midnight, he left the Crescent. The hunched beggar disguise had the desired effect, letting him slip through the thin crowd at the entrance to the Crescent unnoticed, including past two priestguard soldiers. Despite the late hour, he spotted no fewer than four more priestguard patrols as he navigated the city streets, causing him to hurry to the cover of the shadows more than once. He had never seen the city like this. *Could they possibly still be looking for me?*

When he reached the Fisherman's Quarter littered with stooped houses and shops on a low bluff above the half-crescent beach, Badu finally had to stop. He collapsed in the shadows on the porch of a net stringer's hut. His body ached and his breath came in quick, shallow rasps. For days, he had done nothing but sleep and recover. The most he had walked was the twenty steps between the hidden room and the main parlor at the Crescent. *What am I doing?* he asked himself for the hundredth time. Something beneath the pile of nets poked his back, and he shifted, knocking a clay pot from a wobbly table. It smashed loudly on the porch. *Shivv!*

Heavy boots sounded on the sandy cobblestone just a few measures away as a priestguard patrol meandered past. Badu pressed himself back into the dark corner of the porch and froze. One of the soldiers glanced up at the porch but plodded on.

Badu readied himself to rise, forcing his aching body to comply. This hiding like a scared skupp would never do. He removed his beggar's cape and stood to go, but as he did, the door to the hut flew open and a shape staggered from the house. The stocky old woman with a wrinkled leather face lifted a lantern and peered off into the yard. Standing just five paces behind her in the shadows, Badu didn't breathe. As she turned, he knew he would be spotted. He reached for one of his poison darts, but something stopped him.

"I'm sorry to bother—" he said instead.

The woman yelped, spinning as she finally spied the stranger on her porch.

"I just stopped to rest."

"No spot for beggars here!" she squawked, shooing him off the porch. "Take a fish off the drying rack out back—" she offered but froze as her lamplight fell on his face. She frowned and tilted her head. "Wait. You're who they're looking for..." She started backing up toward the door.

Do it! a voice snapped inside, his fingers still pinching the poison dart. It was the right move, ruthless and smart. Badu shut out the voice and held up his empty hands.

"I'm going, I'm going." He staggered backward and hobbled off the porch and across the road. She started yelling for a guard. When he was out of sight, he turned past another set of houses and down a narrow lane paved with crushed shell. Any other night, he would have welcomed the strong moon that cast a shadow, but tonight, he prayed for cloud cover. When he reached the sandy path to the beach, he silenced his body's aching cries and hurried to the water.

Badu ignored the moonlit beauty of the sparkling half-circle lagoon that protected the shore from the angry waves ever thundering against the crescent-shaped reef a cliq out from the beach.

To his surprise, counting the twelfth boat from the left, he found the white rowboat with blue stingray insignia covered in a canvas tarpaulin just as Oster had said he would. He peeled the canvas back to reveal paddles, an oyster diver's pot, the heavy anchor, and a whaler's harpoon. In the hours since their conversation, Badu had begun to doubt everything, including Oster's promise of the provisioned boat.

"I told you it would be ready!" Badu leapt, a jolt of fear lancing through him. Oster rose from his crouch behind the next boat over and moved to the stern of the white boat.

"What am I doing here?" Badu hissed.

"It's perfect, but we don't have time. You've attracted some attention." A shout from behind. Badu spun and spotted three torches through the seagrass moving down the path toward the beach. With a glance out over the black water and a deep breath, Badu joined Oster to lower his shoulder into the stern of the rowboat. The men pushed, sending the boat sliding down its rails and splashing softly into the water.

"Get in!" whispered Oster. Badu climbed in and Oster gave the craft one more shove, sending the boat sliding out into the calm water. "I'll be ready for you!" called Oster, disappearing among the boats.

Badu only shook his head as he sat on the bench and positioned the oars. Silently straining against the waves, he rowed for everything he was worth. His atrophied arms burned, and his palms soon felt like they gripped coals. The wound in his side screamed.

On shore, the three torches had paused. Among the tinmen in their glinting armor, Badu spotted a shadow he presumed to be the old net maker. From the way they moved, they obviously hadn't found Oster.

After twenty minutes of sustained pulling, Badu had to stop. He gasped for air and his entire body felt like it was afire. Blisters had formed on his palms. The three restless torches on the beach had grown to six, and the glassy surface of the lagoon had begun to ripple with an onshore breeze. He would lose progress to this headwind if he rested much longer.

Wrapping his blistered hands in cloth, Badu picked up the oars again and pulled. When he finally permitted himself to stop again, gasping for air like a fish at the bottom of a boat, he saw he had drawn within fifty mounts of the reef. The soldiers on the beach had finally assembled themselves into four boats and were pushing out toward him with strong strokes.

From out here, Badu could see the entire moonlit Fisherman's Quarter, climbing up from the water's edge in a gentle slope, winding streets snaking upward to the plateau and the main city. Even as he watched, dozens of pinpoints of torchlight multiplied and trickled down through the dark streets from the city to the Fisherman's Quarter like raindrops sliding down a sheet of waxed canvas. The alarm had been sounded.

You knew this was a one-way trip, Badu told himself, returning to the agony in his hands as he ripped the oars through the glittering water. He had begun counting the ways he might die tonight, with drowning being the obvious favorite. He was up to three variations on death by drowning, and now counted death by the goon squad pursuing him as number four.

The increased headwind slowed his progress, but Badu was now close to the line of frothy white waves that broke over the submerged reef. The rock formation called the Shark's Tooth stood in black relief against the moon-drenched sea beyond as glowing waves of white foam bowed at its base. *This has to be close.* He closed his eyes, trying to remember the ink drawing and how the Shark's Tooth had aligned with the ravine cutting through the Fisherman's Quarter. After a final survey of the surrounding area, he made a last adjustment, rowing fifty measures upshore.

Like a plunderer's vessel piled high with gold, the pursuing boats sparkled as moonlight and torchlight glinted from the armor and weapons of dozens of soldiers. On the shore, dozens more torch-wielding patrols had trickled down from the city and pooled on the beach. More boats launched. The breeze had grown stiff, and stray clouds now hurried across the moon. Badu didn't have the time or strength to worry.

He hefted the iron anchor over the side, watching the sinking weight rip coil after coil of rope from its basket. Counting as it went, he reached five full counts before the anchor line stopped. Roughly fifty measures down. He swallowed. He had imagined the lagoon to be twenty or twenty-five measures deep at the lowest point within the reef.

"Halt!" came a voice across what had become choppy water. Badu ignored the call and removed the wavesbreath pellets from his pocket. The sight of them ripped him back to some of the last words he ever spoke to Cor. *I'm coming,* he thought.

Without giving himself time to think better of it, he popped one of the pellets into his mouth and swallowed. Twenty minutes wasn't going to be enough. He swallowed the second. If his heart exploded on the way, well, that would make the fifth way he might die tonight.

An arrow flew by his head followed by a scolding shout carried off in the wind. *An angry officer,* he thought. *It means the Farish wants me alive. Of course he does.* The priestguard boats were now only fifty measures away, but the wind had begun to whip over the lagoon. The anchor line groaned. Even within the reef, the water had grown rough. Badu hefted up the rope weight belt and tied it around his waist, groaning under the full weight of the four fist-sized ironstones that hung to it like dangling fruit.

Cold rain spattered across the boat and water, and silent lightning flashed off in the distance. *Lightning strike: number six,* he thought, smiling to himself. Badu ignored the oversized clay vase adorned with heavy weights and a tether line. Oster included it so Badu could carry a pocket of air down to the ocean floor. It was how those brave fishermen who harvested the precious stargazer mollusks stayed underwater long enough to complete their task. But Badu would be going without.

A warm sensation built in his stomach that told him the effect of the wavesbreath was building. *How long do I wait?* he wondered. Sevin told him that once underwater, there would be a frantic moment as his body fought against water entering his lungs. *At least I'll find out for sure if it works,* he thought darkly. Despite the whipping wind and steady rain, the priest-guard boats continued to advance.

"Give yourself up!" came a shout from the closest boat. "We will not kill you." That he believed. *The Farish has something much, much worse in store for me.* He had no intention of finding out what. A priestguard soldier at the helm struggled to keep his balance as the small craft rocked in the waves. Six more soldiers were stuffed in the small boat, causing it to ride low in the water. Through the veil of rain, dozens of lights bobbed on the water, though most appeared to be stalled much closer to shore in the struggle against wind.

His heart raced like a choluk, and his chest burned with fire now. *It must be time.* With harpoon in hand, Badu took a breath and jumped from the boat, chased by a cry from a nearby vessel.

23

UZGÜL

Badu's plan to tread water as he gathered himself before descending proved to be a gross miscalculation. With the combined weight of the heavy metal harpoon and the weighted belt around his waist, Badu sank like a millstone through the dark water. He kicked frantically to slow the descent but to no avail. Looking up at the water's surface as he dropped, he caught the flash of lightning far above, silhouetting the hulls of the boats now nearly on top of his own.

Fire radiated from Badu's gut. He prayed Sevin was right about the wavesbreath. As cavalier as he had felt staring death in the face moments before, now, with the sea above him and the weights pulling him further down, terror came. *"When death becomes a reality, the defiant man's boasting melts into common, ugly fear,"* Garris had once told him.

As he fell, the growing pressure felt like it was pushing his eyes through his head and stabbing an ice pick into his brain. He squeezed his nose and blew, bringing sweet relief as the pressure equalized. But when the pressure let up, his lungs screamed, and his body shook from lack of breath.

Drop it! Escape! a voice inside urged as his breath ran short.

Frantic, Badu dropped the harpoon and pulled his knife to cut the rope belt. *No!* He stayed his hand. *There's death waiting for you above, too.* His feet touched the soft seafloor, sinking into the silt. *Let go,* Sevin's voice instructed him. *Not that I have a choice,* he quipped. His body took over, and he reflexively gulped in what should have been air.

The mechanics of breathing offered brief relief even as seawater rushed into his lungs. His chest burned like it held hot embers within, and he began feeling sleepy as spots appeared in his dimming vision. The sandy seabed seemed to be dragging him down, swallowing his body. *This is what the end feels like,* he mused in a blurred stupor. His body suddenly jerked like a mule had kicked him in the chest. The core of heat in his lungs burst out, radiating through his body, ferrying burning streams of revitalized energy. His vision cleared, and he stood, strong again, relief washing over him.

In the dim light, he spotted the harpoon, planted in the silt a few measures away. Recovering the spear, he surveyed the ocean floor. The hazy blue landscape was vast. *This is like finding a lone skupp in a zipgrass field,* he thought. "Look for clusters of glowing uzum beads," Oster had told him. By some silent beckoning or innate sense, the uzum skate congregated in the sand above their ancient, sleeping ancestral kin, or so Oster's family legend went. Finding a field of uzum, carrying the green glowing eggs implanted on their backs, would be an excellent sign.

Badu froze as a long black shape glided through the water above him. *There's more than uzum down here,* a voice reminded him. *Death by buyuk, the shallow water alpha predator: number seven. Or was that just a common shark? (Number eight.)* Trying to move inconspicuously, Badu strode forward slowly, harpoon in hand.

After nearly half an hour wandering on the sea bottom, scanning the horizon for bright glowing green, he had found nothing. Crabs skittered out of his way, a shoal of squid passed around him, one jettisoning a cloud of black ink, and a few curious fish had swum near to inspect the stranger. At first, drawing on the wavesbreath felt like sucking air in through a fire bellows, but that feeling had receded and his breathing was close to normal, if he could call it that. *Time is running short.* The thought jabbed at him.

The harpoon caught on something and Badu glanced down to free it. Two measures ahead, the sand was glowing ever so slightly, a muted green. He examined the spot. It would have been easy to miss altogether. He tentatively poked the mound with the harpoon and sure enough, a shape wriggled out in a cloud of sand, and an uzum skate burst from its hiding place, the beads on its back now a brilliant green as it swam away.

Fool! Badu scolded himself in a moment of sudden clarity. He now recalled the words of an old diver many years ago who had told him how hard the uzum skate was to find because they almost always burrowed beneath the sand. It was why the fishermen dragged the seabed with weights when hunting for the creatures. Badu had been looking for a sparkling field of brilliant glowing green, but now he realized he would need to be nearly standing atop of the skate to even see the glow.

Something large bumped him from behind, nearly knocking him over. He spun in time to see the long body of a buyuk slip away into the dark. *Shivv!* The dark-blue buyuk was unmistakable with its massive, prehistoric jaws, long sharklike body with the exaggerated dorsal fin, and four stubby crocodilian legs it tucked up when it swam. No predator matched it, at least not this close to shore. The fishermen said they had spotted an old male over fifty measures long within the reef. Zulu, they called him.

This one was young; it appeared to be only fifteen or twenty measures with a midsection the girth of a large hog. Still, buyuk were tenacious and ruthless when hungry. Divers and fishermen alike knew to abandon the hunt when they had been spotted by a buyuk. A good catch would only draw the monster, perhaps two. *"You don't want to be within a net toss of two fighting buyuk,"* Badu's uncle, Nur, a fisherman, had once told him. He tightened his grip on the harpoon.

Spinning around, Badu searched for the shape, but it had vanished in the dark water. *Maybe it had gone?* In a flash of lightning, he spotted a long silhouette thirty measures away moving to his right. Then it was dark again and he could only guess at the creature's path. As he started moving, Badu felt a disturbance in the water, like a soft but forceful push that set him back a step. He peered into the dark, his heart racing.

Lightning flashed, illuminating an enormous gaping jaw that flew at him from the right. Badu instinctively spun away and dropped as he thrust the harpoon upwards with all his strength. He struck something. The harpoon tugged in his hands. *Don't lose it! You need it!* He clamped down on the harpoon and was ripped from his feet, his body dragged through the water by the frantic buyuk. Again and again, the thrashing tail slammed into Badu's side, shooting pain through his wounded abdomen as the flailing creature desperately tried to escape. The buyuk darted up and then down again in a dive, causing the harpoon handle to slide from Badu's grip. In desperation, he twisted the harpoon and yanked.

Suddenly he was falling. He landed with a soft thud in the sand. The buyuk streaked back overhead, turning when it spotted him. *Not good.* Badu readied the harpoon. The only thing worse than an angry buyuk was an angry, wounded buyuk. This time Badu spotted the beast on its approach. Trailing a dark cloud in the water, the buyuk sped straight at him. He had to kill it. If it dragged him again, he might never see the harpoon again.

His grip tightened as he stared down the missile with the gaping jaws that raced toward him. Bracing his legs, he readied himself, visualizing the soft roof of the mouth of the monster. Ten measures before impact, an enormous shadow surged from the blackness and engulfed the wounded buyuk in massive jaws. The wake from the colossal buyuk knocked Badu backward. *Zulu.*

Lying on his back, Badu just waited, not daring to move. Finally, he noticed that the feeling in his chest had changed again. Instead of regular breathing, it now felt shallow and thin. *It's wearing off.* The thought burst in his head. *You're running out of time!*

The lightning storm above seemed to have passed, and the seafloor had grown dark again. Badu rolled over to his hands and knees to stand. As he did, his eyes settled on a faint green glowing mound in the sand before him. He poked it, and an uzum skate streaked away. There, a few measures away. *Was it?* Yes, another mound. He jabbed it and set another skate to flight. Like a child staring intently at an ant and suddenly seeing the busy colony that moved nearby, Badu now beheld it. Hundreds of glowing mounds surrounded him. *Uzgül, you sneaky old sarsmak! I found you!* he declared in triumph. Excitedly he surged forward, sending skate fleeing in every direction as he went.

Even as he did, his chest burned with the rising strain to breathe. Along with the breathlessness came the sinking realization that the glowing mounds appeared to have no end. In his mind, the uzum would be concentrated in the area of a pigpen, perhaps. Yet before him, stretching as far as he could see in every direction, lay what resembled a vast pasture of softly glowing mounds.

He scrabbled forward, frantic desperation now replacing his excitement. The cloud of sand from his shuffling feet grew into a storm around him, glowing green shapes launching in every direction. When he finally reached the edge of the uzum field, he stopped and turned. He had begun to struggle for breath. His limbs hung heavily, and he found his thoughts drifting. Badu called his mind back to the present. *Focus!*

Then he saw it: a gradual slope fifty measures ahead, dotted with glowing bumps.

He trudged forward. Oster instructed him to find the skull sloping up from the monster's back and dig down to locate the crown, a raised circular blowhole. *"It's in the crown that you must plant the harpoon,"* Oster had said. As he neared the incline, the doubt rose. *You are a fool! This entire thing may be a shivving myth. How do you know this isn't just one of a thousand random fevers of uzum congregating in these waters?* His mind drifted to the origin of the odd term for a group of skates. *No! Stay focused!*

At what he approximated to be the middle of the mound, he dropped heavily to his knees and dug. The sand moved easily at first, but when he was three full measures down, he reached hard-packed sand or coral, not moloth skin. He moved and tried again, only to find the same. Speckles danced at the edge of his vision, and fatigue filled him like liquid lead. Struggling to stay awake, he dropped to his knees one last time and dug. This time he hit coral or bedrock after only two measures. *Herf it!* he shouted in silent exasperation.

Returning groggily to his feet, he stumbled forward. A stabbing pain shot through his foot and immense pressure closed on his leg followed by a crunching sound. Jerking back from his hypoxic daze with sudden alertness, he looked down in horror to find his left foot entirely consumed in a great shell up past the ankle. *Trap clam!* Again, a silent curse as he remembered a distant warning about trap clams, those haybale-sized mollusks with the thick wavy shell opening that dotted the seafloor. *"Once they clamp on, they don't let go,"* his uncle, Nur, had also once told him. *"Have to saw your own leg off if ya want to live,"* the weathered fisherman added with a twisted smile and squinted eye. Badu remembered staying out of the water all summer after he had heard the story.

The stabbing pain from his crushed ankle felt muted by the weight of the despair of his failure, the helplessness amplified by the waning power of the wavesbreath that robbed him of breath and thought. Blackness crept further in on Badu's field of vision, and a profound exhaustion flooded him. *What is there to lose?*

Summoning what he knew would be the last of his strength, straining against his crushed ankle that sent shooting pain up his leg, he hefted the harpoon high above and slammed it down into the shallow depression, the only hole he could reach. Nothing happened.

No, I suppose not, he thought darkly. Blackness crowded out the dim green glow of the ocean floor, and Badu stopped breathing.

24

THE ENCOUNTER

As his heart began to fail, Badu sank deep into a void of blackness. From the depth of the nothingness there came a flash, exploding into a crackling, brilliant white.

The seafloor, the ocean, the night was gone, replaced by ubiquitous, blinding white. *How can this be?* Badu looked down to inspect his crushed foot and chased a fleeting thought about a harpoon, but he found his feet and ankles without blemish as he stood on dry ground in sandals, draped in a white robe.

Beneath his feet, the infinite whiteness took shape. Stone. He stood on a broad limestone step. Ahead, three more wide, low steps rose to meet a white limestone wall extending to the horizon in either direction.

Set in the expansive wall, an archway held a set of large, weathered wooden doors. Everything around him shone brilliantly, standing in stark relief against shadow, like a white stone street in full sun seen after stepping from a dark tavern.

"Hello, Badu." The voice came from behind him. He twirled to see a man at the bottom of the steps, also in a loose robe. The man smiled up at him.

A chill ran through Badu. "Father?" he asked with disbelief. The man only smiled. "I'm dreaming."

The man just pursed his lips in a tight smile.

"No." Badu recalled a flicker of an image of him at the bottom of the sea. As realization set in, a bolt of fear lanced through him. "I'm dead." The words felt foreign leaving his mouth. Badu's fear and wonder vanished as he returned his gaze to the man before him. He tightened his fists to balls and clenched his jaw against the years of anger that crashed over him. He had imagined this encounter a thousand times.

"You!" Badu accused, descending the steps to face the man. "You killed her! You killed them all!"

"It's good to see you," was the man's only reply. Asil appeared just as Badu remembered him, not a day older than the last time he had seen his father.

"You were a coward!" Badu jabbed an accusing finger at the man. His searching eyes flicked over Asil's placid expression. *Detached as always,* Badu thought with disgust.

"And you are a... man!" replied Asil with uncontained delight. "But a fighter, a killer." His face lost the expression of elation, delivering the accusation with a sad smile.

"I do what I must," snapped Badu. "What you never did! I fight for what's right. Against the monster that you invited into our home!"

"You killed Garris." Again, the statement held no anger or judgment. It was spoken in earnest sorrow, as if Asil was sharing sad news.

"I... I... It was what was needed," Badu fumbled, hearing how hollow his words were. Shame bubbled up in him, a shame he had never before allowed in. *What you did to Garris was unforgivable,* he accused himself for the first time. *And what has it gotten you? Cor is dead, you have failed—*

"That won't help," Asil said kindly, putting a hand on Badu's shoulder. Badu shook his head wordlessly, his gaze dropping as he pinched his eyes.

A groaning and scraping sound came from the wall, and Badu looked up to see the doors had opened. Through them shone color in unimaginable brilliance: greens and blues so rich they seemed to glow. An irresistible desire pulled him. *The Garden!*

"I'm tired," Badu confessed, surprised at his admission. "I'm glad to be done. Done with all of it."

Asil smiled with amusement. "Oh, it's not over, my boy. Not for you." Badu frowned, a question in his eyes. "But there *is* something that must be done," Asil continued. "You must relinquish."

He betrayed you! Don't trust him. You're nothing like him. The hissing voices flooded Badu's thoughts in a cacophonous swirl. The familiar rage rose in him again.

"It was because of you!" Badu shot back, but he didn't feel his normal fire behind the words.

"You gave in to your hate long ago," said Asil. "You offered your heart as a foothold." Badu wanted to object, to argue, but it was true. As a young man, he had stopped fighting the dark thoughts, and they had rushed in, swallowed him, and become a part of him. "Relinquish," Asil said again.

"I... I..." A tearing feeling burned in Badu as fire and surrender warred within him. "I can't," he finally replied. "I've tried, but I just can't."

Strike him! the voice wailed. *Kill him! Show him what it felt like.* Badu felt his fists begin to clench. *No!* He resisted the mounting wave. *Sezlik merkaz.* Breathing deeply, he un-balled his fists and didn't move. "Help me." Where the words came from, he didn't know. Had he spoken them out loud? From the relieved and joyful expression on Asil's face, it seemed so.

"Is that what you want, son? I cannot choose for you."

Badu felt the darkness, the years of anger and death coiled

within him, the bedrock of rage on which he had defiantly built his defenses. *No! Resist.* He let the thoughts slide from him.

"I do," he replied quietly. Something snapped inside. Like a sack lifted from his head, he suddenly saw with clarity the wretch he had become, the lives he had ruined and the destruction he had brought. *I am filth.* It disgusted him. Tears streaked down his face. He met his father's earnest, eager gaze and wanted escape, freedom from all he had done and all he had been. He nodded. "Help me," he croaked

"So be it."

It happened fast. Asil's hand slid from Badu's shoulder to the back of his neck and clamped on with surprising strength. Badu grimaced, his mind flashing to memories of a scolding and his father grasping him by the neck. Before Badu could twist free, Asil's other hand shot forward and struck him in the chest. Instead of stopping on the surface, the tips of Asil's fingers penetrated his bare chest.

Badu watched in horror as Asil's hand sank deeper and deeper. He wanted to cry out, but he could not. There was no blood and no pain. Badu's body was frozen. He looked up, but his father's kind expression was gone. Fire filled the man's eyes as he stared intently at the point where his wrist disappeared into Badu's chest.

Then pain like Badu had never known exploded within him. The voices roared back in his mind in a tempest of screeching commands and pleading that he couldn't understand. Screams and bellows, calling him to action, to fight to stop this horror, but Badu didn't move.

After many long seconds of excruciating pain, Asil roared and ripped his arm back out of Badu. A flash of cold blasted through Badu's body and he sank to his knees. He ripped open his robes with trembling hands, horrified at the sight of his ruined chest, but his skin was unmarred, showing not so much as a scratch. Asil stood before him in triumph, gripping a short, thrashing black snake that spat flickers of fire as it struggled to strike its captor.

Asil swung the snake, striking its head on the stone ground three times in quick succession. He dropped the lifeless serpent, and as soon as it hit the ground, it burst into flame. Asil looked up at Badu, panting. Their eyes met. Badu searched himself, grasping for the anchor of rage, but to his disbelief, he found in himself only a deep affection for the man. Asil held out his hands. Without knowing why, Badu stepped forward and embraced his father.

As soon as he did, a tremor shook the ground. Badu covered his head against the ear-splitting cracking and roaring. When he looked up, he found himself alone outside the wall, trying to keep his footing as the ground lurched and shook. His father stood on the other side of the archway, surrounded by saturated color. Asil waved slowly, even as a chasm opened in the ground and the archway collapsed. The quake sent Badu to his knees. He squeezed his eyes closed, and when he opened them, he found himself at the bottom of the sea.

The vision was gone, but the shaking hadn't stopped. The entire seafloor rumbled and lurched. Sand billowed in a swirling cloud around him. He was rising through the water, the entire seafloor lifting beneath him. The pressure on his ankle ceased as the trap clam let go, sending fresh pain lancing up his leg. He still couldn't breathe, and his lungs felt like they would burst within him as he rose.

Then Badu broke free from the water, out into the night sky, under the stars. He retched and coughed, heaving again and again as he vomited up the seawater that had filled his stomach and burning lungs. With deep, desperate gasps, he inhaled the rich night air.

The storm that had raged when he dove into the water was gone, replaced by the brilliant moon. He floated out in the lagoon, a cliq away from the beach, but atop some sort of massive island. He spotted his small, boat bobbing in the waves not far away. Then the island moved. A giant waterspout erupted next to his head, shooting a glowing white geyser of seawater a hundred measures into the night sky. Each edge of the island folded up out of the water, sending Badu tumbling down into the valley created in the middle. His stomach lurched. This was no island. It was a creature. A moloth. Uzgül.

The wings of the giant ray beat down in a low roar, slapping the ocean's surface, sending plumes of water into the air as the great mass lifted out of the water and into the air. *No!* thought Badu. *What have I done?* Instead of victory, his mind flooded with guilt and sorrow. *I have woken a monster!* If the legends were true, if Oster had lit the fires, it meant hundreds would die. He found himself scrambling on hands and knees across the back of the moloth to the nearest edge, even as the creature beat its wings again and continued to rise. When he reached what must have been the front of the moloth, Badu threw himself over the edge.

He fell a hundred measures before splashing into the water. The impact took his breath and shook his mind. But he swam. He climbed into the tiny boat even as a great shape blotted out the moon above. Fatigue and pain owned his body, but there was no time to waste. He pulled the anchor and started back to shore, rowing with all he had. *I must warn them. 'Save them.'* In a quieter moment, Badu, Blade of the Nöz, might question these thoughts, but all he could feel was the mounting sorrow, like the weight of the sea above him when he was down below. The weight of the hundreds of souls within the castle.

The shape in the sky moved up and away, flooding the lagoon once again with moonlight. As he neared shore, he spotted the waiting priestguard. The beach was alive with lights and shouts carried across the water. *At least I can warn them,* Badu thought, continuing to pull in their direction.

"The castle!" cried Badu to a trio of boats glided out to meet him. "It's in danger!" Even as the priestguard boats surrounded him, a wave of relief overcame him. *How long did Oster say it would take?* He tried recalling the words. *The moloth would rise high into the sky, circling for hours as it awoke from a century of slumber. There is time still.* "Take me." He offered his hands to the priestguard in the boat beside him, palms up to show he held no weapons. "But you must clear everyone out of the castle!"

"'In the downs happened to you?" bellowed a thick man with a sneer, wearing the stripes of a captain. Badu noted absently that a few of the soldiers beside the captain stared in surprise as well. *I suppose they thought I had drowned long ago,* Badu realized. The captain nodded to the nearest Tszoi brute, and rough hands ripped Badu from his seat, dragging him into the priestguard boat. The beating began.

When Badu opened bruised and puffy eyelids, caked with dried blood that ran down his face, he found himself bound and chained in the back of a wagon bumping along the streets of the city. There must have been two dozen guards in the escort. As they drew him through the street, Kopolians emerged from their dark houses to jeer and shout at his passing. Badu's blurry mind mused at another strange sight: dozens of rats, dogs, cats and skupp fled up the cobblestone street from the shore into the heart of the city. His stomach sank as the cart passed over the bridge to the castle. High on a cliff, far above the castle walls, he spotted a bright spot of yellow. A signal fire.

25

WARNING CRY

The soldiers were deaf to his pleading warnings. Every time the cart passed a servant or a guard, Badu shouted at them to flee the castle. Each cry earned him a strike on the head or face. A collection of priestguard gathered on horseback in the castle courtyard. The animals whinnied, stamped, and circled nervously, pulling against the reins as the soldiers cursed them. One reared up, sending his rider crashing to the ground. Soldiers spat on Badu, and others jeered.

"You have to get out!" Badu pleaded. "Death is coming."

"Oh, we are. Heading to your hideout at firstlight to round up your friends!" taunted a priestguard wearing a commander badge. "We found the, what do you call it? Skirt?" The commander barked an order to gather the pikemen and Tszoi. "We'll have their heads on posts by sunrise." The group laughed. "I think the Farish plans for you to watch the beheadings."

"Uzgül, the great moloth, is coming!" shouted Badu, earning another slap. Men laughed.

"I saw it," whispered a voice full of fear. A slender priestguard leaned in close, his mask only inches from Badu's face.

"The others told me I made it up, but I know what I saw. It blocked the stars. Fish were throwing themselves on the shore."

"You must escape!" urged Badu. "Go now! Get away from the castle!"

"No talking to the prisoner!" barked the commander, jerking the young priestguard away.

The guards whisked Badu below the castle to a third-basement dungeon.

"Dunno what happened to you," sneered the guard who locked Badu in the deep chamber. "But the Farish will be happy to see what we found."

"I won't hurt anyone," Badu protested even as the disinterested dungeon keeper clasped shackles to his wrists and ankles that looked like they could hold a gorgol. Badu wasn't sure he could even lift the enormous chain that secured the shackles to the floor bolts.

"No. I 'spect you won't," chuckled the guard, spitting a wad of chewed ferikökü root on the ground as he wandered off, up the stairs.

Badu tried to find a position on the floor that didn't send agony through his broken ribs, his beaten face, or his crushed ankle. His foot flamed hot from the inside and looked like an inflated blowfish. He tried yelling a few more futile warnings and then finally fell into a fitful sleep.

"Just throw it in there." Badu heard the voice from up the stairs. "Don't think he'll need it."

Badu pried open burning eyes to find a young castle maid gingerly approaching with a bucket. Like an animal handler delivering meat to a deadly beast, she gingerly tossed the wooden bucket at Badu, presumably his latrine, and whirled to go.

"Wait!" Badu cried as the girl reached the foot of the steps. To his surprise, she stopped. "Before you go, I must tell you something." The girl turned slowly as if she thought she might find the Ice King himself in the dungeon.

"Do you have family within the castle?" Badu asked. She turned back and started to leave, apparently deciding against sharing anything about her family with the chained devil. "If you do, they'll be dead within the hour!" Again, she froze. "I can help you," Badu offered finally, dropping his head.

"My... my mother works in the kitchen," the girl said softly, turning again. "And my sister in the boiling room." Her smudged face was fair, blond hair tucked beneath a printed headscarf.

"There is a monster coming for this castle. One I... I woke from the sea." His voice broke and a wave of sorrow bloomed within him. To his shock, Badu felt something he had not for many, many years: tears rolling down his cheeks. "Please, go find your mother and your sister and anyone else who will listen and leave the castle. Right now." Uzgül had risen from the water deep in the night, but surely some must have seen the great shape.

"They say you eat babies," she blurted.

Badu snorted a laugh. He hadn't seen that coming. "Well, that's not true." He offered a smile. "But who I am and what I've done isn't important. You must leave. Save your family."

"I can't release you," said the girl warily.

"No—no, I don't need you to release me. Just save your family. Please, save any you can."

"I heard whispers," she added. "Something darkening the sky over the lagoon tonight."

"Yes!" Badu exclaimed. "And it's coming here. Please. Go!" More tears streamed. "Convince the servants, the priests, even the guards. Any who will listen." Badu was shocked to hear those last words, and even more aghast to discover he truly felt them. He felt a sorrow even for the ruthless, broken soldiers who had pledged fealty to the tyrant clinging to his throne. *How could I ever convince him to leave?*

"Thank you, Beyazi," the girl said, gingerly approaching. Badu looked up at her and smiled, wondering why she called him that. *Beyazi* was the name he called his wrinkled, silver-haired grandfather as a child. She touched his shoulder gently, and as soon as she did, Badu's curiosity was replaced by profound sorrow and a rush of affection for the girl, her mother, and her sister. *What had she been through living in this place? What life had she endured?* A sudden deep knowledge of her struggle and hardship rushed through him as if he lived it himself, bringing tears to his eyes again. *What is this?* The overwhelming tide of grief wouldn't have been any stronger had the girl been his own daughter. Seeing his face change, she backed away. With an awkward wave, she hurried off.

Sometime later, lost in a swirl of thought and still struggling to understand the bizarre feelings churning within, Badu heard the trumpet blast. The first was soft and far off, but soon more trumpets sounded nearby. The muted buzz of frantic shouts and running filtered through the thick stone walls of the dungeon and on the stairs. This was not a routine morning call to sunrise. There was urgency in the blasts, alarm.

Even as he watched, roaches, spiders, and skupp streaked across the dungeon floor. *They can feel him!* A soft growl rose up through the stone floor, vibrations like that of a heavy cart rumbling nearby. Suddenly footsteps rushed down the stairs.

The dungeon keeper appeared followed by a small knot of guards.

"What's happening?" Badu asked, but nobody so much as looked in his direction. "No! Don't come in. You have to get out!" he pleaded. "If you stay here, you'll die!"

"Someone shut him up," called a priestguard.

The hefty dungeon keeper waddled over. "We're gonna have company on account of the storm, old man. And we don't want to hear you spouting your nonsense!" He raised a club threateningly. From behind the keeper, more people were streaming into the open dungeon. *Old man?*

"It isn't a storm," Badu protested. "And if you don't get everyone out—" The man struck Badu on the head with the club. White streaked across his vision and pain crackled across his skull. He covered his throbbing head with his hands in anticipation of another blow, but the short, thick chains caught.

"Last warning," said the burly guard, his eyes gleaming with challenge.

"Where's the keeper?" came an authoritative voice in the threshold to the winding stairs. Badu glanced up to see a decorated priestguard and a dozen priests. The skupp weren't the only ones looking for cover. Badu's eyes fell to the dungeon keeper beside him, whose attention was on the captain. Only inches from Badu's face hung the tarnished brass keyring.

"Ye can make a space over to the side." The dungeon keeper directed the new arrivals to a cluster of crates. More people filed in, growing the group to at least forty, all crammed into the basement dungeon, even as the soft vibration in the stones grew to a steady rumble.

"Is the prisoner secured?" asked a nearby guard.

"He's not going anywhere," bragged the dugeon keeper. "Got 'im in the heavy chain." He kicked Badu, then lifted his club to strike.

A deep boom followed by a tremor jerked the entire room. The keeper lunged forward, nearly losing his footing. Someone screamed.

"What's happening?" a voice called out.

No. No! Badu cried quietly.

The rumble beneath Badu now felt like he was atop the wagon bumping over cobblestone. Another crash from somewhere far above, and the room lurched again. The quiet apprehension of the crowded room erupted into panic. Voices popped like cracking embers in a growing fire, but another sound filled the room. A hollow rushing grew in intensity and pitch. It was coming from the stairwell.

Through the writhing mass of people, Badu met the terror-stricken eyes of a young maidservant standing closest to the stairwell the moment before she was sucked off her feet into the stairwell and out of the room. Shrieks and screams filled the room as the rushing wailing sound grew to a roar and another body disappeared up the stairwell, then another. The frenzied crowd surged away from the stairwell and toward Badu at the back of the dungeon. But it was no use, the force of the invisible hand only grew, snatching more and more victims.

Crates flew through the air and the room swirled with a whipping cloud of dust and debris. Despite their desperate clinging to columns and torch brackets and anything else fixed to the stone, the mighty wind continued to snatch hapless bodies into the open mouth of the stairs. A strong pull tugged on Badu's arm. The dungeon keeper had grabbed the thick chain, the aggressive sneer from a moment ago replaced by wild panic. Even as he did, his feet were lifted off the ground, pulled toward the door.

Badu blindly reached for the keeper, his hand catching the man's belt. The screaming wind was so loud it hurt Badu's ears. The keeper's grip slipped from the chain, multiplying the weight of the belt. For a moment, Badu's hold on the belt was all that tethered the man. Something snapped, and the dungeon keeper flew off, his head slamming into the stone archway, sending his body spinning through the air into the stairway. The roaring wind was deafening, sucking everything from the room.

With a rending crash, a piece of the wall broke away, revealing pink sky beyond. Badu's shoulders felt like they were being wrenched from their sockets against the heavy chain. He couldn't breathe. His back bowed with what felt like an entire team of blue oxen slamming into him from behind. The sharp sound of the wind tunnel from the stairwell gave way to a roaring chorus of rending metal, splintering wood, and cracking stone.

Something shifted, and Badu felt himself no longer pulled sideways toward the ruined stairwell but rather straight upwards, lifting him off the ground. He feared his arms and legs would be ripped off as scorching pain seared his wrists and ankles. Everything around him became a brown cloud of dust that choked him as the wind sprayed him with tiny projectiles. Behind the dust cloud, it glowed brilliantly like morning. Something slammed him in the head, and everything flashed and then went dark.

A GULL CRIED from somewhere far away. Cold, hard rock pressed against Badu's cheek. He pried his eyes open against burning red light. He drew ragged, salty breath into lungs that felt like they had been scraped for hours with a barnacle rasp. As his eyes adjusted, fire burned in every one of his joints. A sharp pain in his left shoulder told him it was dislocated.

When his vision cleared, Badu found himself somehow on an open stone patio overlooking the sea on a gorgeous morning. *Where am I?* He slowly raised his woozy, pounding head and tried to sit up. Heavy chains clinked holding him back. *What?* Badu looked down and, for a moment, could not make sense of what he saw. The bulky gorgol chains still secured his bloody wrists and ankles to the massive iron anchors drilled deep into the stone foundation of the castle beneath him. *Impossible.*

There, alone in the sun, Badu sat chained to the third-basement dungeon floor. The hundreds of measures of castle and the thousands of slabs of stone that towered over him the night before were gone. Completely gone. Sucked up by Uzgül like a tale of old. Stinging tears sprang to his eyes. *They're gone. All of them.* A heavy weight fell on him. He reached for his face to wipe the tears and beheld the bloody claws that were his hands. There in his right fist hung the dungeon keeper's leather belt. Like the punchline of a cosmic joke he couldn't understand, Badu spotted the brass ring of keys still lashed to the belt.

26

COME AND GONE

Shuffling feet responded to the seagull alarm cry. As Badu hobbled up through the dark passage into the Skyrt, a shadow thrust a spear to his neck.

"What do you want, old man?" demanded a voice. "And how did you get here?"

Badu looked up, meeting Ferat's hard glare. The eyes suddenly widened in recognition and Ferat stammered, his mouth moving but no words coming.

"Badu?" asked Salik. Still, Ferat tried to speak without a sound as his eyes darted up and down over Badu.

"You like my hair?" Badu asked with a smile.

"It's white!" blurted Täs. Badu had only discovered as much after he had hobbled out of the city and stopped to wash his beaten face and bloodied hands in the river. The reflection looking back at him was the same strong, young face, if not a bit more marred and sorrowful, but it now wore a head of brilliant white hair.

"You... you're here," replied Ferat, still in a stupor. He broke from his trance and rushed forward, followed closely by the boys. All three embraced Badu at once. He winced at the pain but didn't let go.

"And Cor?" asked Ferat.

Badu simply shook his head, his eyes glistening. "The Farish knew our plot from the beginning. There was no hope." Silence gripped the men.

"How'd you escape?" asked Täs, finally letting go of Badu.

"Well, that's a longer story."

"The men will be overjoyed to see you," said Ferat, his eyes fixed on Badu's. "They've been like a brood of frightened ducklings after the... monster. But first, come, come. Have a bath. Dinner is on the fire."

Badu patted Ferat on the cheek. The moment he touched the man the flicker of a vision flashed through his mind. *Ferat stood draped in chains, some holding bricks and others iron weights. A black dragon flew out of his open mouth.* A tear ran down Badu's cheek. Ferat drew back.

"Your hate has left you," said Badu, his eyes wide with a fresh realization. "That brings me great joy, uyesi. But so much sadness remains. Once you're gone, time will lift your chains."

Salik and Täs shared a confused look even as they helped Badu into camp.

"Bɪᴢʜᴀᴋ! We gave you up for dead days ago!" bellowed Kafa, jumping up from the ring of men at the fire. He wrapped Badu in a bear hug and lifted him off his feet. Badu winced as pain shot through his bruised ribs. Kafa deposited him, and he landed gingerly on his good ankle. "You look terrible," Kafa said with a broad smile. The other men crowded around him, all peppering him with questions.

"Let him sit," ordered Ferat. "Someone, pour him a bowl of stew." With Badu and Corvina gone, Ferat had clearly taken command. "You're lucky, we found a den of bushpig only yesterday." His eyes glittered delivering the news. Badu was starving. He sighed with relief as he sat, taking weight off his crushed ankle, though a dull pain seemed to permanently radiate up his leg.

"Cor?" asked Sevin. Badu only shook his head. His eyes filled with tears again.

Someone thrust a thick clay bowl of hot stew into his hands, which he devoured. After finishing his second bowl and a long draw from the wineskin, Badu began to recount the incredible tale. Several times he had to stop to regain himself as tears sprang to his eyes. He was amazed at the depth of sorrow he felt for all of the fallen; not just Cor, but the prisoners, the servants, the guards. He even felt sorrow for the Farish – not for the despot whose centuries of sins stained the countless broken lives he left in his wake, but for the young man, the one lost to hate hundreds of years earlier. The jagged pauses caused the men to squirm in their seats and exchange awkward glances.

"I'd never have believed a word of it if I didn't watch the whole thing with my own eyes!" declared Heffel.

"We thought a squall was moving in," added Salik.

"Or an earthquake," added Täs.

"But the night was clear and still," said Finnur.

"We all ran to the Ridge," said Heffel, shaking his head.

"I'll never forget that sight," said Ferat, his voice trailing. "Not as long as I live."

"None of us will," added Sevin.

"Herf me! Oster was right all along!" said Heffel.

"It sucked up the entire castle!" Täs blurted turning to Badu.

"I think he knows," chided Salik. Täs sneered at his brother.

"I told you Sarsmak!" the voice echoed off the walls of the Skyrt from the direction of the meal hut. All the men turned together to see Oster nearly skipping up to them. "Badu, you're alive! You did it, you sneaky old fezzi—Ahh!" Oster jumped. "What the downs happened to your hair!" Badu rose and the two embraced.

After another rowdy reunion of hugs and songs, Oster launched into the tale of Uzgül the moloth king and his assault on the black castle, all as witnessed up close, from the top of the cliffs beside the castle. The warrior hero from the tale received a round of cheers and toasts and another song.

"Three nights ago, I saw it in a glimpse," Sevin's quiet voice carried across the firepit, cutting the revelry. "I knew it was a premonition, but I thought the monster from the sky must be a symbol of some kind, a warning of a coming threat. Perhaps an army from the fahyz or attack from the sea. I spent hours and hours searching for the key to this puzzle." He shook his head. "I never imagined it to be a moloth, in the flesh."

"Are we sure the Farish is dead?" asked Heffel.

"He's dead," replied Badu flatly. How he knew, he couldn't quite say, but he did. Unequivocally. He felt the screaming in his soul of each and every one sucked up by that monster. A burning pit of fire had closed, and its terrible flames ceased.

"With the Farish dead, what will happen?" asked Salik. Badu saw seven faces looking to him and realized what they asked.

"You will lead us," declared Ferat.

"The city will be in chaos," added Kafa.

"True!" said Finnur excitedly. "It could be ours for the taking."

"There will be bloodshed," said Sevin. "Many will die." Badu felt the truth behind those words. His eyes watered.

"The Nöz could come out of hiding," said Heffel. "We could add to our numbers. Who would stand against us?"

"Yes!" Kafa stood. "We come out of the shadows."

"Where should we start?" Heffel asked, turning to Badu.

The others looked to him as well. "Topple the zengin? Take the trade routes?"

Badu only smiled. "My brothers. My uyesi. I cannot lead you. I am... changed." Salik frowned. "Whether you feel it or not, many of you are, too. These last years have been dark and full of hate. The raids, the killings." He paused. "It has worn on all of us. More than we know."

"We have killed for justice," said Heffel looking to the others for support. Badu caught Sevin shaking his head. *He knew.*

"No, Heffel," replied Badu, eyes fixed on the fire. "I'm afraid we didn't." Heffel cocked his head. Some others did too. "Those were lies, all lies. Cor was taking direction from the Farish himself." Gasps erupted around the circle. "The only crime committed by our *targets*"—he spat the word—"was opposing the Farish." The men's eyes widened. "Political rivals, dissenters, even one who led a pocket of followers faithful to Yuz. They should have been our allies. We have been doing the Farish's bidding."

"Impossible," floundered Heffel. "The mission details, the debriefs..." He trailed off.

"Carefully fabricated," Badu said.

"Deceivers!" roared Kafa, jumping to his feet and pounding his chest. A choir of angry voices joined him.

"Cor worked for the Far Seer Priest the whole time?" asked Täs.

Badu nodded. "Up until the end. Her allegiance had changed when she betrayed him, but it cost Cor her life."

Kafa returned to his seat, and for a long moment, the group sat in sullen silence. Badu knew the faces of those they had slain danced through the minds of each man, as they did his.

"Uyesi, I have stood at the gates of the Garden. I have claimed the lives of hundreds of souls within the castle."

Täs drew back at the sight of tears.

"I have fought and killed enough for ten lifetimes," Badu continued. "I cannot lead you back into that darkness."

"But we're the Nöz," Täs said, looking to his brother for support.

"He's leaving," said Sevin with flat conviction. Ferat snapped his gaze up to Badu in question. The statement surprised even Badu. He hadn't thought beyond making his way back here. All he saw was the horror of what was behind him. Yet as he weighed Sevin's words, he felt the truth beneath them. He couldn't stay.

Hours passed, as the men laughed and talked and ate, remembering happier days. Badu cried a few more times, and finally, he staggered to the pool to wash and then was helped back to his tent by Täs, where he collapsed into a deep sleep.

BADU AWOKE BEFORE THE SUN. He washed and hobbled to the Ridge. The saltwater breeze tossed his white hair as he sat in the peach glow of the rising sun.

"I've seen lifetimes you will yet live, uyesi," said Sevin walking up behind him. "I've glimpsed your final, valiant days as an old man."

Badu didn't turn around. "How did we lose our way so badly, Sevin?"

"We tasted the darkness, felt the power, the longing." Sevin stepped up beside the white-haired Badu.

"It lurks in the heart of every man, I think," said Badu. "The desire to become a god."

"I'm sorry about Cor," said Sevin. "I know you cared for her."

Badu sat heavily on a rock. "She truly had changed, but it came too late." He looked down at his hands. "She was tired.

Like the rest of us. Ready to be done with all of it," he said wistfully. "She dreamed of escape to the blue hills of Ghiesa."

"I grieve for her," said Sevin. He sat beside Badu.

Badu turned to face the Midlander. "I killed hundreds, Sevin. Maybe thousands." Tears rolled down his cheeks. "Today mothers mourn, sisters wail, and uncles curse the clear morning sky."

Sevin was quiet for a bit. "A picture came to me at breakfast fire," he finally said. "I couldn't make sense of it before now." He stood again, motioning to the rock. "I was standing right here. When I looked up, dark and wicked storm clouds raced toward me from above a frothy and boiling sea. As my fear rose, I realized that the darkness wasn't on the attack but rather fleeing in retreat – chased by rushing color and song. A chorus of victory."

Badu snorted. "I don't feel victory, uyesi. I feel the weight of a thousand stones on my shoulders."

Sevin nodded. "You've crossed the line, uyesi. You now see like I see. And I have begun to see more clearly, like my mother saw. It's a heavy burden to gaze through the walls of man's shallow prism."

"What have I done?"

"Perhaps you give yourself too much credit," Oster's voice started Badu as he walked up beside the two.

"It was *his* plan after all," Sevin smiled and nodded at Oster.

"It was an impossible plan," said Oster. "You and I and the Nöz were but tools. We didn't get here on our own, we couldn't if we had tried. It was in the plan."

"The Farish is dead," said Sevin. "You helped us all escape a storm that was being fanned into a roaring fire before our eyes. The Farish would have consumed hundreds of thousands of souls before the end. Maybe more."

Badu gazed down to the city, past the yellowed domes and golden spires to the blank space where the castle once stood. Its absence was arresting, like the gap in the smile of a child who has lost her first tooth.

"Perhaps so. He spoke of his tether to Kilzhet, of a plan to conquer Yiduiijn herself."

"That future is not ours, and its thanks to you," said Sevin. "Both of you." He smiled, shaking his head in disbelief as he clapped Oster on the back.

The men stood in silence as the blood-stained sky grew to an opulent orange and then a blazing white.

"Come, uyesi," said Oster finally. "Let us break bread together." The men returned to camp. Sevin strode freely across the ancient radial stone paths when they crossed the colonnade. Badu smiled.

"I must tend to my ankle. I will join you at the fire shortly," said Badu, parting with an embrace. Badu hobbled directly to his tent. Closing the flap behind him, he kneeled before his trunk. He carefully lifted the lid and spotted the rolled paper tied with twine. With trembling hands, he untied the string and opened the note.

Badu,

I had hoped to be the one to give this to you when you were ready to receive it, but I'm afraid my time here has come to an end. I will not fill this letter with the ramblings of an old man's sorrow about a time lost or offer any more warnings about the dangerous and deceived spirit that now seems to saturate the Nöz. I have spent many useless breaths on such things. I only hope that your heart will let you see with clarity one day.

I have few earthly possessions, and those used to hurt or kill I will leave behind. But this was left in my keeping by your father. I know you have said you wish nothing more than to toss this bundle into a roaring fire, but I hope you will stay your hand.

Your father knew a truth that the Nöz once knew as well. He longed for you to know the peace and love for fellow man that he held, so I know he would have wanted you to have these.

Fe-al Yuz
- Your Ussa, Garris

BADU UNCLASPED the long canvas bundle and slowly began to unroll it. A vision of the family sword hanging on the wall flashed in his mind as his hands spun the long, rigid shape, peeling its layers back. When he had peeled back the last roll of the package, he found a white robe, sandals, and a long staff with a gnarled wood bulb at one end. Tucked in the fabric was a scroll Badu instantly recognized as his father's worn and beloved copy of *Colorsong—Words to the Colorgiver.*

WITH HIS BLACK nightwrap lying in a heap beside his boots and dagger, Badu stepped from his tent, robed in white, wearing sandals, and holding the gnarled walking staff.

As he slowly made his way through camp, the nözan stopped what they were doing and began to follow him. The loose escort grew and by the time he reached the entrance to the Skyrt, the entire Nöz surrounded him. His departure was an unspoken inevitability.

Making his way from man to man, Badu clasped forearms and patted each on the back or cheek.

Kafa picked him up and squeezed him again, causing a groan. "Sorry," he said, putting Badu back. "Please don't cry again." Badu smiled and rested a hand on Kafa's great arm. As he did, another vision crackled through his mind, this one dark and terrible.

"You must go home," said Badu suddenly, fixing Kafa with an intense stare, the smile gone. The big warrior frowned. "Your blood debt is paid, and your people need you." His words surprised even himself. "Death from the slag. You must leave tonight." Kafa nodded, bewildered, and moved off a step, mumbling to himself.

"I can't say I understand the new you," said Ferat, waving up and down at Badu. "But it somehow feels... right."

Badu nodded. "Words cannot capture the depth of a man's heart." The long-forgotten line his father used to quote from the Colorsong Scroll came unbidden. "You have a new story to write, my friend. Death will not haunt you any longer. You will find a new life over the mountains." Ferat nodded slowly as if trying on the idea.

"You can see the future?" asked Täs. Salik elbowed him.

"No, not quite," replied Badu with a smile. "Just flashes, glimpses of things I know to be true."

"Like Sevin!" said Täs.

"Perhaps."

When he had said goodbye to them all and refused for the third time the offer of a horse or choluk, Badu began limping off, his bad ankle slathered with healing balm and wrapped tightly in canvas by Sevin.

Before he stepped into the shadowy passageway leading out of the Skyrt, Badu stopped and turned.

"Uyesi, to a man, only one life is given. Tomorrow is an elusive promise. How he spends today is the question his heart demands he answer." His head seemed now full of his father's sayings. "I hope to see you all again."

With a parting wave, Badu turned and walked down into the tunnel, his white hair blowing and his flowing robes fluttering in the breeze as he faded like an apparition into the black mouth of the passage.

AUTHOR'S NOTE

THANK YOU so much for coming on this journey! I hope you loved reading the story as much as I loved writing it.

★★★ <u>PLEASE LEAVE A REVIEW</u> ★★★

Reviews are the lifeblood of the indie author. If you've liked this book, it would mean a lot if you could take 60 seconds to leave a review.

Keep any eye out for novellas released between novels (yes, one is in the works right now) and lots of other stories, histories and writings from the world of Yiduiijn.

ALSO BY MAX MOYER

Zodak - The Last Shielder

Revisit Yiduiijn 50 years later, after the fall of the great Kingdom K'andoria and new Age of Governors. The costly wars of men and kings have left a vacuum, an opportunity. The great evil stirs, seeking a foothold, an opportunity to rise. An unassuming orphan will be called into the eye of the storm.

Read on for the first 30 pages...

Available on Amazon:

TEMPEST RISING • ONE
ZODAK
THE LAST SHIELDER
MAX MOYER

PROLOGUE

Hallah's eyes flashed at her husband. "Leave it on a doorstep. Drop it in the river. I don't care! I want that thing out of this house!"

"This is madness!" said Ardon, shaking his head. "That *thing* is a child. My only nephew."

"A nephew you didn't know you had, from a brother you never knew. He may as well be a kin cousin!"

"He's an innocent child! My flesh and blood!" Anger smoldered in Ardon's eyes.

"A mouth we can't feed. That's what he is!" A sip of bandi sloshed from her wooden mug, and she tottered, adjusting her stance.

"Bandi," Ardon growled. "How many cups have you drunk tonight?"

"It doesn't matter," she snapped, regaining her footing. "What matters is the dirt! The ground's been stone hard for seasons; ever since that boy was forced on us. He brought the drought."

"The drought's got nothing to do with him. For Color's sake, his parents are dead! Taking him in was the only honorable option."

"So you've said. But we both remember that night," replied Hallah. "The way the ground trembled the night he arrived. Rumors of a giant, of all things! And the rain stopped the very next day."

Ardon just shook his head.

"What happens to us without crops?" she pressed. "Barst isn't a patient man."

Ardon dropped his face to his hands and rubbed his forehead. "Barst has more money than he could spend," he replied. "I've got but two quarter-seasons to pay. I'm sure I can reason with him. He knows I've been nothing if not dutiful."

"Ha! If you knew anything of duty, your children—your true flesh and blood—wouldn't be asking for food from bare cupboards. Instead, we're running an orphanage."

Ardon flinched at the jab. "Where is the Hallah I married? The girl who used to lie beside me in the leopard grass?"

"She's gone. She and her dreams died long ago."

"Please, Hallah," he persisted, his wedding vow of ample provision echoing in his head. "You know I've been in those fields from dawn until last light tending the silka seeds. And each morning on my knees pleading with the Figure in the Clouds for rain—"

"Silka seeds, the Figure in the Clouds, the Color!" She spat the words with a fine mist of bandi. "Foolish mind rot, all of it! I told you not to buy those cursed seeds. That's two seasons of our wages locked in the barren ground. If that Figure you pray to cares a dither for us, then where is the rain? Can you eat a silkeen scarf?" she slurred.

"Of course not, but prices for threshed silka in Pol Dak are as high as—"

"It doesn't matter!" she shouted. "We have no threshed silka! No food! We have no money!"

"Please," urged Ardon, holding up his palms. "The children," he added, glancing up to the darkened loft.

She scoffed, waving him off as she crossed the small room to the shelves. "They've been asleep for hours." She uncorked the bottle of homemade bandiroot broth and poured another foaming cupful.

***

"We gonna starve?" whispered Ergis to his sister, eyes brimming with tears.

"If we do, it's 'cause a Zodak," Alana whispered back to her younger brother. The two huddled close in the dark on the shared straw mat where they had been listening to their parents argue. At seven seasons, two older than Ergis, Alana was the authority on all things. "He cursed us," she added. "He's why the plants is all dead. If we die, it's a-cause of him." She stabbed a finger in the darkness. A few measures away, in a large drawer repurposed as a bed, lay young Zodak, his soft chest rising and falling rhythmically, the only one oblivious to the firestorm.

CHAPTER 1

"Argh. Empty," Zodak scoffed, restringing the orko snare even as his stomach groaned.

Collecting dried zheibak dung patties for the fire, checking the snares for any hapless orko trapped during the night, and collecting armloads of kindling were but a part of his daily chores and duties. When the darkness came and he felt like punishing himself, he'd imagine himself a young rising lord to a royal family, dining at the table of one of the Pol Dak nobles. He could picture biting into a thick steak like those he'd seen wrapped in paper at the butcher's stand in the market or opening a box of pepperfruit carted in from far away. But a young lord of Pol Dak he was not. Instead, he'd have to settle for the stringy orko meat from the oversized haunches of the squawking rodents cooked with earthy potatoes or misshapen carrots.

Zodak leaned his weight into the sapling, clipping it to the tiny snare. A darting movement caught his eye. A shadow the size of a dog slipped behind a thicket and froze. Zodak carefully released the sapling and, drawing himself up, slowly pulled the knife from his belt. He crept a step forward, then another, his eyes ever fixed on the thicket. His foot cracked a twig and three zheibak shot from the thicket. They bounded on springy legs, launching higher than his head with each jump as they glided through the forest like whispers of light, their painted stripes making them all but invisible in the brush. Zodak released his tensed muscles and his shoulders sagged.

The delicate creatures had once captivated him. Five seasons past, he had freed one whose ornate latticed antlers had gotten tangled in the underbrush, he recalled marveling at the beast's bounding retreat, only to meet his uncle Ardon's disappointed longing gaze as the week of meals sped away. That day killed his pity and wonder for the splendid little animals. He soon learned to pin the spindly legs of a trapped zheibak to keep its sharp hooves from thrashing, and swiftly slice the throat to bleed it. Ardon often reminded him to be grateful for the forest's bounty, truly a gift when the poor in the cities didn't have a roof overhead or a warm meal for days.

With nothing to show for his efforts, Zodak turned back to the house. The forest was silent and inviting. *Try it*, a tiny voice urged. After a step, he sank to his knees. He stilled his body and breathed deeply of the morning forest, digging his fingers into the rich soil. "*The trees around us, the earth beneath us, the creatures of the wood, they were all created by the Figure in the Clouds and so they are touched by the Color,*" Ardon had told him a season ago. "*Silence your mind. Let the Color cover you. You'll see the Figure.*" So here he sat, extending his hope again, ignoring past disappointment. He tried to clear his mind, tried to empty it of the unceasing cacophonous swirl of thoughts and memories and fears.

"Hurry with the spate wafers, boy!" came Aunt Hallah's shout from inside, cutting his meditation short.

His head twitched involuntarily, a regular movement of his that now came unbidden. "*Another of Zodak's broken parts,*" his cousin Alana had jabbed recently. She wasn't wrong. He couldn't control the twitching or the subtle shaking in his hands. They had been there for as long as he could remember, only getting worse.

A hundred measures from the house, circled by trees, his eyes closed again against the weak morning light. Even as he tried to clear his mind, the same question pecked at him: *Why not leave? Why not run from this pack of jackals without a glance back?* Every day he felt like a prisoner under his aunt Hallah's cruel watch, tormented by his cousins Ergis and Alana. But was he a prisoner, really? There were no guards watching him, no chains keeping him here. He could easily slip out and never return.

Even as he asked the question, he knew the answer. At sixteen seasons old, Zodak was no child—though undersized for his age, he *had* grown a half measure in the last season—yet he was far from a man. Without family or guardian, he would be vulnerable. This village was too small for him to get away from his problems, and while the city of Pol Dak was plenty large, stories of the child stealers made his blood run cold. Tales told of bands of grizzled hunchbacks, armed with nets and sacks, hired by the Governor to clear the city of urchins and child beggars. It was said they delivered captured children to group homes for education, but fragmented stories of these homes brought nightmares to even the bravest boy. And for older ones, it could be far worse.

The other reason Zodak knew he'd stay was his uncle Ardon. The worst day with Ergis, Alana, and Hallah was tolerable knowing Ardon would come back at the end of it. Zodak deeply longed to call him "Father," but this word was wrong. Too sacred for a nephew, for a bastard. If that word were ever to leave Zodak's lips, Ergis and Alana would make him suffer. *The Wickeds*, as Zodak called them, put on a pathetic façade of kindness in front of Ardon, but when he was gone, their potent venom came out.

Zodak shook his head, again seeking silence, digging fingers deeper into the earth the way Ardon had taught him, feeling for the Color. *This is foolish.* He brushed the thought away, listened to the breeze dancing through the trees, and quieted his mind.

A bird's cry carried from far off. Silence.

There! Had he heard something? Sensed it? A scrap of feeling, a faint thrumming from beneath his fingers, through the soil. Or was it imagined? He quieted himself, receding deep inside, listening for the quiet voice.

"The wood, boy! Now!" Hallah's cry came again from the house, shattering the moment.

With a deep breath, he abandoned the failed ritual and rose, wiping dirty hands on his pants. *Stupid! It never works,* he scolded himself. *There's nothing out there.*

Zodak heaved the long pole to his shoulder, finding the midpoint that would balance the bundle of sticks in front and the basket of spate behind. The stiff spate wafers carried only a hint of manure odor and the impressive pile of sticks stood as evidence of his morning efforts. Walking back to the house, he chased visions of the city of Pol Dak: the lords, street rats, and the child stealers.

He was so lost in thought that he didn't notice the unusual log standing upright on its end in the middle of the path near the edge of the woods, or the curious flecks of blue that speckled the bark. He absently raised a boot to the top edge of the log and pushed hard. Instead of giving way and rolling into the underbrush, the log stood fast. A burst of energy shot back against Zodak's kick, knocking him backwards. He fell to the path, his basket and kindling crashing to the ground.

What? Zodak crept forward cautiously on hands and knees, inspecting the odd-looking log in the middle of the path, the blue bark glittering. As he stared at the log, water began to seep up out of the end grain onto its surface.

Strangely, it neither ran off the sides nor soaked into the wood. It pooled into a shallow dome before his very eyes. Then the water began to vibrate. He drew back, startled as tiny peaks appeared on the surface, like a round of dough pinched by an invisible hand. Zodak stared, transfixed, as a small pyramid of water arose from the center of the pool and transformed into a small figure. Before him stood the form of a person made entirely of water, no taller than the head of an axe. The form shimmered translucent blue in the morning light.

Zodak blinked rapidly and smeared an eye with the back of his hand, trying to return to reality. *Am I dreaming?* He shook his head, trying to clear the vision. Yet there the watery form stood, defying all his senses, a tiny figure with smooth, delicate features. Then it spoke.

"Zodak."

He leapt backward and looked around wildly to see if anyone else had witnessed this vision. An electric tingling flashed through him. *It knows my name!*

The figure raised a diminutive arm towards the boy. "Your call has come," said an ethereal little voice that cooed like a dove, hollow like wind sweeping over a bed of reeds. "You are needed."

"How... what *is* this?" he stammered.

"You have questions, young one. But know this: you are not alone. You never have been. And you shall have company every step, whether you perceive it or not."

"Every step where? What *are* you?"

"Your journey will not be an easy one. Much will be asked. Much will be taken. But in you, there is courage and strength."

"What? What journey?"

"Patience, young one. Patience," replied the creature. "Your call has come."

"Zodak, how's the gathering coming?" Ardon's familiar

voice came from the house. The liquid figure collapsed into a pool of water, then ran off the edge of the stump.

"Wait! Come back," Zodak called after the puddle that even now soaked into the earth surrounding the log.

Ardon strode from the house, his tall, strong frame moving to the boy in an effortless glide.

He laid a hand on Zodak's shoulder when he reached him. "Everything okay— Oh, looks like you had a stumble?" He surveyed the path. "Goodness, you've collected a lot this morning. Let's get it inside." He stooped to gather the kindling, but Zodak didn't move. Ardon noticed Zodak's face for the first time. "Are you all right, son? You look like you've seen a ghost." He smiled, but Zodak's expression didn't lighten. Ardon's smile faded. "What happened, Zodak? Was it Ergis again?" A flash of anger danced over his face.

Zodak looked up into Ardon's inquisitive eyes. "No, not Ergis. I... it's nothing," he muttered, and began gathering wood, shaking the vision from his mind. He knew how ridiculous his story would sound.

Ardon put down his stack of wood and gripped Zodak's shoulder. "I don't think nothing happened," he said. "What is it?"

"You wouldn't believe me. I'm not even sure if I do..." Again, he trailed off, staring at the log.

"Try me," said Ardon.

With a resigned sigh, Zodak quickly recounted the fall and the words of the sprite. Even as he spoke, he saw his folly. He asked too much of a grownup, or anyone, to entertain such a fanciful tale. "I probably imagined the whole thing," Zodak added quickly as he hurriedly returned to gathering the wood.

Ardon didn't move. "I'm not so sure," he said, shaking his head.

"You're not?" Zodak slowed his gathering. He had already convinced himself the whole thing had never happened.

"This world is filled with mystery, both visible and hidden." Ardon put a hand on Zodak's shoulder. "Many people don't believe anything beyond what their own eyes see. They're small-minded, afraid of the unknown. But the Figure in the Clouds made our eyes and hearts to see so much more. Maybe He sent a messenger." He stood up and walked over to the log.

"I've never seen blue bark like this," said Ardon, rolling the log over.

The bark sparkled with sapphire flecks. Under their gaze, the blue faded and disappeared, returning the log to an unremarkable brown.

"You see?" said Ardon with a knowing smile. "Mystery."

"The spate for the fire, boy!" came Hallah's angry cry. "You'll feel my belt if I find that you—" Hallah had marched out the kitchen door into the dewy grass to the edge of the forest. "Oh, Ardon... I didn't know you were out here." She offered a shallow smile and nervously flattened the front of her skirt. "We've been waiting on the fire all morning. Would you please have him bring the wood?" his aunt asked in a tight voice. She avoided speaking directly to Zodak whenever possible.

"It's my fault, Hallah. I've kept him. We'll bring it in now." Ardon winked at Zodak. "Come on. Load me up," he said, ruffling Zodak's hair. Ardon shouldered the pole while Zodak secured the kindling bundle, and the two walked back to the house.

Aside from their occasional snickering, Ergis and Alana were uncharacteristically quiet during breakfast. Whatever hidden joke they shared, it would certainly come at Zodak's expense. They knew he had spent time with Ardon this morning, and they'd almost certainly punish him for it on the walk to school. After breakfast, the children fastened their boots, and Zodak heaved the leather bag full of school supplies over his shoulder.

"Let me look," insisted Hallah, inspecting Alana as if she

was a prized auction bull. At almost eighteen seasons, Alana should have aged out of the school experiment already, but so far, Hallah's desperate search for a suitor for the sour girl had been fruitless. "This is a mess." She tugged at Alana's thick dark hair.

"It's fine, Mother."

"Hardly," Hallah scoffed. She herself went to great lengths to ensure her carefully manicured appearance. "Now remember, chin up to avoid those terrible neck rolls."

"I'll make sure not to look downward today," Alana quipped. The girl shared a few of her mother's attractive features but was not as fair. She also possessed some of the hard angles of Ardon's face and an "offensive beak of a nose," Hallah often reminded her.

"I doubt you do much of that anyway," Hallah said, spinning the girl to inspect the back of her drab dress. "If you did, you might accidentally find yourself reading your school materials." Hallah gave a pressed smile as Alana rolled her eyes and stormed off. Ergis, a head taller than Zodak and dozens of doka heavier, shouldered past him on his way out.

Zodak took a breath and then he stepped through the door, out of the safety of the house. Out from under Ardon's shield of protection.

CHAPTER 2

Zodak accompanied Ergis and Alana to school every day, but not to learn. Like the others in Laan, the family was allotted just two students in the experimental school established by Barst the overlord to bring Pol Dak culture to the agrarian village. Though Ardon had promised each season to find a way to enroll Zodak, the spaces were few. At his age, Zodak was already growing out of the program. He knew the mines were more likely his fate. For now, though, Zodak went to serve his cousins. They certainly couldn't afford one of the massive golyath snails and cart—only one family in town could—so he carried their tablets and bags, brought them lunch, and walked them to class.

Ergis and Alana walked ahead of Zodak, without so much as a glance back. *This isn't good,* he thought. The straight driveway to the main street, still in view of the house, served as neutral ground, but once out of sight, Zodak was on his own.

Alana whispered and giggled to her brother, but Ergis remained dangerously silent. Ergis, whose name meant "valiant knight," fell woefully short of his title. Bossy and tubby, at almost seventeen seasons, he stood taller than most men, with an unkempt shock of black hair always hanging over his brooding eyes. When they were younger, Zodak could recall a handful of happy moments when he and Ergis had laughed or played together. But even those sunny memories often ended in anger or pain, and the seasons had washed away any remnant of friendship. Zodak had outdone Ergis too many times, beat him at some little game or contest. As the joyful moments grew fewer, the hatred festered, until every interaction became a strategic assault in Ergis's war of aggression.

"Look!" Alana stopped, pointing at the spider weed beside the path.

"Hmm?" grunted Ergis, his cold anger stifling his full participation in her charade.

"It's a little goblin made of water, and he's talking to me! He's telling me secrets!" Alana put her palms to her cheeks in mock surprise. Embarrassment and then anger stabbed through Zodak. "He said I'm not alone. Oh, you don't believe me, do you?" She pouted.

His pulse quickened and his hands trembled with fury. *You fool!* he scolded himself. The Wickeds had overheard the morning's events.

Ergis puffed his chest and screwed up his face into a scowl. "Why, of course I do, my half-breed, cursed *son*." Ergis spoke in a deep voice mimicking Ardon. Even in charade, Zodak knew the last word tasted bitter on Ergis's tongue.

"The water goblin said I am to be king of the Midlands," sang Alana in falsetto, clearly relishing Zodak's torment. "He said I will be a hero."

"Now that's going a bit far, my little bram dropping." Ergis furrowed his brow and stuck out his lips in ridiculous exaggeration. Thespians these two were not. "I can bear your lies only for so long, you little bastard. No matter how many water goblins are in your head, you'll never be a king. Just a cursed bastard!" Ergis wrapped a meaty arm around Zodak's shoulders and clamped down on Zodak's neck, pulling him into a headlock. Zodak lurched forward, yanked into a bowing position as Ergis squeezed hard, cutting off his air and pinching Zodak's folded ear painfully. Zodak dropped his bag and thrust Ergis's arm over his head, pulling free from the hold. Ergis and Alana exploded in shrieks of laughter.

Seasons of rage bottled inside Zodak bubbled over. He screamed as he snatched up the heavy leather bag with the slate tablets and hurled it straight into Ergis's face with a satisfying crunch, knocking the larger boy to the ground, blood showering from his nose.

Then Zodak turned to face Alana. "You're a selfish poison dart worm!" he snapped. "You know our father loves me, and he can't stand you! Who could? You're the most pathetic, horrible person I've ever met!"

Alana burst into tears and collapsed in a heap on the ground.

So went the fantasy in Zodak's head. He had played dozens of scenarios like this over in his mind, but as always, he remained silent under their jabs. Instead, he stood panting, his ear throbbing as he stared into the eyes of the Wickeds, fighting off the rage that welled within.

"Come on, hero! What's wrong?" taunted Ergis. "You gonna cry?" He swung to cuff Zodak on the back. Zodak dodged to the side, avoiding the blow. Ergis had earned the satisfaction of Zodak's tears in seasons past, but those days were long gone. Instead, Zodak lifted the school bag, his eyes still fixed on Ergis as his body fought to keep the shaking at bay. *Throw it! Hurt him,* the voice inside goaded him.

"Is carrying our slates to school your big journey?" taunted Alana.

"Careful," warned Ergis, looking around. "He's not alone!" Now Ergis joined Alana in laughter. Zodak knew the worst danger had passed. After a long minute, the cackling finally subsided.

"Don't you dare tell lies to our father, boy!" hissed Alana. "Play with your slagging wood fairies in your mind, but don't you bring your cursed pathetic little world into our home!" Zodak dropped his eyes under her barrage of words, hurled like darts. "Even a little sich moth like you can see your extra mouth to feed is killing our father."

The shame and embarrassment welled in Zodak. Alana wielded her biting words with precision compared to Ergis's blunt abuse. Her rants only encouraged Ergis.

"That's right," he added, moving close to Zodak. "If I ever hear you talk that foolish mind rot again..." He grabbed Zodak's shirt front and raised a meaty fist. "Even a stupid sich like you knows these woods got nothing but trees, orko, and skupp. No slagging goblins, no water creatures, no magic gnomes. Keep that scat in your pathetic empty head." He cuffed Zodak hard on the back of the head and let him go. The surge filled him again. Zodak clenched his teeth and ripped away from Ergis's grip.

"And Father doesn't need to carry your lies with him down into those horrid mines," added Alana, fixing Zodak with her challenging stare. "Don't worry, you'll be marching with him soon enough."

Still, Zodak said nothing. Trying to explain himself would be a fool's errand, and any retort would only make the situation worse.

"The goblin-loving moth can't even speak for himself," Alana taunted. "Lots to say when you're whispering your filth to Father, though."

Zodak tightened his grip on the heavy school bag, staring Ergis down. *Do it!* the voice shouted. It had been seasons since Zodak had fought back, and a part of him relished the opportunity. Zodak knew Ergis was afraid, afraid of one day unleashing the darkness deep in Zodak, fed by seasons of insult and abuse. Hallah had once promised him that the day he laid a hand on her children was the day he found himself in the woods. Whether just another of her manipulative childhood stories or a true promise, Zodak didn't know.

"That pill isn't worth the scratch on your knuckles," Alana said to Ergis. *She knows it too,* Zodak realized. Ergis hesitated long enough to show he had made up his own mind and then spat at Zodak and turned to go. Zodak sighed with relief, smearing off the spittle with his cuff. The teasing and jabs would no doubt continue. The intimate moment with their father was too rich and painful a prize to squander. But for now, Zodak had succeeded. He had survived another walk to school.

The dirty mustard-colored schoolhouse hadn't had a fresh coat of paint in all the seasons since the experiment had begun. *A building just for learning, like in the big cities.* "A waste of time for growing children who should be learning a craft or helping in the fields," many complained. The first season only three students attended, but the trickle had grown to a steady flock of children who congregated there each day. Viera Folba, one of Laan's only inhabitants with two names, was brought in by Barst himself from Pol Dak for the schooling experiment. Some villagers said his vision for an "oasis of culture" was a thinly veiled scheme to recruit for his growing krius mining empire. Ms. Folba had very much been an outsider when she arrived, but most in Laan had come to appreciate her teaching and the school itself as a luxury for such a small, sleepy farming village.

Zodak situated Alana and Ergis in the classroom with their slate tablets and chalk sticks. Then he was excused to the stable until classes ended when he would return for their things. Most days, only a few children gathered in the stable with Jup the grounds hand to shoe horses, stitch saddles, or learn simple carpentry and farm work. Most were either too young for school, third children, or children of families indebted to Barst, and therefore declared ineligible for school. Hallah, it seemed, didn't care much what Zodak did as long as he was out of the house.

Zodak had only been to the stable a few times when he discovered the hallway storage closet behind the classroom. Exhausted, he had slipped in to catch a nap, but once inside, he found the wall planks had flexed and bowed over time, making a slit between the closet and the classroom. From his secret spot, he could watch the entire class.

That first day Ms. Folba taught on the enthronement of Kaen the Great, urchin turned king, and Zodak was hooked. He never returned to the stable. From his cramped haven he absorbed Ms. Folba's every word, even without being able to see the leather books passed around in the class. The other children casually glanced at the sketched charcoal pictures on those pages before passing the book, but Zodak closed his eyes and imagined every detail of the scene. The smoke from the villages razed in the Great Seaborne Battle burned his nostrils. He could hear the trumpet blasts announcing the arrival of the Seven Judges. The wind atop Atlas Peak in the Direth Range blew and tussled his hair and he tasted the cool mountain spring water where the spade fish spawned. He longed for the next season when he could walk in as a real student as Ardon promised.

Today, though, his mind was not on the lesson. His thoughts flitted back to the water sprite. *Was it even real? What is my call? Or am I truly crazy?* He had heard about the tailor's apprentice, who swore he was seeing his dead ancestors walking about in the dye shop. The boy was sent off to Pol Dak and two seasons later had still not returned.

"And in what season was the Octarch Queendom established?" Zodak heard Ms. Folba ask. Silence. *Seventy-nine seasons into the Second Span,* he thought. She had taught this only last week. Ms. Folba was thirty-five seasons, although, with her hair pulled back into a tight ponytail and the hints of urban flair in her dress, she was sometimes taken for younger. She had a soft, kind face with warm eyes when she smiled, but she had never married. In response to the students who regularly asked, she would say she had married the love of learning.

"All right then, in what Span was it established?" she asked patiently. *Second...* thought Zodak. Still uncomfortable silence.

"Third," blurted a child near the back.

"Not quite," replied Ms. Folba. "The Queendom became disrupted and fell during the Third Span, just before the Goblin Swarm. But actually, it was established a good bit earlier."

"There's no such thing as goblins!" cried a child.

"Well, history is actually full of accounts that they do exist," replied Ms. Folba levelly.

"H'ol Chazkar controls them's minds," chirped a mousy girl from the back.

"Jelda!" gasped Folba, her face suddenly drained of color. "That name is never to be spoken." She gripped the desk to steady herself.

"Why?" replied Jelda. "'Cause yer afraid the Ice King is gonna come back?"

"Those are just dumb stories made up to keep us from traveling!" declared Alana. "The wicked Judges invented the Ice King to keep control over all the people."

"Where did you hear that, Alana?" asked Ms. Folba, her voice brimming with alarm. "The seven noble Judges forged the peace in the Midlands that has endured for hundreds of seasons."

"My mother has a cousin in the Venerable Council in Pol Dak," said Alana, lifting her chin. The class murmured admiration. Actually, Morzi, the daughter of Hallah's aunt, had been a servant in the washroom of one of the Council members until she was caught stealing silver spoons and thrown out of the

Sisters' Keep. "She told my mother about this conspirity," Alana proudly declared. Zodak rolled his eyes. Ergis and Alana were among a handful of students who challenged all accounts outside of their reality. History class was largely a wasted hour because it invariably broke down into arguments among children infused with their parents' uneducated politicized views of the past. From the way her mouth tightened into a thin line, it was clear that Ms. Folba, who had studied royal lineage and history herself at the Institute of Forgotten Learning in Pol Dak, fought to keep from joining the obtuse debates.

As the class drew to a close, Ms. Folba announced, "I have a special project for you all." A few groans. She paused patiently. "You will each have a writing assignment." Now muffled whispers rippled through the class. "To complete the assignment, I will be giving you each a black coal marker...and paper." The questioning murmur turned to excitement. *Paper?* Zodak perked up, and then just as quickly sank back into disappointment. Paper was a treat. The students did all of their writing on slate tablets. Nobody in the village other than the money counters wrote on paper. Writing paper belonged to the elite city folks and in old leather books, not in the hands of country children. But sure enough, Ms. Folba, ever a devotee to knowledge and learning, produced a short stack of writing paper.

"You must each write about an experience you have had. You can describe something that made you feel happy or something sad. Choose whatever you like. Have fun with your writing. It should be just like writing on your tablets, but you'll use both sides of the paper like this." She demonstrated how to keep the letters in line. The large room was full of whispers and squeals as the twenty-two children lined up to get their coal markers and two sheets of paper each. "I will collect your papers in three days," concluded Ms. Folba.

Zodak burned with envy. He had practiced his writing along with the other children during class on a broken piece of slate he had found in the closet, but he could only imagine writing on real paper.

"This is stupid," complained Ergis, returning to his desk with the supplies.

"I don't know. I think it could be fun," said Alana. There was a gleam in here eye, replacing the typical scowl.

As the classroom cleared out, the stable children shuffled in, collecting the tablets, chalks, and supplies. Zodak moved especially slowly. He desperately wanted to try writing on paper. Asking Ms. Folba for the supplies was out of the question. He wasn't even a student. His eyes roved from desk to desk, but none had been left behind. His mind raced. Ms. Folba collected her things up front, and without knowing what he would say, Zodak found himself walking towards the front of the room. As he approached Ms. Folba, he froze.

She glanced up. "Ahoi. May I help you?"

His throat was suddenly dry. She smiled patiently. After what seemed like an eternity, he croaked, "Pa—per."

"Oh? For Ergis. I see," she said, shaking her head, handing him the supplies.

Zodak didn't speak. He clutched his prize and slowly backed away. Glancing over his shoulder, he carefully slipped the paper between the two tablets in the bag and pocketed the coal marker before nearly skipping out of the room.

"What's taking so long, skupp?" Ergis's bulky figure blocked the doorway.

Zodak's breath caught. "Uh, n-nothing." He felt the weight of the marker in his pocket. Ergis looked him up and down, his accusing gaze finally settling on Zodak's face. Zodak averted his eyes, praying for the silent inquisition to pass. Ergis peered over Zodak's shoulder into the classroom.

"Psheesh," he finally grunted, shaking his head as he walked away. Zodak breathed again.

CHAPTER 3

For the next two days, Zodak slipped away every chance he could to work on his story. Writing on the fragile paper was like handling a dried snakeskin. Marking the paper while holding it on his lap like a tablet was very difficult. He finally found that laying it down flat on the worktable in the shed worked much better. He knew exactly what he would write about: the water creature from the woods. He would pour every detail he could remember about it, and then he would burn the paper so Ergis could never find it.

Ergis, it appeared, had completely ignored the project until Ms. Folba announced that any student who failed to turn in their story would be required to read aloud to the group. That night Ergis hurriedly wrote a sarcastic and sloppy story about when he had won a first-place ribbon for growing the largest fire squash for the Harvest Festival. Conveniently excluded were the details that he had actually won third place, had stolen the squash a day earlier, and consequently had his victory denounced and his ribbon reclaimed.

To Zodak's surprise, Alana seemed genuinely excited every time she discussed the project, though he hadn't actually seen her start writing. Despite Hallah's dismissive comments, Alana continued to share the details of the story she planned to write.

The classroom hummed with excitement on the second day. The students chirped and chattered about their stories and their adventures writing on paper. A few had ripped their paper and needed a new sheet. Bluef, a stocky boy with a slow drawl, had somehow burned both sheets and the marker and he had the charred paper to prove it. Most, though, eagerly shared the snippets of writing they had completed. As he sat in his closet, Zodak cursed himself for leaving his story back in the shed. How he longed to pore over every word.

On the way back from school, Alana hurried ahead of Ergis and Zodak.

"Why do you even care so much about this stupid project?" he overheard Ergis call after her.

"I don't know," she admitted, slowing. "It just somehow makes me feel...alive or something."

"Boring as pith if you ask me," huffed Ergis.

"Maybe," she replied airily. Once at home, she skipped off and went straight to her room. That night she missed dinner, claiming a stomachache.

"Wouldn't hurt her to miss a meal now and then anyway," Hallah had said. From the candlelight dancing on the ceiling over the curtained-off section of the house that was Alana's room, Zodak guessed she was working on her story late into the night.

On the morning the assignments were due, Alana was dressed and finished with breakfast, reading her story when Zodak went out to get the morning wood and spate. He couldn't remember the last time that had happened. She usually stumbled into the kitchen irritable and half-asleep, hurling sharpened insults, shoveled food into her mouth, and tromped off to school.

"Good morning," he said, immediately regretting opening his mouth at all and bracing for the barbed retort.

"Good?" she replied. "It's a trimidious morning!" Again, he waited for the attack. She must have sensed his hesitation. "It's the day we turn in our stories in class," she explained. "Ms. Folba gave us real paper. It's...it's amazing." She spoke fast as if trying to catch the thoughts. "Before I knew it, I was at the bottom of the page. And then the second." She was nearly breathless. Their eyes met and Zodak quickly looked away. An awkward silence landed as they both sat in the foreign, intimate shared moment.

"Are you going to Far Market tomorrow?" she blurted suddenly, changing the topic.

Zodak had no idea what to make of Alana. She had never spoken to him like this. "Yes," he answered carefully. In all the excitement, Zodak had completely forgotten about his upcoming trip to the town of Komo. He felt proud of his responsibility to buy provisions for the family and usually counted down the days to the trip, though he never understood why Hallah granted him this gift. But whatever the reason, she entrusted him with the family's money, their horse, and the cart across the rocky vale to the river town of Komo.

"Lose a dither of this money and you'll never set foot outside the house until you're old enough to be shipped off to the mines!" she warned on his last visit. But Zodak considered her routine threats a small price to pay. He made the trip only every mooncycle. Most of what the family needed came from the local market. Yet Hallah demanded fine herbs, oils, and the occasional fabric whenever she had stashed enough of Ardon's money to afford it. Laan produced no such finery.

"Oh, good." She clapped her hands together. "Mr. Kanes gave me a corq for helping him pickle his pig turnips last week, and I was wondering if, well, I was hoping you could buy me a blue scarf when you go. Dyna at school got one and said they only cost a corq."

Zodak turned the question over in his mind, searching for the trick or insult. *Will she claim she gave you two? Or that you stole her corq?* That seemed unlikely, even for her.

"Okay..." he answered guardedly.

"Really?" she chirped.

"Mm-hmm," he answered, now looking around for Ergis. But they were alone.

"Great!" Alana beamed.

"What's all this?" Hallah's voice cut in. "Where's the wood?" She shot a glance at Zodak. "And what's gotten into you?" She turned to Alana.

"It's this writing assignment, Mother. It... it feels like drawing back a heavy curtain letting light and color rush in."

Hallah snorted. "Foolish indulgence if you ask me. You have better things to do than playing make-believe on expensive paper."

Zodak grimaced, backing through the open door.

"I don't know," said Alana, finishing off a bite of cold cheese and rusk bread. She dashed out to finish getting ready for school. *What's happened to her?*

Before collecting the wood, Zodak slipped off to the shed to get his treasured story. He wouldn't turn his paper in, but he hadn't brought himself to burn it yet. The words from the encounter with that strange water creature came alive again on the pages and now haunted him anew. Today he would read and re-read his story again and again, relishing every word. Zodak swept aside a dusty canvas sack and lifted a wide floorboard out of place. Ever since discovering this secret spot a few seasons earlier while patching a skupp hole, he had used it to hide his most precious items. Most were boyhood treasures only to him. Among them, three colorful glittering stones from the stream, a very old glass lens, and a smooth silver ball just larger than an almond. Zodak carefully removed his paper from the hiding spot and replaced the board. He unrolled the story on the worktable just to look at it once more.

"What are you doing, half-wit?" Ergis darkened the only doorway to the shed. Zodak's stomach twisted.

"Just... putting the axe away," replied Zodak, not turning.

"I heard no chopping," accused Ergis, stepping into the shed. "Why are you at the worktable? You came in here yesterday, too."

His back to Ergis, Zodak slowly rolled his papers, his heart galloping.

"I asked you what you're doing!" Ergis's hot breath was on Zodak's neck.

As subtly as he could, Zodak slipped the roll under the front of his heavy linen shirt. "Nothing. I told you." Zodak turned around to face Ergis, trying to look calm. Ergis pushed him aside, searching the table. Zodak moved to step around Ergis, but Ergis blocked his path.

"Why are you rustling about in here before school?" His dark eyes searched Zodak.

"I'm not," replied Zodak, again trying to step around Ergis, only to be cut off again.

"Then what are you doing here, worm?" Ergis pushed Zodak, causing him to stumble backward.

"It's nothing," insisted Zodak. He lowered his head and again tried to shuffle past.

"What are you hiding there?" Ergis asked, reaching for the slight bulge in Zodak's shirt.

"Nothing!" Zodak lunged forward and shoved Ergis with all his might. Unlike Ergis, who rarely exerted himself, Zodak had grown strong from his many daily chores. The push launched Ergis backward. He tripped and fell to the ground against the shed wall, a shock of his messy black hair flopping over his eyes. For a moment he just sat, stunned. Zodak hadn't raised a finger against Ergis in many seasons. *What have I done?* The look of fear flitted from Ergis's face, and his cheeks turned from white to bright red.

He jumped to his feet, rage in his eyes. "You," panted Ergis.

"I... I'm sorry... I—" Zodak stammered, holding out a hand.

"You will be sorry. Just wait!" he seethed and turned and ran out of the shed.

Zodak shook uncontrollably. He had dreamed of and dreaded the day he would stand up to Ergis, but it felt nothing like he'd imagined. He hadn't thought or planned. It happened too fast. He simply reacted. Ergis couldn't know about his story. Zodak carefully removed the roll of paper, put it in his coat pocket, and walked back to the house.

Ergis didn't say a word on the walk to school. A thick icy wall separated the two boys. Ergis hid his shame and anger expertly, yet Zodak knew how he loathed being humiliated. Once, a small village boy named Simpeon landed a lucky blow as he flailed about in a pathetic attempt to shield himself from Ergis's merciless bullying. The punch bloodied Ergis's nose and drew laughs and jeers from the knot of onlookers. Ergis didn't retaliate in the moment but fell into a dark brooding silence until a few days later when Simpeon's beloved pet ram died mysteriously. Ergis never claimed responsibility or gloated, but Zodak found the empty bag of weed poison and feed in the shed. The very day Simpeon shared the tragic news, Ergis snapped back to his boisterous, impetuous self.

Alana, meanwhile, appeared a different person, changed somehow. She didn't offer to carry the slates or compliment Zodak on his outfit, but a new, unfamiliar glow covered her. Even her face seemed free of the morning shadows and persistent scowl that normally clung to her like bogmoss. She spoke excitedly, talking to no one and waiting for no answer, then whistled a melody of some sort. Her high spirits couldn't lift the cloud over Zodak, though. He feared his inevitable punishment for the clash with Ergis. The attack could come anytime, maybe today, maybe in a month, but he would hold nothing back. It would be terrible. Zodak was in danger.

As soon as they arrived at school, Alana hurried inside to show Ms. Folba her written pages before the other students arrived.

"I'm afraid I didn't finish my story," Zodak heard Alana say as he entered the classroom. "Actually, it felt like I had only just begun when I ran out of room..." Zodak caught Ms. Folba's surprise, but her eyes twinkled.

"Oh, I know that feeling," she said, reaching into her desk and removing at least five more pieces of paper. Zodak pretended to straighten the desk as Ms. Folba drew close to Alana. "I don't have enough for the entire class, so you mustn't tell the others." Alana nodded, wide-eyed. "Though I think it important that you finish your story," Ms. Folba added. Alana gleefully snatched the paper and slid it under her tablet, just as two other children arrived.

After setting up, Zodak hurried out the door towards the stables under Ergis's searing glare. As was his routine, once outside, he turned back to the road and circled around the schoolhouse. He slipped through the building's side door and glancing around furtively, cracked the closet door, and stepped inside. Blades of light from the classroom cut in through the cracks in the wall. Zodak had turned a crate upside-down as a makeshift table, and carefully unrolled his story. When most of the children had arrived, Ms. Folba began collecting the stories. The students shuffled to the front of the class, chatting and giggling, sharing in the grandness of the accomplishment.

"Anyone who likes may read their story to the class tomorrow," Ms. Folba announced.

Zodak could have finished reading his story in a few minutes, but he wanted to savor the experience, to re-live the encounter with the water creature. Reading and re-reading every sentence, he returned to the woods, to the magical encounter, whether real or imagined. He was picking through the second page when his thoughts were interrupted.

"... we'll finish talking about the Tszoi people and the Nomadic Nost Clans after lunch," said Ms. Folba. *Lunch?! Could it be lunchtime already?* It was just as Alana described it. His story had sucked him in, and he had completely lost track of time. He would have to leave the rest for after lunch. Snatching up the wax cloth bundle with the children's lunch, he crept from his room. Today they would have biscuits and salted orko jerky with a chunk of cheese and a misshapen apple each. Zodak had the same, but saw there was no orko for him, and only the most meager slice of cheese. But today nothing could topple him from his joyful perch. He peered out of his hide-away, slipped out, and pulled the door closed behind him.

He hurried into the multipurpose room where the children settled into lunch. He handed Alana her meal and nearly fell over when she said, "Thank you." In all the seasons living under Ardon's roof, Zodak couldn't recall anyone other than Ardon thanking him for anything. His service was almost always met with a snide remark or complaint.

"You're... welcome," faltered Zodak. Ergis still fixed Zodak with the cold stare, yet he said nothing as he collected his food. He took Zodak's apple as well in a subtle, but clear declaration: the war had begun.

Zodak didn't need the apple today, though. His story would be his food. After delivering the waterskin, he hurried out, skipping ahead of the other stable children. He checked over his shoulder and scurried down the slender hallway. But as he rounded the corner, he stopped short. From a few paces away, he could see the door to the closet, his closet, was wide open. He always closed it. And it looked like someone, or something, was moving inside. Zodak's stomach twisted. *I'm found out. No... No!* Fear welled up and burning tears flooded his eyes.

He had been so careful to conceal his hideout, the only escape he had from his grueling days. *What if I'm caught?* he had wondered many times. They would throw him out of class, that was a given. But the thought of being relegated to the stable every day felt like a prison sentence. Hallah would positively erupt. But much worse than all of that was the shame it would cause Ardon. The entire town would hear of it: Ardon's stableboy breaking into school. He took an unsteady deep breath and crept a step closer. As he approached the opening, a figure stepped out, nearly colliding with him. It was Ms. Folba.

Zodak's breath caught, and his mind spun. *Should I turn and run or start talking? Spouting excuses? Or I could just break down and tell the truth.* As he opened his mouth, fumbling silently for words, Ms. Folba walked right by him, not even glancing up. Zodak released the breath he had been holding. But then he noticed what had her so transfixed. She stared intently at something she held in her hands. *No,* said Zodak silently, gripped by a new terror. Ms. Folba glided down the hall as if in a trance, a perplexed expression on her face. She was reading his story.

KEEP READING

Zodak - The Last Shielder
Revisit Yiduiijn 200 years later, after the fall of the great Kingdom K'andoria and new Age of Governors. The costly wars of men and kings have left a vacuum, an opportunity. The great evil stirs, seeking a foothold, an opportunity to rise. An unassuming orphan will be called into the eye of the storm.

Available HERE on Amazon

ABOUT THE AUTHOR

Max grew up roaming the streets and exploring the deep dark forests of Washington D.C. terrorizing neighborhood wild game and putting his brother Eli through various club initiations. He now resides just outside D.C. with his wife and four kids (lovingly referred to as the "Treehouse Gang"). The Treehouse Gang and the rest of the family are, without a doubt, the biggest fans of his writing and creativity.

As a day (and sometimes night) job, Max runs a boutique law firm supporting amazing founders building, growing and selling inspiring companies. In the off hours (read: early in the morning before anyone else is awake), he loves getting lost in his writing.

In his limited free time (see above about running a law firm and raising four kids), he loves playing/skateboarding/trampolining/fishing/skiing with the Treehouse Gang, Crossfit, riding his classic motorcycle, woodworking, drawing, painting, watching great movies and playing board games.

The Tempest Rising Series is Max's first published fiction.

Want more? Sign up for the newsletter and come join the adventure: https://www.maxmoyerwrites.com/join